AF091989

Return of Atlantis

Atlantis Rising 2
Amy Cip

Chapter 1

Queen Aura watched from the window as a great dragon swept past Atlantis' tallest tower, his wings outstretched and neck held high. Sunlight flared off his scales, and for an instant, the air itself seemed to breathe again. He moved with such effortless grace it was as if the beast was meant to be there all along. Her heart skipped a beat.

Before Ember arrived, it had been years since she'd seen a dragon—and almost as long since she'd stood on solid ground. Both filled her hope and terror in equal measure. She'd forgotten how volatile dragons could be—and how unsteady the ground could feel under her feet.

So far, Draco was the only one, but there were more out there. She was sure. Things were in motion with the return of Atlantis. No one could yet pass through Atlantis' gates. They had warded the city carefully when it fell from the sky, where it had been cursed for ages, but the gates would have to open sometime.

Whether that would save them—or destroy them—Aura couldn't say yet.

She sat by the same window she had spent countless hours when Atlantis hid in the sky—wishing and praying that they might one day return to the ground.

In the last few years of their isolation, she had often seen Sierra on the steps of the castle. She'd heard the girl's pleas, but never known how to help her, not until Ember arrived.

And then there was Aurelia, no longer orphan now that her father had returned. Casius—once her loyal guard and now known to the world as Shepherd. He'd sacrificed everything to bring Atlantis home, and that sacrifice had separated him from his daughter. Until now.

Time moved slower in Atlantis, but Aura guessed Aurelia to be in her late teens. She had raised the girl as her own, and once she'd come of age, made her a lady-in-waiting. Now Aurelia paced in the adjoining room, her grief still raw. She had taken the King's death hard. Aura feared how Aurelia's reunion with Shep would go. She sensed anger in her old guard— rightfully so. He had been cheated out of so much. They all had.

Queen Aura sighed and ran her hand over the gauzy curtains, tracing where the fabric had frayed after so many years in stale air. Beyond the city was no longer the relative safety of the clouds and sky, but land—and danger. Atlantis had fallen near the sea, and she watched its whitecaps catch the last light of sunset. Another army was massing at their borders. Perhaps not

Zyah but there were always enemies. People had always been jealous or afraid of Atlantis and its power.

It was the bane of her reign to broker peace. She'd barely begun, and already she was so tired. So far, the enemy hadn't tested their wards—but it was only a matter of time.

A sharp wrap at the door broke her thoughts.

"Enter," she called.

Javiar stepped in, cautious as ever. She was in her dressing room furnished with an ornate sitting area, dresser, and a desk. The wood had been white once, but like everything it had yellowed. A torch flickered, illuminating a large tapestry of Atlantis's better days—a joyous festival that was a long-forgotten memory.

"Your Highness," he said, bowing with hesitation. He needn't have. She already knew what was in his heart. Javiar was a loyal guard—and an even more loyal friend. She noted the thinning gray at his crown, his chest-length beard, the kindness of his brown eyes, and the pity in his brown eyes.

"They need leadership," she said, letting the curtain fall, and hiding the sunset where pink clouds darkened. The dark would bring ill tidings.

He cleared his throat. "Actually, the King is...."

At his pause, she turned. Her usually confident guard wrung his hands.

"Disappearing," he finished.

Her brows lifted. "Disappearing?"

So much had happened in the last few days. Atlantis had returned to the ground after centuries, but it's return came with a price. The King had been cursed. When Atlantis came home, he had taken his last breath. Their relationship had been complicated, but she mourned him.

"You should come see," Javiar said. He wore the same uniform of the King's guard—crisp white shirt, red cloak. *Queen's guard*, she corrected herself.

There was no King to guard now. What would become of them?

She rose slowly, uncertain of what the night would bring. She'd been so eager to return home—all of them had. But now, Atlantis was afraid again. Would they be welcomed or shunned? Would there be another war? Would magic, this time, be lost for good?

Javiar joined her at the window. What he saw, she couldn't say—danger, perhaps. He was always watching for it. This time, he was right to be afraid.

"The people seek counsel," he said, softly. "They are frightened. Confused."

Aura drew a deep breath. King Corin had left so much to her in his final years. Then, her hands had been tied. What would she do now, unbound?

"They're right to be," she admitted, turning away. She had no one but Javiar. She'd been too cautious to seek other counsel while the King lived. But times were changing. Outside, a faint murmur of unease rose outside the castle.

"What of those who brought us back—Shepherd and the others?" Aura asked, glancing toward Aurelia in the adjoining room.

On the ground, lights approached—too fast to be horses. The sorcerers had told her of horseless carriages, even ones that flew. They'd avoided them before, but now there was no choice. Blue and red flashes blinked against the horizon, unable to cross the wards. Somewhere, the dragon roared.

"They are inside the gates," Javiar said. "Keeping vigil for the King. But they wish to speak with you."

"I'll bet they do," Aura murmured. Her heart swelled with a mix of fear and excitement. The sight of those strange machines stirred something in her she hadn't felt in a long time. She reached for Javiar's hand and squeezed.

"It was the right thing," she said—half question, half statement.

Javiar smiled, lifting her hand to his lips. "It is done now, my Queen. The only way is forward."

His eyes sparkled with excitement, maybe even joy. Atlantis had been cursed for too long. Freedom called to them. But first, Aura had to give them permission. Tell them it was safe. Lie.

"And what of Zyah's wife, Maryse?" she asked.

He released her hand. It hovered between them for a moment, and she yearned to reach out for his comfort again.

"She has disappeared," he admitted.

"Perhaps like King Corin," she wondered.

"Perhaps," Javiar agreed, skeptical.

She touched his face, his beard rough under her hands. "Always so cautious," she said, meeting his eyes. It wasn't something she'd done in so long. If she'd approached the King in such a way in the last century, he'd have scolded her. She learned to keeping her gaze lowered. But now she allowed herself a moment of boldness.

"Thank you, Javiar, for your loyalty—and your honesty—these many years. I truly trust and cherish your kindness."

His cheeks picked up a hint of blush. "It is my honor," he said, bowing his head slightly.

Aura turned and led the way out of the sitting room, stopping at the back door. She cracked it open. The girl sat cross-legged on a chair, brown eyes wide as she gazed out the window. Her blonde hair favored her mother. Aura had known the fortune teller well enough. Her dark eyes, though—all Shep.

"They have magic here, too," Aurelia said, turning those brown eyes on Aura. "They fly, and they move so quickly. The lights are so bright."

Aura's heart swelled. She had raised the child as her own, worried what this reunion might bring—for Aurelia, for Shep, and selfishly, for her.

"Yes," the Queen said softly. "And until we know what kind of magic, I'd like you to stay here."

Aurelia's expression fell. Aura lifted a hand in warning.

"For your safety," she added.

"I am stronger than that," Aurelia protested, standing to her full height—almost as tall as her father. "Please, let me see this new land. These wonders."

"Soon." Aura squeezed her hand. "For now, be careful."

"Careful." Aurelia muttered, huffing as she sank back into the chair. The torchlight caught a single tear on her cheek. *Better she cry,* Aura thought *than let her anger fester*.

"I'll return shortly," Aura said, but Aurelia didn't move her eyes from the window this time. The Queen had guards on the child. She was special—perhaps too special for this world—but it was too late now. Things were in motion that couldn't be undone. Soon, she would meet her father and learn her true story.

The Queen's gown whispered across the floor as lanterns flickered to life. The magic of Atlantis held steady—even here. Lights bobbed overhead, casting restless shadows along the halls. Most of the servants and guards were outside—where the danger waited, and the future, too.

A breeze came in the window. She paused before the great doors.

"I'll need your counsel more than ever," she told Javiar, not daring to reach for his hand this time, though she wanted to. Her eyes carried more than words: a question, a plea.

He stepped closer, hand on the hilt of his sword. "I will defend you to the death," he said softly. And there were more to his words than defense.

Aura's breath caught. She could have said more. Done more. Instead, she nodded and stepped through the doors—into whatever awaited them next.

Chapter 2

Paine nudged the King's body as it lie prostrate on a table. Once, long ago, he'd sat upon a throne in this very room and ruled the city. Tall, wide windows on the left overlooked the city from the top of the hill, though they were shrouded by heavy red curtains now and the thrones sat empty. Tables had been pushed to the side of the wide room, and only a few chairs had been scattered haphazardly around him, lying in state.

Long ago, the King had chosen to raise the city. Since then, though, he'd been nothing more than a figurehead, hidden in his tower, afraid to return Atlantis—afraid of this own ending.

Ember hoped it wasn't just fear for his own life that kept the city aloft for so long. Deep down, she believed he'd done it for his people. As he should have. She wasn't sure the world would be kind to them.

She looked at his body—calm, peaceful... fading. Actually fading. And she hoped, at last, he'd found peace.

"Maybe this is what happened to your other friend?" Paine said, cutting into Ember's thoughts. Her voice echoed in the carnivorous room—it was too big for only five people.

The rest of the city, even the palace guards, were outside taking stock of what had happened, and feeling the weight of solid ground beneath their feet again. If Ember had to guess—and she was good at guessing moods—their feelings ranged from relieved to awestruck to fearful to outright terror. They needed a leader.

Though the King looked more regal in death than he ever had in life, Paine's finger sank farther than it should have when she touched his shoulder. His body was fading—literally dissolving out of existence.

After Atlantis had returned to the ground, Paine, Ember, and Shep had gathered in the throne room, joined by Ember's sister, Sierra, and Captain Hawk. Each dealt with the city's return in their own way. They'd achieved what they set out to do—but at what cost?

"Maryse?" Ember asked, tapping her foot. "She was hardly our *friend*." Zyah's wife fought against magic for centuries, and Ember had thought it was more like a parlor trick when her body faded out of existence after Atlantis returned. Much had happened quickly—the least of which, the government had been called in. The city was surrounded on all fronts: air, water, and land, but because of the wards, the world couldn't get close. Ember was worried what they'd do when they did get through. Her dragon took it all in stride. Draco was showing off: doing rolls and roaring for the assembled governments—the internet must have been loving it.

"Maryse did disappear," Hawk said, his voice aloof yet casual. But Ember detected truth beneath it. He wasn't wrong. Maryse's body was there one minute, gone the next. Ember was almost certain she had still been breathing... but this? She looked at the King's tragic form.

"Not like this," Ember said softly. She took the King's hand—bones the only solid thing left—and placed it on his chest. What a burden he'd carried for so long. He hadn't carried it well. He'd made mistakes. Terrible ones. But he had returned them all the same. She patted his hand. "He's going home... wherever that is."

Shep, who had been pacing, paused to give her a smile. Something she had sorely missed. While he was here holding Maryse off, she and Sierra had been in Atlantis negotiating with the King to let them return. Hours had passed, but it felt like weeks since she'd seen him. She could still read his deep brown eyes, which reflected amusement, and maybe concern. Beneath it all, like a steady heartbeat (if only he had one), love. A flick of his curly hair fell in his face.

"Maybe home is farther away than Atlantis ever was," he said. They'd talked about home before, but now it seemed to mean more, with the King's body fading.

"Yeah, maybe the moon," Paine joked. Ember could always count on her friend to lighten the mood. They'd grown close since meeting aboard Hawk's flying pirate ship. Rescuing survivors of Atlantis had once been Paine's life mission. She remembered meeting the fiery redhead in the kitchens. What would she do now, on the ground? Stay here in Atlantis—or see the world?

"Look," said Sierra, holding the curtain back as she sat at the window. Her blonde hair shimmered in the fading light. She had been trapped in Atlantis so long by Maryse, while Ember thought her sister was in a coma. Even then, Sierra never gave up. She still carried the same light heart. Once, it had annoyed Ember, the way sisters annoy each other. Now, all she felt was overwhelming love—and the need to protect.

Following Sierra's gaze, Ember saw Hawk's ship approaching. Its silhouette cut an impressive form against the night—flying pirate ships tended do that. Though it passed through Atlantis' defenses easily, lights flashed behind it and jets streaked overhead.

Hawk grinned—another sight Ember had sorely missed. His usually pulled back hair hung loose, a reminder of how exhausted they all were. "I'll see that they land," he said, with Sierra and Paine offering to accompany him.

Sierra gave the King a once-over.

"I never liked him," she said, her face scrunched up in an unusual frown. "But I forgive him." The King had trapped her as much as Maryse had by refusing to acknowledge her. Did he make up for that in the end, when he returned Atlantis despite knowing he was cursed to die? That remained to be seen.

"His legacy is complicated," Shep agreed. He looked like he wanted to say more, but he'd only just met Sierra.

She smiled at him, eyes crinkling. "You could say that."

"Be careful," Ember told them. The three left, leaving her with Shep and the fading body of the King. Atlantis was defended by strong magic, but who knew what might be thrown at them? So far, no one could approach. It would fall to the Queen to meet them—wherever she was. Grieving the King, perhaps, or taking a moment alone. She was complicated too. Maybe everyone was?

Shep pulled a chair up beside her, their knees touching. It was such a different sensation from the King's fading body—Shep's touch was real, warm. Energy pulsed between them—it had since the moment he'd walked into her store. She tried to look down, but he wouldn't let her, tipping her chin up with his fingers and keeping his hand there.

"Home," he said, "is where his soul is at peace."

She smiled. That was as much for her as for him. There were so many questions crowding her mind: What happened to Maryse? Where was the Queen? Would Shep find his daughter, left on Atlantis all those years ago to proctor the island's return?

She took his hand and closed her eyes. Was her soul at peace? So much had happened in the last few months. She'd been dragged out of her old, predictable life—a life that had been stable, but at peace? No. Now she was surrounded by danger. Adventure. The unknown.

"Perhaps the definition of peace is different for everyone," she said, opening her eyes to take him in. Once, she feared trusting him, but now, she'd given him her heart. Fear lingered beneath it, but she chose to believe.

He leaned in, pressing their foreheads together. She needed his reassurance more than she realized. He still smelled of the wind and the sea, and the same adventurous twinkle danced in his eye as when he'd been on the ship—seeking Atlantis but protecting Ember at the same time. That both things could exist in one man was beyond her understanding. She'd already learned so much from him. He had changed her life.

"This is home," he said breathless.

She tangled her fingers in his and kissed him—not the way she wanted to, the celebratory kind saved for when they'd be alone and she could forget about Atlantis, their struggles, and their journey—but a kiss of gratitude, love, and maybe a little distraction. She pulled back. The King's body had faded even further, and so had the sun. By midnight, he'd be gone. There was so much to do.

"We have to—"

He pressed a finger to her lips and shushed her.

"It will happen in time," he said—and he was right. Every time she'd tried to rush something it had only made things worse. But she looked at the King's body. Was he to be buried? How? Her attention shifted to the door where she could hear the murmurs of the city. Finally, back to Shep. She reached up and moved his fingers gently.

"Your daughter," she said, her voice soft. Tears built from the weight of all they'd been holding back. Somewhere out there, the baby he'd left waited for him.

"Aurelia." His tears mirrored hers, though his carried more relief than sorrow. She'd always been able to read what people didn't say—a blessing and a curse. He nodded. "I'll find her," he promised, leaning in to brush a soft kiss against her lips. "There is time."

Time. Such a strange thing. It stretched endlessly when she was alone, running the bookstore—days bleeding into years, all the same. But now? It never seemed like they had enough of it.

She forced a smile. "And what are we going to do with that time?" she asked, feigning innocence. He recognized her playful tone, but before he could answer, the Queen entered—Javiar close on her heels.

She made a strong impression. Ember had only met her once before—back in Atlantis, when they'd broken into the castle to convince the King to return them. Aura had played a pivotal role then, and Ember had known even in that brief encounter that she was stronger than she let on. She could see it again now, in the proud set of the Queen's shoulders. But the deep shadows under her eyes betrayed her exhaustion. They were stark against her pale skin, yet with her blonde hair loose and curled at the ends, you could scarcely look past her luminous blue eyes. She was beautiful in an ethereal way, and Ember didn't mind standing in her shadow.

Ember and Shep stepped aside, giving Aura room to stand by the King's side. She touched his shoulder gently, her slim fingers hovering above his fading form. Her eyes misted, and Ember looked away, granting her the privacy of grief. Whatever the Queen had to say to the King she said in silence. Did she forgive him—or simply let go?

After a long moment, Aura patted his hand. "We should let the people see him," she said softly. "His sacrifice."

She met Javiar's gaze, and something passed between them—something deeper than words. "So they know he was more than a monster."

"I'm sure he was no monster," Ember said quietly, wringing her hands.

Aura's answering smile was sad. "He alone is responsible for his legacy. But I will have them see all of him." She straightened, her tone firm. "Javiar, get the room ready. Have it guarded."

As the Queen began issuing orders, Ember moved to the side. Outside, Hawk's ship had landed on the courtyard, drawing a crowd. Hawk stood among them, speaking to the people of Atlantis, who gathered in growing numbers to listen.

Ember threaded her fingers through Shep's. "Your daughter could be out there right now," she said, her pulse quickening.

He swallowed. "I don't know what she'd look like. How old she'd be..." He trailed off. "Her mother..."

He never finished his thought. The Queen's quiet authority had transformed the room into a rush of motion. Within minutes, the King's fading body lay in state—ready for the people of Atlantis to say goodbye.

The Queen paused beside Ember. "They need a ceremony," she said, her gaze lingering on the King. "And I will give them one. What happens after this..." She let out a weary sigh and shrugged.

"We will have to greet the world," Ember said, suppressing a shiver.

"You will help with that?" the Queen asked.

Ember nodded, though she was no ambassador. Sierra would be better suited—she could charm anyone. "When you're ready," she said.

The Queen nodded as if it were already decided. "Let them in," she told Javiar. "Let in my city."

She took her place on one of the twin thrones—the other conspicuously empty. The people would pass before her to offer condolences, then past the King's body. *They'd better hurry*, Ember thought. He didn't have much time for goodbyes.

She tugged Shep's sleeve. "There's one place I'd like to go before we get started," she said. She'd felt the pull in her heart since they'd landed. She and Draco had never had a proper reunion.

Shep smiled. "Of course."

He took her hand and together they slipped her out the back door—where her dragon waited.

CHAPTER 3

Ember's connection with Draco wasn't a typical friendship. She'd tried to explain it to the others—all but Shep, who had once had his own dragon. No words could capture their connection. It was a heartbeat. A tether.

During her time in Atlantis, when they were apart, she could sense Draco out there. She'd wished he could have been with her, but that job had fallen on her and Sierra alone. Ember knew she couldn't always pick the battles she fought, but she sure as hell better learn their lessons. She'd learned she could do hard things—difficult things, almost impossible things even, and she would need that lesson as they returned the magic of Atlantis back to the world.

Her excitement rose as she and Shep weaved through the castle. She was learning her way—but just barely. They took a wrong turn and found themselves in the kitchen, where they helped themselves to a snack. Then they backtracked to the most breathtaking view of the ocean, and her home island visible in the distance. The lights shimmered faintly in the moonlight. But this wasn't what she had come for. Shep, however, lingered at the window.

"What I'd give to see Actuous again," he said, his gaze far away. She paused, her heart pulled in two directions. This was his homecoming far more than hers. Here was where he was born and raised—and here was where he had sacrificed his own future to bring them home.

"What was she like?" She stood behind him, watching the moon rise over the water. Here and there, warships dotted the waves.

"Blazing red," he said, laughing. "With a temper to match." He pulled his gaze away from the window. "I tempered her—but just barely. In those days, dragons were the source of most magic. They had power. Purpose."

"What happened to them?" she asked. She'd known Draco was the first dragon to be seen in years, but not how—or why. *The King's brother*, she assumed.

"They disappeared one day." His shoulders fell. "There was a battle far away between Zyah and a neighboring village. Corin wouldn't send troops, but the dragons decided on their own. It was like..." He stopped, taking a deep breath. "Like a cord had been severed between us. She didn't die. She's just... *gone*." He looked back to her apologetically. "It's hard to explain."

She took his hand. "It's not. I get it."

She wondered what it would feel like to remove her tether to Draco. *Like something was missing*, she supposed. "Do you think she's out there somewhere?" she asked.

Shep frowned. "Perhaps," he said, but the implications of that were frightening. He put on a faint smile. "But we have other things to attend to first." He brought her hand to his lips and kissed it gently.

They slowed their pace as they walked through the castle, admiring the beautiful busts and tapestries, all in rich reds and golds, telling of Atlantis's long history. Her tie to Draco pulled her with every step, and finally they reached a side door.

She peeked out and spied the whole city in line to see the King, candles in hand. Lights fueled by magic dotted the line above them in dancing colors that somehow stayed muted and respectful. Low murmurs of conversation carried, with some singing. Beyond the line, she caught a fluff of purple as Draco fluffed his wing in the courtyard.

Shep dropped her hand so she could run over the cobbled square, down the steps, and past the fountain. People turned to watch her, but she didn't slow. There would be plenty of time for greetings later.

She ran right into the side of her dragon, avoiding the sharp parts of his scales and sinking herself into the soft, downy fur underneath. Draco let off a contented sigh. She'd come to know his feelings, even read his mind when she was attuned to it.

"I'm sorry," she said, voice muffled. She'd told him she wished she could have taken him, but she wasn't sure he understood. For all his bravado, Draco was still young.

He twisted his long neck so his golden eyes were level with hers, then gave her a big lick from toe to head. She laughed awkwardly. Dragon drool was not something you wanted on you all day.

"I take it I'm forgiven, then?" She patted his soft nose, and Draco closed his eyes. She felt his forgiveness in her heart and dipped her head to meet his.

"I promise," she told him. "From now on, together." *Though how is that was going to work?* Could people on the mainland see him now that magic was returned? What she wouldn't give to go back and see all the people on the island who'd called her crazy.

"It is good to see you again." Shep gave the dragon a bow, and Draco nodded in return. They'd had a good relationship on Hawk's ship, though Ember suspected Draco opened a hole in Shep's heart. Another hole. There were so many.

Draco had grown so his nose just fit in both her hands. He would cut a fearsome form if you hadn't known him as a baby, chewing up placemats in her store. She wondered if the stories she'd read aloud had stayed with him—the far-off lands they had explored together in the pages of a book. The magic. The mystery. His eye twinkled. He would be no ordinary dragon. There were others out there.

You should stay close by, she practiced talking in her mind. *I don't know what they'll do on the mainland.*

Draco responded with a huff and an image of them shooting at him. Ember frowned.

"Please be careful," she said. She looked back at the city. "And don't eat the horses."

Draco lifted his head and snorted in laughter. It called the attention of a few townsfolk who began to wander over. Between their King lying in repose, a flying pirate ship, a dragon, and their return home, they were all dazed. Draco again smiled. Ember hugged the beast, though her arms barely reached around his neck.

"Let's show them what you can do," she said. She turned back to Shep, watching them from the shadows. His expression was unreadable, a fact that often drove her mad because she could read almost everyone. *Was he thinking of his daughter, or did he just need time alone?* She had learned to ask. It was the only way to get in his head.

Before she could, though, he broke out in a wide smile.

"Go," he said, gesturing to the dragon, who had lowered his neck so she could climb on. As Draco grew, it was becoming more difficult to mount him. They'd need to devise something, but for now, Shep cocked his head while she paused with her hand on his hide.

"Just be careful of the missiles and stuff."

Now he was teasing. Between her magic and Draco's, no missile would touch him. Shep took a step closer and touched her shin. "Be safe," he said. She frowned.

"I know," he continued, "safe is boring. But please, today, just be safe." He kissed her forehead.

"We'll be safe-ish," she replied. She needed to connect with her dragon, to sort things out. Shep had his own lessons to learn.

"Will you go find her?" she asked, referring to his daughter. "I could go with you."

His expression darkened—a curious reaction.

"I'm going to walk the city. Clear my head." He waved his hand toward Hawk's ship, anchored a foot above the plaza. Most of the crew had already come out and were mingling with the city.

"Maybe welcome our shipmates."

She eyed him, but there was no use arguing. "Okay."

She hugged him tightly, then climbed onto Draco—a sensation like going home. She buried her head in his back, feeling the warmth of his fur. Shep stepped back, watching them lift into the sky. Whatever was on his mind was lost in the sensation of flying.

True to her word, she was careful. Draco stayed near the city, never flying higher than the tallest tower of the castle. He circled, his curiosity nudging Ember. She wasn't keen on flying over those warships or tanks, which seemed to multiply by the minute. So many blue and red lights blanketed the horizon that she could barely see the little island she once called home. She had a strange homesick feeling for the bookstore and hoped she'd see it again someday.

"Let's give them a show." She patted Draco's back, who roared in approval. A cheer went up in the crowd. Ember leaned forward, letting go completely. Wind rushed past her face as she soared, laughing, alive, free.

CHAPTER 4

Shep left Ember with her dragon—their reunion both beautiful and painful. A reminder of all he'd lost.

He rubbed his chest where his heart would have once beat. What would his daughter say when she learned what he was? What would *any of them* say when they discovered the price he'd paid to bring their city home was his very soul? Could he face them?

He walked the once-familiar streets of Atlantis, keeping to the shadows. Every corner breathed a memory.

Shep passed the shop where his wife had once kept her apothecary. He'd loved her, then—or thought he had. She'd been wise beyond her years, mystical, beautiful. She died bringing his daughter into the world. Some things even magic couldn't fix.

The park where they'd met lay empty now, everyone gathered in the square. He sat on a swing and listened to the distant sound of celebration.

Above, Draco made circles in the night sky. Wind whispered through the trees. The swing creaked softly as Shep pushed himself with his toe.

Things were familiar yet unfamiliar—like walking through a memory. The air had changed from something light and airy to something damp and guttural. Paint peeled from houses. Fruit rotted in a gutter. Signs of neglect and sadness were everywhere.

He got up and moved on.

Shep had never been one for fortune-telling. The mages and the sorcerers saw what *could* happen, but he always believed it depended on choices—on the unpredictable nature of people. People surprised him all the time. Or they didn't.

He turned down what passed as an alley in the city, still wide and well-lit by bobbing lanterns even under the moonlight. A sign reading *Fortunes* blinked in red, a crystal ball glowing beneath it. He laughed—half at the appropriateness, half at the gaudiness.

He didn't remember the shop from before, though time had stolen so many things from him. On impulse, he drew the curtain back and stepped in.

He gripped the curtain in his fist, angry at himself for considering this unstable magic, but the feeling inside the shop was quite different from the outside. He stepped into a small sitting room, not unlike the back area of Ember's bookstore, with all its rugs and books. Two cushions framed a small, empty table.

Lamps, pillows, and blankets in every color covered the space. A fireplace glowed in a soft, low flame.

Shep smiled, remembering the first time he'd seen Draco in the bookstore. When he glanced toward the window, though, there was no chimney or smoke—only cold air pressing at the glass. He let go of the curtain and stepped fully inside.

"Hello?" His voice came out rough. He'd never gone to a fortune-teller on the island, and the last time he'd visited a mystic on the ground, well... he'd been turned to a vampire. His trust, understandably, was thin.

On the table, a tray appeared—a teapot and two cups, both steaming.

"I see you've finally made it."

A woman entered. She was one of those whose age was impossible to guess—anywhere from girl to young adult. Dark hair bound with a colorful headband, cheeks flushed pink, her eyes the color of the moon on a night like this.

He turned to leave.

"This is a mistake," he muttered.

She caught his arm. Her grip was firm.

"Stay a bit," she said. "I've been waiting for you."

I bet you have, Shep thought.

"Why are you still here?" he asked. "Why not in the square with everyone else?"

She sat cross-legged on a pillow, her skirt billowing softly. "I'm not so enamored of this world as most of them," she said. Her voice had an odd, lilting accent—curious for someone trapped here for so long.

Despite himself, Shep lowered onto the cushion across from her, waving off the tea.

"I've seen it all play out," she said as she sipped. "Long road for Atlantis, but they're tough people. They'll make it, all right.

Make some things better, some worse. That's the way of it, isn't it?"

She shrugged and produced a set of cards from the folds of her dress. At her gesture, Shep nodded for her to begin. She started to shuffle.

"I have my reservations too," he admitted. Now that Atlantis had landed, he wasn't sure what came next. Were they even safe?

Thinking of his daughter sent a sharp ache through the place where his heart had once beat.

The fortune-teller noticed. Her expression softened as the cards slowed in her hands.

"My name is Grace," she said. A card slipped free of the deck. She placed it facedown on the table. "And I am sorry for your pain."

Shep frowned. "You know nothing of my pain,"

He tried to make it sound flippant, but his voice cracked. He imagined his heart was splayed out for the world to see—cold and still.

She only nodded. "I have a gift," she said with a sad smile. "I can see people's hearts—their struggles, their pain. Once, I called it a curse. I fought it. I made terrible choices—ones that had repercussions."

Her gaze drifted to a shelf where there was a photo: a younger version of herself beside a girl in shadow. "Ones I cannot ever take back. But you—" she looked back at him, "—you think you've gone down that path, but you haven't. Not yet. You can still come back. There is penance for you. There is hope."

Shep balled his fist to still its tremor. He leaned in as she drew another card and set it beside the first.

"If I believe what you're saying, it's impossible," he said quietly. "My choices... are irreparable. Finite." He wavered. "Devastating."

He hadn't told anyone the whole story—not even Ember. Especially not her. He'd learned to deal with the hunger. He fed, not to kill. Yet sometimes, especially in the beginning...

Yes, he'd taken lives. Bad ones—thieves, robbers, and murderers. But weren't they entitled to the same mercy he sought? That made him a hypocrite at best. At worst, a murderer.

Grace smiled faintly, laying out a third card. "Nothing is finite in this world. I'd have thought you learned that by now."

She set the deck aside and sipped her tea, her silver-gray eyes never leaving him.

"And your choices?" he asked.

"Mine require penance as well," she said. "Why do you think you're here?"

He gave a short, incredulous laugh. A black cat slipped through the back room, cast him a disapproving glance, and vanished beneath a curtain without so much as a mew. He thought he saw the flutter of a wing.

"Okay," he said, bold now. "Since you know so much about me... tell me what your cards say."

Perhaps it was the act of confessing, or merely hinting at his secrets. Perhaps it was hope—the promise of absolution. Freedom.

Grace flipped the first card. "The past," she said, mouth wrinkled at the corners. She frowned. "Great sadness and loss." She looked up from the five cups depicted and scrutinized him. He felt that it wasn't the cards she was reading—it was him.

"You think you've made such grievous choices," she said, "but you've done them for love. That is what will save you."

Before he could answer, she laid the next card.

"Curious," she murmured at the picture of a man hanged by his feet. "Your situation is not as you think. You feel swallowed by this sadness... unable to move past it." Her gaze flicked to the figure on the card. "Perhaps you think you're unworthy, but there is more to your life than you think."

A breeze ruffled the scarf over her shoulder, though the room was still. She flipped the third card—the Wheel of Fortune.

"As I thought. A great destiny awaits you, Casius. Shepherd."

His eyes narrowed. In his experience with mystics, it wasn't worth asking how she knew him. She could have employed any number of tricks—but he knew magic when he felt it. This place was teeming with it. He leaned forward, tenting his hands.

"And just what does destiny have in store for me, Grace?"

She leaned back, her expression mixed. He glimpsed sadness for what he carried, hope for the future. Ember wasn't the only one who could read people. She smiled, though it didn't quite reach her eyes.

"Don't you know?" she said. "Destiny is whatever you make of it." She gathered the cards in one swoop. "Something tells me, Shepherd, that when the time comes, you will know what to make of it."

The sparkle returned in her eye—but in his mind, he saw the wheel of destiny turning. Many turns still lay ahead. *Hardships,* he guessed. More and more and more.

She stood and hesitated. "This... is not in the cards, but it's a feeling—and I've learned to trust such feelings."

She scooped up the cat that Shep hadn't noticed had returned. It regarded him with aloof green eyes, hinting at its own magic.

"There is love, too," she continued, "but like all such things, only if you accept it."

He tried to scoff, but he'd lived long enough to know the truth of that—and the difficulty. Reaching into his pocket, he drew some bills and coin that might be useful. "How much do I owe you?" he asked, thoughts lingering on love and destiny.

"'Tis I who owe you." She mimed a bow best she could, balancing the cat in her arms. It fluffed its fur in mild irritation. "We will see each other again. Soon, if I'm right."

He nodded curtly. He knew better than to argue with a mystic—he'd been with one. He paused, resting his hand on the curtain. "Do you know..." he began.

She laid a hand over his. The cat jumped out of her arms.

"She will forgive you, Shepherd," Grace said, "though it's not her forgiveness you seek. That heart of yours is deep enough for everyone else. Use it to forgive yourself, and you may find it beats again."

He sucked in a breath, but she only winked.

She let go of his arm, and in a flounce of skirts, disappeared in the back room. Only the cat remained at his feet. It mewed, though what that meant, Shep couldn't guess. He touched his chest. It was a metaphor, he was sure. His heart couldn't beat again—but what if...?

He briefly let himself get swept away by hope. Yet hope carried a powerful, and deadly current. If he did not navigate it correctly, he was as likely to drown as to live happily ever after.

And when had someone like him lived happily ever after?

He released the curtain with a shake. The mystic's shop vanished into the cold Atlantian night. Behind him, a plain storefront reappeared, a single light flickering above it. He wasn't surprised to see the cat follow him out. A mist had started to fall.

He turned on his heel and headed back to the square—and to Ember.

CHAPTER 5

Night rolled over Atlantis like a slow fog, and still neither side made a move.

Ember landed Draco near the steps of the palace without flourish, his claws striking the cobblestone once before he settled. Lanterns twinkled over the thinning line waiting to see the King. Though his body faded, the crowd lingered. The cheer and merriment Ember once associated with Atlantis was gone—replace by fear.

A little girl clung to her mother's skirt, staring wide-eyed at Hawk's ship, its shadow cutting across the plaza in the moonlight. The markets stood dark and shuttered. Somewhere far off, a siren wailed. Otherwise, a hush blanketed the crowd, even with the sight of the dragon.

Draco lowered his neck so Ember could climb off. He whined softly.

"It'll be okay," she whispered, though she didn't believe it.

He rolled to his side as a curious group approached. Across the square, another group gathered around Hawk's ship, anchored theatrically a foot above the ground. It was low enough for Ember to pull herself up.

Hawk's ship never ceased to amaze her. Magic hummed beneath her feet. The deck gleamed, spotless as ever, but the crew shuffled around aimlessly, murmuring to one another. *Fear*, she thought, *was contagious.*

Shep emerged from the residences and crossed the plaza, his head bowed, lost in thought. Lanternlights played over his dark hair in amber tones—perhaps that was magic too.

He spent so long chasing the dream of reuniting with his daughter, yet now that he was here, his heart was conflicted. Would his daughter accept him? Would she even know him? Dreams are one thing, but reality was often far different.

Near the ship, a man and a small child stood gazing up in awe. Shep smiled as he approached, pointing out her features, as if it were his own. In a way, it was. It belonged to all of them.

His smile faded as their conversation deepened. After a moment, he pressed a coin into the man's hand and nodded. Then he turned and approached the ship from the stern, climbing aboard.

"The mood in the city is curious," he said, putting an arm around Ember's shoulder. She leaned into him. His presence was the opposite energy as the city—warm, inviting, strong.

Hawk's stomach rumbled. He shared a look with Shep.

"Perhaps the morning will bring better tidings," he said, though his tone suggested he didn't believe it.

Dark clouds rolled in from the west. A storm was brewing—one they couldn't escape. Hawk's ship swayed in its bindings. His face had gone pale, and not just from the wind.

Ember glanced between the two men. Shep had reluctantly turned Hawk into a vampire after he'd been—*technically speaking*—killed by a hellhound. Shep pretended it didn't pain him, but it did. She knew he blamed himself, still searching for a cure. But Hawk? He was so new to this, she couldn't help but wonder—*how did they feed? how did they stay in such control?*

"The Queen will sort this all out." Sierra appeared from below decks, her gaze drifting toward the castle steps where the Queen had just been. Only a handful of lost Atlantians remained, murmuring as they waited to see their King, whose body had become little more than shadow. He'd passed to another realm—sacrificed for their return. *Cursed, perhaps.*

"Is she tired of the ground already?" Ember asked, watching Hawk battle with the rigging to keep the ship on the ground, while Paine secured the other anchor. They barely managed to get it down while the crew had warily joined the crowd in the city.

Hawk sighed and brushed his blond hair from his face. His patchy beard made him look younger. His face was pale, but his lips flushed red. "She does not seem to wish to be grounded," he said. He scanned the city. "I can say the same for us all."

His gaze met hers, the blue in his iris hinting of adventure ahead. "They're restless. They sense danger, though that should have passed. What is it about this place, Ember?"

He gripped the rail and looked out over the citizens who lingered below, keeping their distance. "This isn't at all how I pictured the city's return," he murmured. "I hesitate to even set foot on the ground. Something does not feel right."

Ember followed his gaze from the castle, only the top windows catching the golden sunset, down the rolling hills to the markets, and finally to a sliver of sea where flashing lights dotted the waves.

"I feel it, too," Ember said, turning back to Hawk. "I thought it was Shep's unfinished business, but..." She caught sight of the Queen on the castle balcony. Aura quickly turned and went back inside. "Perhaps it will ease when the King is gone. His disappearance is an ill omen."

"More than that, I think—" Hawk said, but Sierra interrupted.

"Hungry?" she asked, tossing Ember an apple that she dropped on the ship's deck. Paine picked it up.

"She's tied down as best she can, Captain," she said, taking a bite, "but she's not still."

The ship rocked, though there was no wind. A whistle cut through the air, followed by a flash of light that illuminated fear on Paine's face. The streak shot across the sky, followed by dozens more. A loud alarm blared. *Something had breached the city's magic defenses.*

"Take cover!" Hawk yelled as missiles rained down. Panic swept the square. One scream became many, and people ran through the streets, dodging the assault. Bombs exploded on impact, some hitting the square. One struck the ropes holding the ship, and it listed sharply to the right.

Ember had a moment to decide. Shep reached for her, and she jumped, landing beside him in the square. He untied the ship to give Paine, Hawk, and Sierra a chance. Hawk flew it off into the night before she could even wave goodbye. Draco took flight. *One dragon against so many enemies?* Ember urged him away from the battle, and the dragon turned to follow Hawk's ship with a mighty roar.

The assault continued, tearing through the city. Some struck the castle, rocking its very walls. Shep pulled her along, dodging debris and fire.

"Not the castle," he yelled over the screams. His eyes scanned the square, then met hers. "As far outside the main city as we can. Hurry."

But Ember didn't hurry.

"Your daughter," she reminded him, tugging his hand back.

"I don't even know if she's alive, Ember," he said as a missile hit the spot where the ship had been moored, throwing debris and smoke into the air. "But we are, at least for now. Hurry!"

He guided her through the twists and turns of the city as if he'd never forgotten its layout. The assault was lighter here, but it was still dangerous. Atlantians cried in the street. Many glanced at Ember and Shep as they ran past, as if they were responsible—and they were. *Heavens, they were.*

"We never should have—"

"Not now..." He slowed, eyeing a curious mystic shop. A sign with a glowing orb read *Fortunes*. A soft chant floated from behind the curtain, and the smell of jasmine wafted out. *So inviting... almost forgot the carnage...*

Until a scream tore through the air. Shep looked up the street to the fields, where small fires had broken out, back to the shop.

"There is something about this place," he said, apology in his eyes. "I cannot explain it, but I think this is where we should go."

She took a deep breath. Hiding in a burning field wasn't her idea of safe, but this building seemed so... exposed. The noise of the city felt muted, as if they were in a bubble. *Yes, she felt it. But did she trust it?*

"You've been here?" she asked.

"Yes," he said simply. But it wasn't assurance she read on his face. She saw fear instead—not of the attack, but something else, something deeper.

"I trust you," she said, though inwardly she felt the bubble around them starting to implode. They needed safety, and quick.

He shook his head. "I'm not sure you should," he said, but he stepped toward the building, and the curtain parted for them. "I am no angel, Ember..."

She took the first step in—and only just in time. A building crumbled next to them. "I'll take my chances," she said, stepping across the threshold to a different time and place entirely.

CHAPTER 6

Ember could live to be a thousand, and still be amazed by magic. Perhaps it was because she'd grown up without it—seeing a magic dragon when no one else could. Or maybe it was the imagination in her—but this... what she stepped into was beyond anything she'd ever seen.

The door was no ordinary door. It was a portal. She'd stepped through them before and felt the same dizziness then push as she emerged through a fog. A light mist hung around them. A silver moon lit their path through the dark. Slick grass covered the hill beneath their feet.

Shep stumbled as he emerged. The sounds of the battle faded, replaced by chirps and sighs of a soft wood.

"I know this place," he said, turning in a circle. The doorway was still there. They were not cut off.

"What the hell?" Ember said, tugging his hand. Their friends were still in danger. The whole city was. "We have to go back," she said, though the faint smell of a deep, wet wood tempted her to stay.

"Why?" Shep asked, his eyes narrowing on a little trail that ended in a cottage. Lights glowed from within, smoke trailing lazily from the chimney. The woods pressed in—dark and deep, but not threatening. Magic hummed in the very trees, as if it had been born there.

"I've sought this place for lifetimes," he said, balling his fists. "Why here? Why now?"

She'd never seen the look on his face—anger and fear intertwined.

"Is it an illusion?" she asked, reaching to touch the pine. It felt real—from the slight prick of the needles to the cool dew clinging to her fingers. She rubbed a needle anxiously between her thumb and forefinger, glancing back through the portal. In her experience, it wouldn't close—but she wasn't willing to take the risk. Her friends were back there. Her dragon was back there.

"Shep..." she cautioned, but the same magic that pulled him forward tugged at her, too. She could feel it. There was something here. Magic could be fun and spontaneous, but it was also in tune with the turning of the world. It wouldn't have opened this door without reason. Maybe there was something that could help Atlantis. Stop the attack. Broker peace. A long shot for sure, but she'd faced longer.

A tear slid down his cheek. She brushed it away with her thumb. "What is this place?" she asked. A bird called in the distance. The breeze whispered through the leaves.

He turned to her. "Mirabal—the witch who turned me. This is her cottage. The place I sought for lifetimes." His gaze lingered on the cottage, filled with longing. His next words were so soft they were almost lost. "Perhaps there is a cure. A reversal. For Hawk, at least…"

Ember took his hand, cold against her skin. She'd seen how the decision to turn Hawk haunted him. Hawk had been technically dead—and if Shep hadn't intervened—their captain would have been lost. Even so, there were days she knew Shep would have preferred death to this fate. But they were here now. Atlantis had returned. His daughter was near. The details of all those things were complicated at best.

Ember swallowed. She felt the pull of Draco behind them, the echo of his bond pressing at the edges of her mind, but the portal still shone onto the street in Atlantis. It would wait.

"Then we should see," she said. She tucked a strand of her dark hair behind her ear and squeezed his hand. Lifetimes ago, Shep had found dark magic in this cottage. It extended his life and allowed him to find and return Atlantis. It had given him the possibility of seeing his daughter again—but he'd paid dearly for it. The witch's "gift" had turned him into something else—something that fed on blood.

Vampire, she corrected herself. She hated the word. It brought up scenes of pop culture, both sparkly and terrifying. The truth was more morally gray, and less sparkling.

"Yes," he said, but he hesitated.

She took the first step down the dirt path. There were well worn wagon ruts with weeds popping up. The road didn't look well-traveled—but it had been traveled. This place connected to somewhere real, though there was no way to know where.

She only knew it was night, though even that could have been an illusion. Overhead, clouds rolled past the stars and moon, casting an eerie glow, but the cottage lights still shone to guide them.

As they drew closer, the sound of humming drifted towards them. Shep was startled by a black cat that darted out with an indignant meow. He watched it disappear back toward the portal with a "hmph." The cat was the least of Ember's concerns.

An older woman sat on the porch. Though pull of magic was unmistakable, the only thing she held were knitting needles and the beginnings of a scarf.

"Harder than it looks without magic," she said as they approached. She was a middle-aged woman closing in on old. The black in her hair was whiter, and lines had formed on her face, but her blue eyes still twinkled. She set the knitting aside and stood.

"It's been a long time," she said to Shep.

He clenched his jaw. "Remove this curse."

She shook her head. "You begged me," she reminded him. Somewhere in the woods, a wolf howled, and Mirabal's gaze flickered toward the trees. "We haven't much time."

She took a step toward the cottage but pinned Shep with a stare. "You can waste that time being angry or you can come in and figure out how to save Atlantis. My daughter brought you here, but we don't have much time."

"Grace," he said, his features finally relaxing. "Of course."

Ember glanced between them, confusion etching her brow. "Grace?"

He offered a half smile. "I met her when I walked Atlantis. There was a shop I didn't recognize…"

Mirabal ushered them in as the wolf howled again—closer this time. Ember cast one last look at the portal. Was that fire she saw on the other side? Mirabal was right. They didn't have much time.

Shep closed the door behind them as Mirabal moved slowly to the hearth, stirring something that smelled deep and tangy. The wooden table beside her was cluttered with books, papers, and jars. Across the cabin was a small sitting area and cot decorated with pillows and blankets. Light bobbed from above in a muted yellow. A fire roared in the hearth. The warmth spread to Ember's bones, making her tired.

Mirabal sank into a cushioned chair between the kitchen and living area. "I've found something that will sustain me—something other than blood." Her tone was weary but proud. "But it comes at a cost." She gestured down at her aged body.

"I'll pay it," Shep said quietly.

Ember moved deeper into the cottage. Magic hummed through the air—alive and curious. Every surface seemed to sparkle with potential, from the sleeping nook buried under a stack of books and blankets to the kitchen where the cupboards and tables were filled with jars and spells. She picked one up and held it to the light. Black stones sparkled like captured starlight.

"Take one," Mirabal offered. "It will shine in the darkness."

Despite herself, Ember opened the jar and held it between her fingers while they spoke.

"There is a cure?" Shep pressed.

Mirabal laughed—a dry, knowing sound. "A cure? No. Maybe. Perhaps. The cure, they say, lies in the merging of both worlds—in harmony, in balance. If you can achieve that, you're more powerful than I imagined." She tilted her head. "I saw it in you that day you came here. And still, maybe..." She let the words drift away.

Ember felt the tug of her dragon. "Shep, we need to go back..." she urged.

He nodded but sank to one knee before Mirabal—the same way he had when he first begged her for extended life. Ember's heart tightened. *What would he be willing to give up now?* "What it will take to sustain me, I will take that," he told her, clasping Mirabal's hand. "But that is not why I am here. That is not the path meant for me, is it?"

The black cat slipped through a side door and wound itself around Ember's legs. She bent to pick it up, its soft purr vibrating against her arm. It wasn't like Shep to be so open. *He used to tell her they decided their own fate.* But destiny—destiny was something different entirely.

Mirabal squeezed his hand. "It is a possibility, yes. But one that fades with each passing day." Still, her eyes were sharp. "Bringing the world into alignment is no small fate."

She struggled to get up and walked to her cupboards, shuffling jars. Ember tapped her foot, still holding the cat, its tail brushing against her arm.

Mirabal turned, holding two small jars. "The sustenance is no secret," she said. "A small red seed that grows in the deep woods, mixed with certain spices." She handed him the first.

"That's all?" he asked.

She shrugged. "Magic can be simple," she said.

She lifted the second jar, unscrewed the lid, and drew out a single small, precious stone. It was as white as the stone in Ember's pocket was dark.

"It's not great magic, this stone," Mirabal said. "But it will shine when you are on the right path. Attached to the lightness." She pressed it into his palm. "For when you question your way. I have nothing else to give you," she said softly. "Except advice."

Her tone deepened, the words pulling weight. "Not everyone can bear a fate this heavy. Try not to think of it every waking moment. Try not to let it crush you. You are only a man, Shep—and even now, there are moments to savor. To laugh. To feel joy. Even after all you've taken on, all you've lost."

She touched his cheek gently. "There is your daughter," she said, meeting his eyes so intimately Ember looked away. "But there is also love. Do not lose sight of that."

When her hand fell, Shep brushed away a tear.

Mirabal turned to Ember. "You are exactly as I imagined you."

Ember cleared her throat, unsure what to say. "I'm just an orphaned bookseller from a small island," she joked. "Mostly along for the ride."

Mirabal smiled, eyes crinkling. "You are much more than that—and you know it, deep down." She pulled Ember into a hug. Up close, Ember recognized the bitter scent of the seeds. She'd seen them before.

"This will not be our last meeting," Mirabal said, "but time grows short. Good luck—and run. The wolves are close."

The cat leapt from Ember's arm as she raised an eyebrow as Shep. He cracked the door open peering into the dark.

"Run?" he asked.

"Run," she confirmed.

Ember caught one last glimpse of the cottage—the flicker of firelight, the smell of fruit and spice, the echo of something she didn't yet understand—and then Shep pulled into the night. The wolves already howling.

CHAPTER 7

Ember didn't look back as the wolves nipped at her heels, nor did she bother to turn when she and Shep jumped through the portal. Something told her they couldn't follow. There was enough to deal with on this side.

The smell of the wood faded, replaced by the sharp sting of smoke. The shop they stepped into was empty, as if nothing at all had been there.

"Hmm." Shep turned as the portal flickered out. "It was her daughter I met here. Grace." He ran his hand along the wall, as if to convince himself it was real. A piece of paint flicked off.

Night pressed against the windows. Moonlight washed the room in a pale glow, giving everything an eerie, abandoned feel. The whole city felt silent and hollow. Ember strained though the door and listened. Nothing. When she reached out to Draco, she felt only peace.

She leaned out the doorway. "It's quiet," she whispered. Other storefronts were dark and no one was about. Smoke curled through the streets, empty and ominous.

Shep wrung his hands. "The attack is over," he guessed, though his frown deepened. "Let's hope the damage is minimal."

"The damage has just begun." Ember fell in step beside him. She'd never paid much attention to politics—one ruler was usually as good or bad as the next—but she couldn't help wondering who would greet a magical city that had dropped out of the sky.

"We must get to the Queen," he said. "Send an envoy. Broker peace."

Ember pressed her lips together. He really hadn't been paying attention, had he? What envoy could fix *this*? Yet, she had no better plan. She took his hand anyway and let the contact steady her.

The city was too quiet. It felt as if everyone held a collective breath. *Sleeping*, maybe, though there was no way she would be sleeping under such circumstances. As they neared the larger homes closer to the castle, the hush only deepened.

Ember's pulse quickened. She reached out to Draco and felt his heartbeat, but no response.

"Something's wrong." She let go of Shep and wiped her palm on her pants.

He only nodded. The look on his face told her everything she needed to know. Something wasn't just wrong.

It was worse.

They approached the square and stopped short. Atlantians splayed out across the courtyard. For one terrible moment, Ember thought they were dead.

Shep knelt beside a woman, found her pulse, then looked up. "She's sleeping." His gaze cut toward the castle.

Hawk's ship was gone. and Ember took a small comfort in that—her friends had taken flight, and Draco with them. Still, the sight before her twisted in her chest. Dozens of citizens scattered across the moonlit stone—men and women in wide shirts and flowing pants, the familiar Atlantis attire. Ember glanced down at her own leggings and a t-shirt and felt that old sting of not belonging She'd been out of place her whole life.

"Maybe now your Queen will surrender."

The silence was so absolute that the voice carried clearly... along with the sharp click of boots approaching.

Shep stood guard, but what did they have to fight with? Atlantis didn't look like a well- armed city. Shame on them for returning the city so ill prepared.

A woman approached them from the far side of the city. She sidestepped the bodies in her brown boots, her skirt swishing around her. She was young, Ember guessed, no older than them—though magic could be deceiving. Her dark hair was held back by a headband. Ember's eyes swept over the young woman's features—the tilt of her head, the wide eyes that seemed to reflect the moonlight—an old habit of cataloging strangers running through her mind. There was something vaguely familia about her, a hint of the woman they had visited in the woods, though Ember couldn't place why.

"What do you have to do with this?" Shep asked, confusion in his voice.

"A question for a question." The woman stopped far enough away that no fists could fly. "How did you avoid the sleeping spell?"

Ember glanced between them. "You know each other?" she asked, a cold breeze cutting across the city. It was winter in Maine, after all. She shivered.

"Grace." He risked a look at Ember, silently begging her not to ask too many questions. "The fortune teller."

"Oh." Ember said nothing. The daughter of the mystic. She wondered how Shep would handle this revelation.

"As to your question..." He took a step toward Grace. "We were indoors. Protected, perhaps?"

Grace tipped her head back and laughed. "That's not how magic works," she said. "But it's okay. You keep your secrets, and I'll keep mine. As to your question—I made a deal, and you're damned lucky I did. They were going to annihilate the place. I know Atlantis' magic is strong, but it would have fallen eventually, and all these people you're looking at wouldn't just be sleeping."

Ember looked around her, thinking of Shep's daughter. "I..." A lump caught in her throat.

"I think 'thank you' is the phrase you're looking for," Grace said. Ember noticed she carried a firearm unlike anything she had seen before.

"It's not," Shep said. "Wake them up."

Grace again laughed. "I don't think you understand how this game is played." She aimed the weapon at him, and a red light pulsing from its tip. "Take me to the Queen. She's the only one who can sort this out."

Ember finally unfroze, stepping between Shep and the weapon—much to his annoyance.

"What makes you think we know where she is?" she asked. Grace eyed her up and down.

"She better not have been on that pirate ship. We shot them down over the ocean. There's a rescue operation going on, but..." She shrugged, watching Ember carefully.

It was a game, all right. Perhaps they'd been shot down. Perhaps not. She couldn't react.

"I sincerely hope that's not true," Shep said, ice in his voice. "As for the Queen, I'd check the castle."

Grace blew a curl out of her face. "As you know..." She turned to Ember. "The castle is the most protected. A pillar in space and time. I doubt I could get in. They could bomb this whole place to the ground, and it would still stand." She flicked a glance at Shep. "I hope they don't though. Believe it or not, I'm on your side. I'm here for other people. Just help me find the Queen—and give her a message."

"And then you'll wake them up?" Ember asked, her mind still on her friends. She tried to look at the sky, but all she saw were stars and clouds. Draco was far enough away their connection was dim, but still there.

Grace sighed. "I am bound by oaths you know nothing of," she said, her voice heavy. "But I will do my best."

"Your best?" Shep repeated. Ember tugged his arm.

"What else are we supposed to do?" Ember asked. Could her magic wake them, she wondered. She couldn't risk it now. God only knew what that weapon was.

Shep set his jaw. Ember saw the fight in him. The defeat.

"The castle, then," he said. "But not with that." He gestured to the gun.

"This?" She waved it, pointed it at the sky. It made a comical *pow* noise and lit up. "A prop. They got it at the dollar store."

Ember rolled her eyes. Magic was the weapon—magic and strategy. They could attack this woman, and then what?

"Clever," she said, sarcasm threading her voice.

"Go," Grace responded. "The sooner we sort this out, the sooner I can go home."

Ember weaved through the sleeping bodies, taking care not to step on any. She followed Shep to the steps of the castle where more citizens strewn about. She wondered where home was for Grace. Was it here, in Atlantis? Did she want Atlantis returned to the sky? Or was it back in the woods with her mother?

She looked back at Shep, pale in the moonlight. Could there really be a cure? It plagued him, she knew, especially since he was forced to turn Hawk. She swallowed. Would she know if he were dead? Paine? Sierra? No. She decided Grace was bluffing. Ember might not know where the girl's home was—or even if she had one—but she knew what it was like to long for a place to belong. Loneliness drove people to do terrible things.

The steps were slick with dew. So much had happened since she first spied the Queen. When she was in the Shadow Realm with Sierra, she'd gotten her sister back. They'd returned Atlantis—but at what cost?

CHAPTER 8

Inside the great hall, Javiar shifted the curtain to peer out the vast windows. Little light remained. The sun had gone down, and the moon cast only shadows, which were picked up by the lights flickering in the hall. It gave the room a sickly, uneasy feel—or perhaps that was from the remains of the King's body, which had lain in state until it disappeared—a complication the Queen wasn't expecting.

"My lady, they approach the castle." He let the curtain fall. Except for Aurelia, Javiar was the only one left in the castle with the Queen. *It was brilliant,* the Queen thought, *the way they had gotten everyone outside to cast their sleeping spell.* The castle would have protected them—but then what? They were still stuck.

The Queen had seen it already, both in her mind and out the window. She sometimes knew things before they happened. She could sense people's moods, their feelings. It was the only thing that had kept her alive during King Corin's worst days. She had not seen this, though. Somehow, the girl—Ember—and Shepherd had avoided the spell.

She looked at Aurelia, who yawned. The Queen had kept the truth of her parentage for so long. Aurelia knew her as a foster mother, and as of her father? She probably assumed it was the King. Lies upon lies.

The girl had known nothing but life in the sky. What would she think of this world, with only rumors and fear, attacks, and sleeping spells? There was so much the Queen had missed on the ground—the mountains, the oceans, birds, butterflies, the people—all of them. The good and the bad. No, she had made the right decision to return, or rather the decision had made itself. All they could do was move forward.

"It's that man again." Aurelia looked over Javiar's shoulder, her cheeks flushed. "The one that was in the Guard. And the dark-haired woman with him. And...someone else."

The Queen's ears perked up. "Someone else?" She crossed to the small window, peering down at Shep and Ember climbing the steps below. A woman followed them. "I've never seen her before," the Queen said.

"*An outsider?*" Javiar frowned. An outsider who cursed her city and put them to sleep? They were at her mercy, and that was not a place the Queen liked to be.

"I wonder what she wants," the Queen said, her voice tight. Perhaps it was a good thing they sent a woman—maybe things had changed in the centuries? But the look on the stranger's face was anything but welcoming. From what the Queen sensed on the ground, magic had left the world like a dying breath when Atlantis rose. No, they would not be happy to return it back. They would be afraid.

She smoothed down her dress and clipped back the sides of her blonde hair. She couldn't meet them with anger or aggression, though she had every right to. That had been the King's way, and it had got them banished to the sky. No, she would have to rely on kindness. Diplomacy. Strength.

"Aurelia, I need you to wait in my rooms," she said. The girl's mouth opened her mouth to argue, but now was not the time for family reunions. "*Please.*"

Aurelia shot her a sharp look. "I think we're well beyond worrying about my safety." She crossed her arms, but the Queen could not relent. The girl had grown up part of the royal family, yet she did not know her full story. And Aura was afraid that Shep would look at his daughter and know.

"I promise I will explain it later," she said.

The trio reached the great doors and rapped three times.

"I've heard that before," Aurelia muttered. She moved slowly across the hall, her dress trailing. The Queen watched her carefully. Aurelia had known she was orphaned, but never why. There was more to the story than anyone else knew. Her mother was more than a close friend—she was family. Aurelia was next in line for the crown. Aura had tried to shield the girl from the burden of that knowledge. A burden so heavy it had destroyed the King, but Aurelia had been raised to be kind and empathic, strong but empathetic. Maybe she was that way before the lessons of blood and lineage. Her mother had been, and her father too.

A voice called from behind the wooden doors. Entry was impossible—not just iron bars made sure of that. Still the Queen couldn't let her city slumber while she hid in the castle. She smoothed her dress down and exchanged a look with Javiar. Hiding had been her husband's way. Not hers.

"Let them in," she said. Javiar pursed his lips, silently dissenting, but he obeyed.

The room was wide and empty, a hall once used for dinners and balls. The thrones were in another room, so she couldn't meet them from a place of power. She'd have to settle for honesty. Peace.

"Your highness."

Shep nodded as Javiar opened the vast doors, letting Ember step inside, then the stranger behind them. Ember moved cautiously, as her sister might have, her eyes scanning the hall with wariness. The woman behind her, though—curly hair pulled back with a long skirt and tall boots—walked in as if she owned the place. No hesitation. No caution. And yet, she looked familiar.

"We have some unfortunate news from the city," Shep said, gesturing back, but Javiar was already closing the door.

"They're asleep," Ember added.

"I see," the Queen responded. "I assume there is a reason for this? A power play?" She studied the newcomer, who smiled in a way that reminded her of a snake—a slow, deliberate curl of the lips.

"That's a good guess," the woman said, "though I am only the messenger. I go by Grace, Your Highness." She mimicked a curtsey.

"Grace," the Queen acknowledged, searching her memory for anyone like this woman in her city. "What demands have you?"

"Demand is such an ugly word." Grace ran her hand over the back of a chair. "There are many who have been waiting for your return. Calling you." She looked to Shep, then Ember. "We owe you a debt of gratitude."

Ember rolled her eyes. "Right," she said. "Waiting... so you could bomb them and destroy them?"

Grace shook her head, curls bouncing. "That's not us. In fact, we want to team up. Atlantis didn't have the only magic left in the world. It's just been well hidden. Waiting for a beacon, you might say."

Ember felt the roar of her dragon flying further away, and urged him to stay safe and hidden. To take care of the others.

"Tell me more," the Queen said.

"We hadn't the magic to change the world alone. Not even to improve it, only in small bits and pieces. To save people." Grace's eyes flitted to Shep. "But it cost us greatly. We were hunted. Killed. Burned on pyres. Stoned. Chased by Zyah—yes—but the rest of the world shunned us, too. Your friend Hawk saved many, but the rest of us went underground."

The Queen paled, almost the color of her dress. "I had no idea," she whispered. Javiar rested a hand on her shoulder.

"No, you wouldn't, would you?" The girl tipped her head, gray eyes twinkling. "You left," she accused. "But those of us who remained were called witches. Not so much these days," she added, gazing wistfully out the window, "but times have a way of coming and going. The mob will be back again, unless we can stop them."

"What would you have me do?" the Queen asked. "Wake my city. We will defend you."

Grace laughed, twirling a curl between her fingers. "If only it were that easy. I come with a message, is all. I have a gift—finding portals, traveling them. Jumping places, even times." Her expression fell for a moment. "Different universes sometimes. Frightening ones." She replaced the mask on her face. "Even more frightening than here. There is someone who can help us. Who's been waiting..."

Shep stepped between them. "We will not meet this person until the city of Atlantis is awake again."

Ember held him back. "Listen to her."

The Queen studied Grace, so assured, yet clearly afraid. She wondered of what. "Who is this person?" she asked. She suffered the same insecurities but hid them better—she hoped. There was only one she knew that was that powerful.

"Better if you come with me." Grace turned, moving toward the great doors behind her. There was no portal here, only the hushed, sleepy breath of the city. But somewhere beyond, a portal waited—vast, unknown, and pulsing with power.

CHAPTER 9

Aurelia had never been the kind of girl to wait in the wings, especially not now. Her heart raced as she watched the trio approach from the upper balconies. She and the Queen had played a game where the Queen pretended not to know what Aurelia was up to. Or maybe she truly didn't. She certainly didn't know half the things Aurelia had done.

It wasn't entirely her fault. The Queen was taken with the King. Everyone had been. His tyranny was far and wide.

Aurelia herself had almost been caught conspiring against the empire more than once. Those weren't the only times she skirted disaster. She was popular with the King's Guard.

She leaned in, thankful for the protection of the shadows. The trio moved further into the hall, speaking in low voices. Each radiated strong magic. Aurelia recognized Grace immediately, though not the reason she was here. Grace tipped her head if she was aware she was being watched. Aurelia shrunk back.

Grace.

Aurelia had met her on the edge of the world—their world, anyway. Atlantis was an island, and when it rose, natural buffers—walls in many places—remained, though some crumbled. The back stables had no protection at all. Aurelia had seen the Queen there often, but it was too guarded to go on her own. Aurelia had found other ways and other places.

The city had grown in a tangled series, maze-like, winding. The other edges of the city were streets that tapered off. Empty lots. Hills. Brush. Aurelia smiled at the memory. She'd memorized them all. Like the Queen, she'd tried to jump off the island—only to find herself bounced back. It was one of those times she'd found Grace.

An unfamiliar face in this place was quite a shock. Especially one balancing along the top of the crumbling wall while Aurelia leaned forward, craning her neck to catch a glance at anything. The land. The ocean. The world. But what she'd really been searching for was herself.

"Don't do it!" Grace called out, though a wide smile brightened her face. Her curly black hair was held back by a band—just as it was now. Aurelia had looked up with tears streaking her cheeks, and somehow the girl had drawn a smile out of the darkest of corners. She'd seen her face before, but she'd thought it was a dream.

"And why not?" Aurelia wiped her tears with the corner of her dress, which turned grungy from climbing. "We're stuck here." She motioned around to a brambling field, empty of even animals. It had been as close to autumn as Atlantis ever came. it wasn't like the seasons turned here, but some of the leaves had a yellowish tint.

"Because you'll just end up in the same place," Grace said. She hopped down beside her, shirts flowing around her like a waterfall. "Change isn't as easy as just jumping." She snuck a look at Aurelia. "Preparations must be made."

Aurelia smiled despite herself. "You've tried it?" She searched Grace's gray eyes for a hint of the sadness she found in her own heart, but found none.

"In a manner of speaking," she answered, rummaging through a saddle bag that had been slung over her shoulder and produced, to Aurelia's surprise, a cloth bag of the biggest, juiciest strawberries she'd ever seen.

"Magic?" Aurelia guessed. They could grow almost anything the city could remember, though those memories were beginning to blur as the years passed. She took a strawberry and pressed it between her fingers. Plump and juicy. She took a bite.

"Of a sort." Grace smiled again and ate her own. Her gaze drifted over the edge of the island.

"You're very good at answering questions with questions," Aurelia said. She wiped her palm on her skirt. The stain was still there to this day. "Why haven't I seen you before?" She wasn't as surprised as she could have been. She knew magic could do all kinds of things. It could project into dreams. Change people's looks. Mask their true identity or intention. Surely this girl didn't have natural eyes the color of the full moon. It could be her mother in disguise, but Aurelia doubted it.

"I haven't made myself seen," Grace said. "See you around, Aurelia."

She got to her feet and dramatically took a swan dive off the side. Aurelia didn't panic. Not really. She'd done it herself. The first time was quite dramatic. After that, the sensation was more nausea inducing but less intense. She'd find herself right back on the wall.

She sat and waited for Grace to reappear.

But she didn't.

And Aurelia was left with a single question echoing through her mind.

How had Grace known her name?

CHAPTER 10

Only Ember and the Queen followed Grace to negotiate with whoever put the city to sleep. Aura wanted someone to stay back and watch over her city, and it made no sense for them all to walk into what could be a trap. Javiar argued loudly that it made no sense for *any* of them to walk into it, but the Queen held fast. And she was brave. Ember had watched her from the shadows long enough to know that.

Ember herself had little to offer. What did she know of magical cities and sleeping spells? Even the politics of her own world were foreign to her, though she was able to add enough to be useful. Would they be meeting the president, she wondered? The Pope? *Who was even in charge of all this?*

"A dagger in the boot." Shep tried to outfit her, but Grace stepped between them.

"No weapons," she said, lifting her shoulders in a dismissive shrug. "Not that they would work. Just take my word. She'll be okay."

Shep grit his teeth. "Tell us where this leads."

Grace waited by the door. "Not my story to tell," she said. Her gaze studied the wide room, stopping on the upper balcony. "I'm just the messenger," she said softly. "We're all pawns in the end, aren't we?"

"I am no pawn." The Queen drew herself to her full height. She carried no blade, but her mind was sharper than any Ember had seen. Whether that would help them was another matter entirely.

Ember looked at Shep. "Pawns?" Her smile was small but real. It had been a hard road, but every step had led them here. They had returned Atlantis.

"Or fate," he said. He tried to smile and pulled her in for a quick kiss. They had laughed at fate before. Ember didn't believe she was *chosen,* but she did have magic in her. For the most part, it had only made her life complicated, but now her future felt nothing like her past. Doors were opening that she had no idea existed. *What would come of this magic*, she wondered. She flexed her fingers.

"And Draco?" she asked Grace as she drew back. She felt him pushing at the edges of her consciousness, restless and impatient.

"He'll have to wait," Grace said, her back to them. The dragon wouldn't like it, but he'd survive.

"Let's get this over with." She released Shep's hand, fully expecting to see him soon.

"Take care of my city," the Queen said.

Javiar nodded. "We will do the best we can."

Grace's gaze swept the room once more before she turned. "As you say, let's get this over with." The scene beyond the wide door was no less jarring. The moon hung high, casting enough light to see half the city asleep on the stairs. It looked like a massacre, unless you bent close enough to see their chests rise and fall slowly.

"Sweet dreams, my city." The Queen bent to brush the hair back off a young woman. "What magic can enchant an already enchanted island?" she asked.

Ember held a breath. She'd felt the pull of Atlantis when they returned, but this was different. It wasn't magic that she felt—but something equally as powerful. A force. Something fought, and that something put the island to sleep.

"Come." Ember led the Queen toward where Grace threaded through the silent crowd. She had little time to study the Queen, but she remembered what Sierra had said: Aura was strong, but frightened. Ember saw no fear at the moment. The Queen moved with pensive determination. Sad, if she had to guess. She had just lost her husband.

"What was it like?" Ember asked softly, "In the sky."

Aura stepped over a cobblestone as they walked toward what were once the gates of the city. "Costly," she said with a faint smile. Then she asked, "What was it like on the ground? What am I walking into? This world, Ember—has it lost its soul?"

Ember considered. She had always felt her home island had a heartbeat. She'd felt it on the mainland, too. It wasn't magic, exactly. It certainly wasn't even wholly goodness. She'd seen her share of anger, meanness, and heartbreak. "It's complicated," she said at last. The Queen nodded as if she understood.

The gates still stood, undisturbed by time but slightly disturbed by their descent and landing. They were permanently cracked open. Grace could just slip through. She was shaded in blues and reds from faraway sirens. Spotlights glinted across the field beyond, but they didn't touch the city. When Grace slipped through the doors, she vanished.

Ember sighed. "A portal?" Her stomach flipped.

Aura pressed her lips together. "We have little choice."

She went first, her boots disappearing into a shimmer. Ember looked around—the emergency vehicles far off, the helicopters in the sky. It smelled like gunpowder and aggression. She could feel the weapons poised against them and decided to take her chances. She held her breath and stepped... into the same scene, yet from a distant angle. They dropped right into the army's encampment.

"What the hell?" She stumbled over a tree root. Flashes of reds and blues blinded her. Radios crackled, people shouted. She wrapped her arms around herself, feeling exposed in only her leggings and shirt. The Queen seemed even more vulnerable, thought at least dressed with more poise. Grace moved through the chaos like she belonged there, though attention followed her every step.

Ember spared a glance at Atlantis. She'd taken to thinking of it as her city. She'd walked its streets enough to know the basics of its layout. From the sky, it had seemed magical but faraway. Here, it commanded attention. Its walls were vast, impenetrable. Castle spires pierced the night sky, lit by an internal yellow glow, almost as if the city had a soul. Pride swelled in Ember's heart—until the Queen pulled her along.

"She is mighty." The light reflected in Aura's blue eyes. Ember couldn't guess what the Queen was thinking, but her own heart carried fear. Aura shifted her gaze to Ember. "But she will have to wait," she said.

The camp was settling around them in uneasy ripples. Whispers. Points. Angered glances.

"*Your Highness*," someone snickered.

The Queen had no crown, yet she carried herself with a presence that needed none. Ember wanted to punch him for his scorn, but the Queen carried her head high and followed Grace to a wide tent in the middle of the encampment.

"A tent?" Ember asked, raising an eyebrow.

Grace turned back. "Your arrival has put a lot of things out of whack."

She held a flap open. The material was sturdy. Ember felt the energy shift immediately. Not a portal. Some sort of deeper magic, and not the good kind.

Behind her was the modern world, buzzing and electric. But inside the tent Ember glimpsed a roaring fire, impossible in its warmth and color.

The Queen paled.

"How is this possible?" She stepped lightly past Grace into what had become a giant room, with guards stationed around two chairs at the front. A great fire roared in the corner, and what Ember could only describe as courtesans of old lounged between carpets and couches.

"What is this?" Ember asked. Heat gathered at her temples and sweat trickled down her back.

"The most basic explanation is that magic is balanced on the head of a pin, and you've tipped that pin." Grace glanced over her shoulder and smiled at Ember. "Not that it's a bad thing, but like I said—everything is out of whack. Space and time itself, even. This..." She raised a hand. Somewhere an animal growled and the hair on the back of Ember's neck rose. "This doesn't even exist right now."

She threaded them through the crowd, which was less menacing than the one outside, but just as skeptical.

"So this is from a long time ago?" Ember asked, bumping into a woman with a powdered face, holding a fan. The woman blew her a kiss.

The Queen answered before Grace could. She straightened to her full height. "Very long."

On the thrones were a man and a woman. She faintly recognized one as a younger Maryse—impossibly younger. She must have lost fifty years of age, appearing to be barely more than a girl. Beside her sat a man with dark, bushy hair and a matching beard, along with a man in an army uniform who looked every bit as confused as Ember felt.

"It seems we have gotten ourselves in a predicament," the man in the chair said. His smile was wide, and beside him Maryse gazed at him with open affection.

The Queen swallowed. "Zyah." She nodded. "Maryse." The court tittered. "I'm afraid I am at a loss." She paused. "Time has... bent?"

"Time has bent, indeed." Zyah rose and gestured for the man in uniform. "We have bent it. General..."

The General stepped forward. "We've been working on a way to bring magic back into alignment. It involves a lot of complicated..." He looked up apologetically. "Magic?" He shrugged. "A portal has been opened, a chance to right the past."

"The past cannot be changed," the Queen breathed.

Ember worked out all the possibilities time travel would open—each one more terrifying than the last.

The General shared a look with Zyah and smiled. "You're wrong," he said, turning his glance to the Queen with a mixture of amusement and assurance.

"And I'll tell you how."

CHAPTER 11

Aurelia pressed her face to the rails, but they'd stopped talking. Her mother thought she was stupid, but she wasn't. She'd heard the name before. *Shepherd*. She twisted a lock of her hair and pressed her back against the hallway. None of the guards were there to see her. They were all asleep.

"Shepherd," she whispered. She leaned closer, watching him escort the Queen and Ember to the door with Grace. There was something familiar about his eyes, something kind that she could feel even from there, but then, she'd always been a reader of people.

And Grace. Grace. Had she been played? They'd met several times since that first time, each time talking of things that were important and things that weren't. But never Grace's origins, never who she truly was. She wasn't from Atlantis. Aurelia knew that much, but she had trusted her. With her heart. With her questions, her secrets. Her fears. Her yearnings. Her body, even. And now—Grace was here negotiating peace. It was more than betrayal. It was a heartbreak, sharp and raw.

She'd had enough of hiding. She sprinted down the spiral steps, hoping to catch them, but each step felt longer than the next, and when she reached the bottom, she collided with Javiar. He grabbed her shoulders and looked down at her with a frown.

"Your mother said…"

"I know what she said…" She tried to look around his broad shoulders, but Grace and the others were already gone. Panic sparked in her chest. "I can help them," she pleaded.

"You can help by staying here and staying awake." He sighed. "Perhaps the observation tower?"

She wrenched free. "I am not a prisoner!" she shouted. Yet her words clanged inside her. *Wasn't she? Hadn't she always been? Hadn't they all?*

"Aurelia!" he called, but he was a step too slow. She'd spent her whole life slipping past guards and patrols and she knew every corner of the island, every blind turn, every echoing stair. Her legs were longer than his and her strides quicker. She crossed the room in a breath, his heavy boots and muttered curses pounding after her.

A small, breathless smile tugged at her. It was past time she outran them, but when she got to the door, someone else stopped her. She ran straight into Shepherd.

His hands lifted to steady her, though she'd always been good at stopping. She leaned past him to the scene outside—the sleeping bodies on the steps, the moon slipping in and out of the clouds, the strange and eerie stillness. Overhead, she felt the absence of the dragon, who had flown off after the attack. Ember and the Queen were gone. And Grace with them.

She sighed.

"I could have helped," she murmured, mostly to herself. She was too late.

Shep raised an eyebrow. "And you are?" His gaze swept her face, lingering on her eyes. She was no wilting flower. She met his stare without flinching, though something in him tugged at a memory she buried long ago. He had been younger then, and she was no more than a baby.

"I am called *Aurelia*." She lifted her dark eyes to his. Someone gasped. Whether it was Javiar or Shep or even herself, she couldn't tell. A pulse of energy cracked through the room.

"Aurelia." His voice broke on her name. "I thought..." His gaze drifted to her hair, light and curly around her shoulders. "I thought you'd have darker hair." A quiet, disbelieving laugh escaped him. "Many years ago, it was my color..."

She studied him. She had, indeed, been born with dark hair, or so the stories said. They'd stopped photographing long ago, days blurred when nothing changed—and no one needed reminders. But she had found a few hidden pictures once, tucked away where no one would think to look.

A woman holding a dark-haired infant.

A man nearby, looking on with sadness.

"You?" she asked. There was much in that single word, but Javiar answered before either of them could. He touched Aurelia lightly on the shoulder.

"The Queen wanted to be the one to tell you," he said. He looked at Shep with sorrow in his eyes. "Many years have passed. You must understand..." He trailed off.

"I understand that she has grown into a beautiful young woman," Shep said. A tear formed in the corner of his eye. "She is safe. Thank you. Thank you for that."

Aurelia looked from one to the other, trying to fit the fragments of her memory into the life she knew. The stories her mother had told her. "Who are you?" she asked.

Javiar answered instead. "It is a story that should be told from the beginning." His gaze drifted to the windows, but the world outside had fallen silent again. "And it seems we have time."

"Aurelia..." Shep repeated her name in a way that made her feel like he'd said it a thousand times in her absence. And somehow, she'd heard them all.

"The study," she said, rubbing the chill bumps along her arms. She would've welcomed a warm fire, and perhaps even a stiff drink, though this man didn't seem the sort to let his guard down.

Javiar led the way across the wide room. Shep made almost no sound. She thought he was used to slipping through the world unnoticed, but she noticed him. She bit her lip to prevent turning back, but his reflection in the glass caught her: worry mixing with fear, relief, and familiarity in his expression.

The tapestries on the walls told Atlantis' rich history. They didn't boast of conquest or war, as she'd heard of the cities of old. They spoke magic and love, of a city once united. She paused before one with dragons soaring through the air. She had seen the new dragon in the city, yet she had felt his presence in her heart long before. Dust muted the brilliant colors of the tapestries, long neglected, yet Aurelia felt a swell of pride. There was more history to weave here. Perhaps she couldn't go with Grace and Ember, but there was work to be done in her mother's absence. She could feel it.

Javiar opened the wide wooden doors to a scene straight out of a storybook. Her mother had always kept the study immaculate. Books lined the walls between the tall windows overlooking the city, where the lights of the mainland flashed as a warning. They lit the desk in the far corner, currently covered with journals and art supplies. Her mother's ledgers were safely locked away—a history of Atlantis when it was in the sky. Aurelia had been allowed to read some. Each day held hope. Each day carried disappointment.

Javiar used a flick of magic to start a fire in the hearth. Shep paused beside one of the wide couches, but he didn't sit. He studied Aurelia as she closed one of the curtains, shutting out flashing lights from the mainland.

"Do you have a problem?" she bristled as he studied her, but there was more to this man than she knew. His magic was strong, but something deeper tugged at her.

"I have many problems." He grinned, then gestured for her to sit. He exchanged a glance with Javiar, who gave a single, solemn nod. Shep perched on the side of the couch. Aurelia remained standing.

"I was once of Atlantis," Shep said.

"I'd guessed as much." She felt steady enough to round the couch and lean against the far arm, smoothing her skirt.

"Your mother asked me to stay behind. To help Atlantis return. I had no idea it would be so long..." He tipped his head, studying her again. "Hundreds of years, and yet you..."

She touched her face, suddenly self-conscious. "And me... what? I was barely a child then. I don't remember being on the ground."

His smile slipped away. "There are many things you don't remember, I assume. You were a child when I left. It took everything in me to leave you, Aurelia." He stood, nervous. "I ask your forgiveness. I ask your grace. I brought Atlantis home, but in doing so, I lost the one thing that mattered to me. You."

She went pale. "What are you saying?"

"I left my daughter here to save the city," he said.
Behind them, Javiar shifted.
"You. I left you."

CHAPTER 12

In her quest to return Atlantis, Ember Weathers had befriended a dragon, met space pirates, and fought magicians. Time travel, however, was a complication she had not been expecting.

She'd known Maryse as an old woman. Her husband—currently sitting on the throne in his prime—was supposed to be dead. Or at least she believed him to be. She'd never known him alive, and yet here he was: broad-shouldered and strong, with dark bushy hair and a matching beard. He didn't look as though he were about to die.

"I don't understand." Queen Aura's voice was tight as she looked from one to the other. Ember had expected the cramped interior of a tent. Instead, she found herself in a castle hall, vast and imposing, rivaling even the halls of Atlantis. It was made of wood, with tall windows that let in a gentle flood of light. A fire roared to their right. Zyah and Maryse wore pelts of animal hide. Ember shivered.

"Come now." Maryse whispered something to the General, who nodded once, and lead the rest of the audience out of the tent. She waited until they were gone and stepped down from her throne. Ember bit her fingernail.

"Your questions can be more precise than that." She approached Aura. In her younger days, Maryse's hair was a strawberry blonde, braided and pulled back, though waves escaped. Beneath the pelt, Ember glimpsed her colorful style, but the lines on her face were gone and her blue eyes shone.

"It has been a long time for you," Maryse said to the Queen, a smile across her face, "but for me, mere months. You've aged, my friend, but gracefully. The magic of Atlantis still protects you."

Aura regained her composure and swallowed. "I'm afraid I can't say the same." She looked at the King's brother, leaning forward on his throne. Dark in hair, eyes, and countenance, Ember could not read the look on his face. Was it menace?

"Who are you?" Ember blurted out.

Maryse laughed. "Finally! A question I can answer. Would you like to take it, Grace?"

Grace stepped out of the shadows. "They are who they say," she answered, her voice flat. "Prince Zyah and Princess Maryse."

"Back from the dead," Aura whispered. The King's face darkened further.

"I do not wish to know my fate in your world," he said, "for I am here to create a new one."

"You're late, then." Aura's lips pressed into a thin line.

Zyah opened his mouth to answer, but Maryse cut him off. She took Aura by the elbow and led her up toward the side door on the dais that Ember hadn't noticed. "There are more comfortable places to talk. I think drinks are in order."

Ember glanced back. Through the shimmering doorway, the encampment flickered briefly into view. Somewhere Shep was in the castle, safe, she hoped. But Sierra and the others? Had they flown off forever? And the city itself—what had become of it?

Grace touched her lightly on the shoulder. "They're safe, for now," she said with more empathy than Ember thought she had. Grace's features fell for a moment, revealing a flash of deep fear. "I left someone I love deeply there as well," she said, "but this was the only way."

Ember raised an eyebrow. There were always other ways, she wanted to say, but she knew that was a bullshit platitude. She understood what it felt like to be cornered by circumstances. "Okay," was all she managed, though beneath everything, she was dying to know how this had come about. Was there truly no end to what magic could do?

Maryse led them with Zyah at her side. He was hardly the villain she'd heard stories about. Grumpy, perhaps, but who wouldn't be after being flung through time to save a city that had shunned him? Ember hesitated at the doorway, but it was only a plain stone arch that led to a study.

Another fire roared to their right. Windows on either side opened to impossible fields with rolling hills covered in flowers. Leather-bound books lined the walls, their spines etched in languages Ember couldn't read. She itched to touch one, to see whether the pages whispered, but instead she hovered just inside the threshold while Maryse, Zyah, and Aura claimed seats around the room. Aura beckoned her in.

Grace stood by the door.

"We recently became aware of the fate of Atlantis," Zyah began. His voice was deep, and sure. Fine wrinkles gathered at the corners of his eyes. "It may not be my favorite place, but it was once home," he said. "And I'd not have it destroyed."

Ember snorted. "Funny, because you're the one who destroyed it," she said. Aura tried to shush her, but Ember pressed on. There were probably rules about changing the past and she disregarded every one. "Your army threatened the city to the sky, and you hunted the survivors."

Zyah let out a long breath and exchanged a weighted look with Maryse. "It is as we feared," he said quietly.

"And what exactly did you fear?" Ember stood, taking a step forward, fist curling. "The disappearance of an entire city? The annihilation of the survivors?" Ember stood, thinking of Hawk and his friends. Of her, and her many lifetimes if Shep was to be believed. Of Shep, and all he'd given up. She balled her fists.

"That was not us," Maryse said. Her voice was plain. She stared into the fire, but gave nothing more.

The flames reflected in the Aura's eyes. She didn't look surprised or amazed or even angry as Ember was. She only took in the room—colorful rugs, the long curtains shifting with the breeze, Zyah standing with no sign of aggression.

"You knew?" Ember asked. Her legs gave out and she dropped into the nearest chair, but Aura didn't look her way.

"Tell us," Ember said. "I need to know who cursed the city and its survivors, and I need to know from you." Aura glanced at her, sorrow clouding her features, or perhaps guilt. If not Zyah, then who?

Zyah cleared his throat. "My brother," he said. "Yes, I was coming to challenge his throne. I'd heard whispers that he was losing his mind. That his rule of Atlantis had grown unsteady.

That his Queen was the only one holding the city together." He met Aura's gaze. She denied nothing.

"It was an army I gathered, yes, but it was meant to force Corin to step down. He was ill." Zyah's voice softened. "He was ill, my lady, was he not?"

He met Aura's eyes again, and this time she looked down, a tear slipping free.

"I don't understand." Ember looked between them. "The darkness massing on the shores. The stories. The traders who came back talking about razed cities."

Maryse interrupted. "All plants by the King. It is frighteningly easy to manipulate a narrative when you can sway people's emotions. He sent bands out to terrorize traders. A few kills here and there, and the stories grew on their own. He fanned the flames... then watched them burn."

"Did you know?" Ember asked. Her voice shook despite how softly she spoke. "Did. You. Know?"

Aura shook her head. "I knew the King was ill, but I did not know how ill until we had taken to the sky—and by then it was too late." She lowered her gaze. "I believed his cruelty was aimed only at me. But then I saw what he did to the mages who crossed him. How he threw them into prisons. Cut out their tongues." She swallowed. She didn't tremble, but she seemed... smaller.

"On behalf of the entire city, I'm sorry." Aura looked up and met Maryse's gaze. She reached for Maryse's hand and held it tightly.

"The things we overlook for love can destroy us." Maryse squeezed her palm.

Aura blinked away a tear. "It wasn't love," she said. "It was responsibility."

Ember took a step back toward Grace and whispered, "I'm confused. So, the King was the one who cursed the city himself?

He made up rumors about Zyah—who is actually, what? The good guy?"

Grace gave a thin smile. "It's more complicated than that, but something like that, yes."

"And then Maryse went off the rails and started hunting magic?" Ember asked.

Grace shook her head. "That timeline hasn't happened yet."

Ember narrowed her eyes. "Where do you fit into it?"

Grace shrugged. "My mother's a witch," she said, as if that explained everything.

Ember searched her memory for what she knew about Zyah. He'd died long ago. She'd met Maryse, who was, indeed, off the rails. She'd tried to drag Atlantis down from the sky to destroy it. She'd released the hellhounds and damned Ember in every lifetime. None of that fit the woman standing before her—bright-eyed and steady, untouched by the years that would change her.

Maybe age and magic and trauma had carved her into a monster?

Maybe they truly did have a chance to fix it?

Maryse raised her voice over them all. "And now it is our responsibility to right," she said, settling back into a soft loveseat. For a moment Ember saw the shadow of who she would become. Age would eventually line her face. Her strawberry blonde hair would fade to gray. But the strength and confidence simmering beneath her skin would only grow.

Zyah sat next to her and took her hand.

"We want you to come back," Maryse said. Her eyes shone. "Before the rising of the city. We want you to stop all of this before it happens. Our magic is thin, but there is a small opening."

"Wait." Ember shook her head and looked at Aura. "Wouldn't this mess with everything since? Me? My life?" she asked. She swallowed. "Would I... cease to exist?"

"That is why we are here," Zyah's voice filled the room. He gestured to the books that lined the wall. "The hidden library. All the knowledge of magic is contained here, just..." He gave Ember a crooked smile. "Messy. And complicated."

"Great," she said under her breath.

Maryse folded her hands. "From what we can tell, time will fold, not vanish. You'll still exist, but there may be... other you's." She lifted a brow. "Like Zyah says, complicated."

"Other me's." Ember sank deeper into her chair, imagining a past where she wasn't an orphan. Where Sierra hadn't been locked away for so long. A world where she might see her parents again...

"Tell us more about it," Aura said, leaning forward.

Zyah rose. "We'll tell you. But it's better to show you."

He rose and offered a hand to his wife, ready to lead them further into the castle, and into danger.

CHAPTER 13

Shep had imagined this moment for so long. Would she look like her mother—fair-haired and bohemian—or would she have his dark features? Her eyes mirrored his, wide and dark, but in other ways she favored her mother. He had not been with her mother for long. A matter of months. A dalliance that became something more. He'd thought it was love, then, but in the years since he'd realized he had not known true love until he'd met Ember, and now... his daughter.

But there was something right about their union, something that had brought this child into the world. Leaving her had meant leaving his entire heart behind. He had made terrible choices in the name of returning to her, and now that he stood before her, he wondered if he was worthy of her at all.

"I'm sorry..." was all he could manage, and somehow it took all the air out of the study.

She tipped her head, lips pursed. He couldn't read her. If she was angry, she didn't show it. If she were happy, she hid that, too. She was a girl who held her cards close. *What had she been through*, he wondered, *to learn that kind of restraint?*

"I knew," she said at last. "Through rumors and whispers." Her gaze flicked to Javiar. "The Queen only said she would tell me someday. She is not my birth mother?"

Javiar dipped his head. "No," he said gently. "She wished to tell you when the time was right."

Aurelia cleared her throat. "Tell me now."

And he did.

They sat in the chairs before the fire and Shep—perhaps for the first time in lifetimes—let the entire story flow through him. He didn't shy away from his emotions. He cried when he spoke of the pain of leaving. His voice broke when he told her how close he'd come, again and again, in so many lives. He admitted the despair that had hollowed him out when he thought he'd lost for good. When his body had begun to age and Atlantis still hung somewhere beyond his reach in the sky.

When he reached the part about the witch, he caught the slight flinch Aurelia tried to hide. He continued. He told her what the witch had turned him into and what that transformation demanded. He didn't soften the truth. Not the need for blood. Not the shame of those early years. He didn't shield her from the man he had been, even though the memory still scraped raw inside him.

He told her how he'd found himself again. How he had searched the world for Ember. How he had found her just as Hawk had taken them away. And now they were here.

Through all of it, Aurelia hadn't reacted. In all the years he'd been gone, he had braced himself for scorn. For humiliation. Shame. But none of that came.

He waited.

She rose and crossed to the window that overlooked the sleeping city. She pulled the curtain aside, fingers tightening on the fabric, the only sign she might be struggling.

Shep exchanged a glance with Javiar. He'd known the guard once, though that felt like another lifetime. Javiar had been energetic back then, bright-eyed and eager to prove himself. Good-hearted. A loyal companion to the Queen, and he clearly cared for Aurelia.

Aurelia let the curtain fall. The candles in the corners worked harder to fill the room with light. She pulled her long hair back, drawing a slow breath.

"I'm sorry for what happened to you," she said at last. "But I'm not sure what you seek from me. If it's absolution, I cannot give that." A small smile touched her lips. "I am not qualified."

Shep stood. Tears caught the glow of the fire. "No. Not absolution. If I may... understanding." He paused. "Maybe a place in your life."

She turned toward the window again, toward the sleeping city. "It is not much of a life," she said. "Not yet."

Shep took a chance and stepped beside her. Magic hummed faintly in the air. She was a healer, like her mother—he wondered if she knew. He looked out across the ocean, wondering where his friends had flown off to. He had dreamed of this place and this moment, held it close through lifetimes. Yet standing here now, he felt unsteady. She owed him nothing. Not love. Not even understanding.

He began to turn away, but she touched his arm.

"I may not understand your decision," she said, hesitating. "But I know what it is to love someone. To make difficult decisions." Her eyes misted. She blinked away the tears away with practiced ease. He wondered how many times she'd done that. How many moments she'd faced alone. And his own heart cracked under the weight of it.

"I'm so sorry, Aurelia," he said. "I did what I thought was right."

"There is no use in *sorry's*." Her smile was soft and sad. "But a wise woman once told me tomorrow is a new day." She gestured toward the window. "And it is almost tomorrow."

Javiar cleared his throat. "And there is hope, my lady."

She nodded. "There *is* hope."

He watched her, hope blooming in his own heart. He pressed his palm to the place his heart once beat. "If there is not a cure..." he began.

She laid a hand over his.

"Then we will search until there is," she said. "Hope is strong. The Queen taught me that. She was my mother, in all the ways that mattered. But I would like you to tell me about the times before. About my birth mother. About..." She tipped her head. "You."

The crack in Shep's heart widened, but this time it let in relief. He let out a breath.

"I met her in the market," he said. "And she was magic."

CHAPTER 14

Sierra paced the deck of the ship, which hovered safely away from where Atlantis had landed, and hidden in the clouds. Every cell in her body screamed to go back and fight, but one small ship of space pirates was no match for the entire might of the government. She paced the ship, stopping at the bow. The wind caught her hair, blowing it off her face. Dawn bled into the horizon, pale and hesitant. Below the wispy clouds she could just make out the whitecaps, but it was the sound—not the sight— that gripped her.

Draco was wailing.

The dragon's cry carried through the sky like a wound torn open. He wanted to be with Ember.

Hawk had flown them far enough that the last threads of their magic would protect them from sight. Even so, they had to dodge patrols and flights. Sierra never realized how much work it took to hide an entire city. The King had kept it from them—or rather, the Queen. Magic was complicated, and this world was less and less able to handle it.

She shuddered, imagining what those governments would do with Atlantis now that it had fallen back to land.

"Couldn't sleep?" Hawk appeared by her side, the reddish tint in his eyes betrayed the same sleepless night. He wore the casual uniform of a space pirate: loose pair of pants and a t-shirt. His blond hair was tied back, and the beginnings of a beard roughened his jaw. He rubbed his chin, glancing at the first rays of the sun spilling over Sierra's shoulder. Despite the old stories, the light didn't seem to bother him.

"Who can?" Sierra asked, turning to watch the pink sunrise filtered through the clouds. Everything seemed unreal, like a dream painted across the sky.

"They used to say red at night is a sailor's delight." Hawk said, leaning on the rail. "Red in the morning is a sailor's warning."

Sierra snorted. "As if we need any more warnings." There was a deceptive calm to the morning. Perhaps she should take the warning and turn back, but so many choices had already been made for her over the past years. No. She would not run.

"No, we have plenty of warnings. We just don't heed them," Hawk said. His gaze was fixed on the horizon, yet his eyes seemed distant. "I've been thinking about how we can help."

Sierra straightened. "Me too," she admitted. "But I'm at a loss."

A sly grin spread across Hawk's face. "I have some ideas," he said. "Well, one. One idea. And it's terrible, really. And risky. Likely to fail."

"I'll take those odds," she said. She wasn't sure if it was the sun lighting up his face or the possibility of actually doing something. It had crested the horizon, a narrow slit at first. Insignificant, almost an afterthought—but it never took long to dominate the whole sky. Maybe hope was like that, too. Small at first, then growing, spreading. She leaned in. "*I'm listening.*"

The grin on his face was wild. She envied it. "The dragons," he said, waving an arm over the side of the ship as if that explained everything. She tried to follow his thought. Draco was close by. She felt him—not as strongly as her sister, but she felt him. And on the edges of that, something else. Something bigger.

"Yes?" she prodded.

He gripped the white rail. "They're the key to everything. The gateway to all the magic in the world. All that's left, anyway."

"Hawk..." She placed a hand over his on the rail. It felt strangely familiar, as if they'd held hands in another life. "They're gone," she said quietly. Hawk had been born after Atlantis was raised. He knew the lore, but he'd never known a world of magic. Neither had she. Still, the stories—they were incredible.

He raised an eyebrow, his blue eyes twinkling in the early sun. "Are they, though?" he asked. He pulled his hand out from under hers and gripped it firmly. His passion was evident in its slight tremble. "Tell me you don't feel it," he said, glancing toward the bow where Draco had flown closer. "There are more. I know it."

Sierra sucked in a breath. She *had* felt it. Something strong, pulling across a veil, straining to break free. "I feel it," she admitted.

"What are we feeling?" Paine crossed the deck, rubbing the sleep out of her eyes. Her orange hair was hastily tied back, and she wore a warm sweatshirt.

"Dragons," Hawk whispered, almost vibrating with excitement.

Paine's gaze settled on the horizon, her expression far less enthusiastic. She was the anchor of more than the ship. Anchors could steady—but they could also hold back. Sierra waited, silent, still, for the decision. Much rode on Paine's opinion.

"Yes," Paine finally agreed, her voice steady. Her gaze swept north. "There are more. I've felt them. But finding them would be difficult."

"Yes," Hawk said, his grin widening.

"Almost impossible," Sierra added.

Paine gave a stern nod.

"Fun." Hawk rubbed his chin. "Adventurous. Difficult. Risky, but fun. Definitely fun."

Paine batted his shoulder with a hand. "Oh, stop," she told him. "You had me at fun."

Sierra laughed—a sound so rare lately that it seemed to lighten up the whole ship, though it was only those three on board. Hawk and Paine caught her enthusiasm and laughed along.

"North, then?" Hawk asked, wiping a tear from the corner of his eye.

"I don't know. What do you think, Draco?" Sierra asked. The dragon had flown close enough for her to see the gold in his iris, a twinkle that mirrored Hawk's. He opened his mouth and roared—a sight that had become fearsome as of late. Not fearsome enough, not yet... but with enough of them...

"I think he's on board," Paine said. "Shall we prepare for a long journey?"

"I don't know how long the journey will be," Hawk said, shaking his head, "but I'd say we should leave immediately."

Sierra took one last look at the city, cloaked in early morning fog and glittering with distant blue lights. She longed to descend and fight alongside them—alongside her sister, Shepherd, and the Queen—but sometimes the battle was best fought from afar. She certain this was the right way.

"Take care," she said to her sister, and the city proper. Hawk steered them north, and Draco followed.

CHAPTER 15

With each step, Maryse took them farther into the castle. Ember felt the strings connecting to her old life stretching thin. She could barely feel Draco anymore—only the faint thud of his great heartbeat, and the pain trembling through it. Was it as much pain as Shepherd felt? Or Sierra? She could only guess. Sierra had fled a city cursed—a city that once imprisoned her. And Shep... Shep was being the protector, as always. He couldn't protect them from this, but she wished he were here.

The castle changed around them. Wood gave way to stone, and stone to moss. They passed doorways and long hallways empty of everything but the occasional torch. Zyah pulled one from its sconce and handed it to Aura. He held his own in the front, and Ember felt their path lead downhill. Aura lit the way behind them, but her steps were in shadow. Ember had forgotten if it were day or night. Exhaustion pulled at her—the same exhaustion pulling at the people of Atlantis. She almost wished she'd been cursed like them, if only to sleep through all of this.

A growl rumbled out of one of the tunnels, echoing through the darkness.

"What was that?" Ember asked.

"The hellhounds," Maryse called back, as if the word meant nothing. "We've caught and caged many of them. Don't worry, they can't get out."

Ember shivered, remembering the hellhound in her bookshop. No wonder it had chased them that day. She looked back and saw the Queen's worried face. "It was Corin all along?" she asked. "He sent the hellhounds after the survivors?"

Maryse lifted her torch, the flame pulling shadows up the walls. "It started that way. I believe he struck a bargain. He would live as long as he fled with magic to the sky, and magic was hunted here." Her expression softened with regret. "I understand that times have changed, and that my husband and I played a part in the twisting of that magic, but those monsters do not yet exist. I only know how things began."

"Who would Corin have made a deal with?" Ember asked.

"A greater magic," Maryse answered. "An old one. One I'd not trifle with, or approach."

Ember thought about it as they descended deeper into the castle—further away from everything she knew: her friends, her dragon, Shepherd.

The tunnel ended in a great cavern. A great gust of cold wind swept through, nearly extinguishing the torches. The light that remained shimmered faintly, revealing a pool at the center of a cavern. Its water glowed a cool, rippled light blue, emanating from under the waves.

Ember knelt at the rocky edge. Her reflection stared back, but it wasn't her. Her piercings were wrong. Her hair was long and frosted. The other her tipped her head, and Ember jumped back.

"The portal," Maryse said, simply. "Step in, and it will take you back."

"Back to where?" Ember asked.

Aura sighed, her gaze sweeping the group. "Portal magic is complicated," she said. "It usually jumps places, not times."

Maryse dipped the toe of her shoe in the water, sending the reflections swirling. Shapes danced across the cavern walls, ones Ember thought she should be able to interpret. Warnings? Encouragement? She didn't know. All she knew what her heart: go forward. The mess of bringing Atlantis back had started a long time ago. If there were a way to fix it—even if it was a trap—she had to try.

"That's true." Maryse stepped closer, taking the Queen's hand. "Much was given for this portal to open." She exchanged a look with Zyah. "Much was lost. It may be our only chance to right the past."

Ember stepped back to observe Grace. *Who was she in all of this?* "What do you think?" she asked. "Being the daughter of a witch and all?"

Grace bit her bottom lip, a flicker of fear. But then, it's not like time travel happened every day. "I think it's risky. Scary." Her face glowed with portal blue light, shifting her features from confident to cautious. Ember's reflection mirrored in her gray eyes, and she suspected fear was there as well. "But there is someone I care very much about in Atlantis. I'd not see her destroyed. Taken by the government. Hunted."

Ember thought about all the survivors of Atlantis, hunted for so many years. Her friends Hawk and Paine. The dragons. "Do you think it could work?" she asked in a low voice as the Queen conversed with Zyah and Maryse.

Grace laughed. "Not really, but what other choice do we have?"

Ember blew her bangs off the side of her face. "I hope we don't get stuck there," she said.

The smile fell from Grace's face. "I think there would be people looking for us," she said, her mouth pursed. "You do not want to mess with my mother."

Ember smiled, remembering her own mother and what she would do in this situation. Her father would say *Sometimes you have to take a risk*, probably with his nose behind a book. Her mom would tut and smile. She stepped toward the water.

"You just walk in?" she asked. The water was cool around her boots, but it didn't feel wet. Instead, it wrapped around her, a hug—or a snake—she couldn't decide. It chilled her from the inside out.

Grace stepped in beside her and took her hand.

"Hold your breath," Maryse advised, "and jump."

"Hold your breath and jump." Grace squeezed her hand. "Sounds like going off a cliff."

"Feels like it, too," Ember said. They didn't jump but walked in slowly, step by step. The portal seemed to stretch before them. It smelled of fresh air. A breeze through the trees. Orange groves. Spice. Ember closed her eyes as the portal overtook her senses—*and fell.*

CHAPTER 16

The portal spat them out in exactly the same place. Despite the water, Ember was dry. The water behind them still sparkled a cool blue, but the air was different—clearer, crisp. It reminded her of autumn at home, when she'd be contemplating a fire in the hearth and stacking new bestsellers for the last of the summer residents to read on their trips home. She pushed the memory aside and focused on the present as the others emerged.

Maryse flicked open a lighter and ignited a torch on the wall. "Technology is handy," she said with a soft laugh, but Ember's attention had fixed on Zyah, who'd turned a shade green. She doubted it was the portal. This was his timeline, and if the stories held true, he'd die soon. Atlantis would fall to his brother, and the curse that followed would echo for generations. There was so much at stake, and Ember was only a bystander.

She walked by his side, searching for something encouraging to say—something her dad would quote about long odds and success—but nothing sounded right. She shivered as she studied his bulk from the side. He raised an eyebrow and shrugged off of his fur vest, handing it to her.

"Take it," he said. "I am used to such weather."

"Is it winter?" She slipped it on. Ahead, Maryse's torch bobbed through the tunnel like a wandering star.

"This season was the only time to open the portal," he said. "Magic is complicated." He smiled this time. "Or so I'm told. As you know, my brother and I wield very little of it. This was all my wife's doing." Pride softened him as he watched Maryse's skirt trail the dirt floor. Grace and Aura followed close behind.

"It's true then?" Ember asked. "The King was jealous of magic? The story says that was you." She regretted the words as soon as she said them. Should she tell him of his fate? Would knowing that change their odds? Their timeline?

He only smiled sadly. "No," he said. "It was not me. My brother always could weave a good story. When people can't control you, they start rumors. They shape what others say about you. It's a tactic as good as any offense I've seen. As you can see…" He swept a hand as if all of Atlantis' history lay before them. "It's spanned the ages. I've become the villain. And perhaps in your timeline I did become a villain. I only hope we can change it."

Ember appreciated the attempt. Her dad would have approved. But *fixing* it? That was harder. "What then?" she asked, thinking of the other Ember she'd seen in the portal's water. Would there be two of her, or none? Would her friends stay as they were? Would her parents be alive? The thought wrenched her focus and she stumbled. Zyah caught her elbow before she fell, but the others were too far in shadow to hear them.

"Ember..." His voice softened. Her name sounded strange on his lips, as if it weren't made for his time. "I cannot promise what the repercussions will be," he said, "but I would not do this if I did not believe with my whole heart there is a better future than the one I saw." He frowned. The light ahead of them got dimmed slightly as it bobbed onward.

Zyah paused. "It is not the domination of magic that we are trying to return," he said. "Not as my brother envisioned. It is balance. Healing. Love."

"It is unfortunate that so much has to be uprooted for that," she said, brushing dirt from her pants. Nearby, Grace paused to wait for them.

"It is not the only time that things have gone astray, Ember Weathers. Sometimes the world must be righted." She searched his dark eyes for signs he was fooling them, but only found kindness and understanding. His gaze could see right down to your soul, into your fears—and fears were not to be taken lightly.

"In my time we say that's two steps forward and one step back," she said, silently thanking her father for the wisdom in his sayings. Zyah laughed.

"Well, this is a mighty step backward," he said. Ahead, Maryse called over her shoulder.

"There is a door!" she said.

Zyah's eyes crinkled the corners in a way that reminded her of Shepherd—kindness and mischief wrapped together. "Shall we go through it?" he asked, tipping his head toward the dark tunnel behind them. "Or retreat?"

Though it was said in jest, Ember knew she could turn back. She could turn them all back. She could tell them it's too dangerous, that their actions might not just change the course of history but the fabric of time. They might all cease to exist. Shep. Paine. Sierra. All of them. Gone.

Or....

She caught Grace's eye in the low torchlight. "Two steps forward," she said, forcing a smile. It wavered. Her mind was afraid, but her heart called the shots, pushing them onward.

"I would settle for balance," Zyah said. He walked with them to the where Aura and Maryse waited by a great wooden door barred with iron. They stood in a semi-circle, the walls pressing in, urging them forward.

"I can't hear anything," Maryse said. "But I believe it is the dungeon." She shrugged. "Portal magic is imprecise. We arrived by walking into the ocean. There was no door."

"How do we leave, then, when we're done?" Ember asked, searching all their faces for confirmation that they would, indeed, leave when they fixed things. No one met her gaze. Aura was the first to lay her hand on the door. Ember felt the ripples of magic, threaded through with echoes of sadness.

"How do we leave when we're done?" Ember repeated in a softer tone. Her words carried back down the tunnel to the portal that had promised her a fractured home—where magic was so feared and reviled, and Atlantis cursed. No, that was no way forward. She stepped behind Aura as she pushed open the door, pointedly noticing no one has answered her.

A musty smell drifted from the circular stone room. It was large enough to line with six cells along the sides, and two hallways that branched off. In the center, two guards slept, their heads resting on tables, drinks untouched. A single torch flickered on the wall, the only source of light.

"Is it the same curse?" Ember asked, holding her hand in front of her mouth, as if the magic that had cursed Atlantis to sleep might be breathed in. Maryse shook her head.

"This is common around here." She exchanged a sad look with Aura, who paled.

"Even then?" Aura whispered, a tear forming in her eye as she looked in the cells. Darkness swallowed their interiors, but Ember heard moans and shuffles. Light flickered down the hallways, but she couldn't tell which led out and which led deeper in.

Behind them, the door closed, becoming part of the stone wall once more. Ember let out a breath as the stones shifted, as if the portal had never existed. It was as she feared. Would she ever get home? She pressed her hand to the wall, trailed her fingers down it's cool, damp stones, and whispered her goodbyes. Not forever, she hoped. Magic achieved incredible things—they were living proof—but to move forward, she couldn't keep looking back.

"I'll be back," she promised. Zyah put a hand on her shoulder.

"I'll make sure of it," he said as Aura and Maryse conferred about which route to take. "I have made many mistakes." His voice lowered. "In both my past, and, as you say, my future. Most of them came down to an unwillingness to fight. A belief that things would fine if I simply left them alone. Cowardice, maybe. It is difficult to believe that one person can make a difference, yet one person can." He rubbed his burly, black beard, thinking aloud. "I should have stood up for what was right long ago, but we can do so now."

He seemed to arrive at a decision. He tipped his head. "I greatly admire you, Ember Weathers. You move go forward with what's right, no matter the cost. It is not something many people can do. Myself included."

Ember looked at the wall and felt faint strings tugging her back. Her heart wasn't broken. Not yet. But it was bruised and afraid. She wanted to tell him there was no choice at all, or that anyone would do the same—the same bullshit woman had been spewing for all of time when someone tried to praise them. Yet he was right. She *was* strong for going forward. She let herself nod.

"Thank you," she said, softly. For the first time in her life, she considered maybe she wasn't "the chosen one" as Shepherd seemed to think. Maybe he hadn't chased her through time. Maybe she was just a girl with a little bit of magic, a lot of strength, plenty of stubbornness, and a strong desire to do what was right. A moral compass that she hoped one day would lead her home.

CHAPTER 17

Before they swept past the prison cells, Queen Aura paused beside one where a prisoner hunched low in the dark. Ember hung back and Grace drifted toward her.

"I don't know how I'm involved in this any more than you are," Grace admitted. She didn't appear much younger than Ember, though with magic it was hard tell. Even in the dim light her skin held warmth, and her eyes shone like moonlight.

Grace watched the Queen murmur to the prisoner, though she kept Ember in the corner of her gaze.

"Love, I suppose," she said with a sigh. She turned as if the motion might steady her. "When my mother found the portal to Atlantis, I slipped in and out. I met someone. She's..." Grace searched the air, as if the words might bloom there. Words for what it felt like to lose and find yourself all at the same time. Words for the kind of ache that could change your entire world.

They weren't written on stone or hidden in the shadows. They lived inside her.

"Like no one else I've ever met," she finished.

"They call it fate," Ember said while Aura called Maryse over to the cell. "Twin flames or something."

Grace laughed so loudly the guard closest snorted in his sleep. Zyah frowned. "Perhaps," she said. "Or perhaps we should not quantify love. We should just feel it." She squeezed Ember's hand. "For what it's worth, I'm sorry. It would have been easier to stay in my mother's cabin and leave all this alone."

"I'll say." Ember squeezed back, though she knew she wouldn't choose the little bookstore over this adventure, no matter how hard, tiring, and heartbreaking it could be. It wasn't just the right thing—it called to her heart.

The Queen turned. "Ember, can you break these bars with your magic?" Her expression fell. "My brother Alistair is inside. I must release him."

The shadow of a man stood by the bars, holding his fingers around the Queen's. He shared her fair skin and noble features, but his pale blue eyes were glazed. The remnants of a shirt that had turned more gray than white shirt clung to his gaunt frame.

"Me?" Ember looked around. Was she the strongest? Grace took her hand again.

"All of us," she said.

Ember tried to pull for her magic. Without Draco it was harder, but together they summoned a flame strong enough to melt the lock. It fought the magic, shaking on the hinges before falling into the dirt. The Queen pulled the door open and hugged her brother.

"The others?" she asked.

"There is no time, and not enough magic," Maryse said gently. "When we change things, it will be different. Please, Aura. Hurry."

Alistair looked at Ember as the others rushed ahead. He tipped his head, wearing the vague, swimmy expression of a wizard whose mind was in another realm. Power radiated from him, but she couldn't read a single thought behind his eyes.

"You," he said. Whether it was a question or an accusation, she couldn't tell. He stared past her, toward the wall they'd stepped out of. "But where are the others? I've seen... I've seen..."

"Come Alistair." Aura pulled him along.

Ember hoped some magic existed that could bring him back to himself, but that kind of healing belonged to a different sort of power altogether.

She spared one last look at the other cells. So many of them, lining both sides of the halls. Zyah hurried them onward before the prisoners could make a sound, but many of them couldn't have made one anyway. She recalled the Queen saying the King locked up his enemies, but this was far beyond that. Ember swallowed hard.

Aura led the way with Alistair, with Maryse and Zyah following close behind.

"What is the plan?" Ember whispered loudly enough for all of them to hear. The tunnels curved in disorienting ways. Torches lit the path here and there, but they seemed sure of their direction. Ember's boots sank in the cold, damp dirt. Grace sneezed behind her.

Maryse paused mid-step and side-eyed Ember. "To change the King's mind," she said. Even in low light, Ember saw her share a look with Zyah.

"How?" Ember asked, the thought of home still on her mind. "Shall we offer him a cookie?"

Grace snorted. Zyah cut in. "We will decide when we get to him. He is not easy man to approach, but perhaps with his Queen here…"

The Queen who is hundreds of years older than the one he knows, Ember thought. Ember might not cross paths with a version of herself—she hadn't been born yet—but could Aura run into her earlier self? How would that work?

They reached a staircase at the end of a hallway, and Ember quieted. She halted for a moment on the bottom of the step, imagining what she would say to her past self. In the end she decided it would be best to say nothing. Not because of the time space continuum—even though that was absolutely a concern—but because the lessons she'd learned had shaped her into the person she was today. And she was proud of that person.

She still desperately wanted to see her parents again, though.

Zyah took the steps first, cautiously, his hand on his sword. Maryse followed, then Grace and Aura, leaving Ember with Alistair. He smelled of the dungeon, and his clothes were rags, but there was a light in his blue eyes as he looked her over.

"They call you the chosen one, don't they?" he asked, shaking his head. His stringy hair hung around his face, but Ember could see it was once the same pale blond as the Queen.

"They try to," Ember admitted.

"They called me the chosen one too." He shrugged his shoulders. The shift of his ragged shirt revealed a bony shoulder and the corner of a sun tattoo. Ember wondered how many times in the past years he'd even seen it. He paused on the stairs. "I think, Ember Weathers, what they mean is you have to choose yourself."

He gave her a thin, weary smile, then slipped up the stairs faster than she thought was possible.

"I didn't tell you my name," she called to an empty staircase. Grace waved her forward.

"Come on," she said. "There's a doorway!"

They emerged in a cleaner stretch of the dungeon where the guards were actually awake. They watched Zyah with their hands on their weapons. He wasn't yet treasonous at this time, but he was certainly suspicious. Zyah made a deliberate show of sheathing his sword.

"His Highness is expecting us." Zyah nodded to Alistair. "He wishes to confer with the magician."

Alistair dipped his head. "I foresee a great battle…" he moaned, then subtly winked at Ember. Theatrics. She couldn't help but smile.

"A great battle?" one of the guards paled. "Where? When?"

Zyah stepped between them. "That is for his Highness alone," he said, voice firm. "Tell no one we were here." He pinned the boy with a stare. The guard looked no older than sixteen.

"Yes, sir." He nodded, shifting his gaze to Alistair. "And we will be ready."

"See that you are." Maryse patted his shoulder gently. And with that, they climbed more stone stairs, and emerged from the dungeons into the castle's basement. It was the same castle Ember been in before in Atlantis—only hundreds of years earlier. The stone was fresher and less worn and the setting familiar.

They emerged into a circular room of stone. More guards and cells lined the rough walls, though these prisoners could call out. They cheered and booed, even sang. Guards sat at a rough wooden table playing cards. Others exchanged banter with the prisoners. Ember thought they might slip by unnoticed, but that would be a different kind of magic—one they didn't have.

"Hey! You there!" One of the men shouted, climbing to his feet. He was the oldest of the crew, with a wide jaw, ginger beard, and round belly. He still clutched his cards as he fumbled for his sword. Ember noticed the card—the seven of swords—which, to her recollection, was not a good sign. She side-eyed Grace for conformation, but the girl was in shadow behind Alistair. They fanned out, with Zyah taking the lead.

"Robert." Zyah nodded, and Robert took a hesitant step back. The sword faltered in his grip.

"We need passage," Zyah said, his gaze locked with the man as if they shared a silently understanding. Ember held her breath. "It's time I speak to the King," he said, softly. A murmur ran through the cells. Even the guards quieted.

"It's treason, Zyah," Robert said, eyeing the Queen behind him, though Aura now was far older than the one this guard remembered. "He is... better, today," Robert added. "Perhaps, in time, he will settle. Perhaps the good in him will win out..."

Aura stepped forward, a measured shadow between them. "Time sometimes has a way of making things worse," she said. "And I do not think that is a gamble you want to take."

"Your Highness." Robert hesitated, then knelt. The other guards and most of the prisoners followed suit. "I just saw you in the dining hall..."

"That is unfortunate," she replied, scanning the cells. "Would you follow my orders if I told you to release them?" Gasps echoed around the room. She looked at Ember with a faint smile. "Might as well start big."

"The King would have my head," Robert said, glancing over her shoulder at Alistair. "I have special orders not to release him," he said, his voice grew firmer. The guards watched nervously.

"I had hoped it wouldn't come to this," Zyah said, drawing his sword.

"It won't." Maryse winked at Ember. She pulled something from of her pocket—herbs that smelled like summer itself. She murmured over it while Zyah and Robert tangled, then blew the mixture into the air. It swirled into a purple cloud, spreading toward all the guards except Robert, who traded blows with Zyah. The moment it touched them, their heads drooped, and their eyes glazed over.

"Put yourself in the cells," Maryse commanded. The guards obeyed as if zombies while she took the key and released the others. Most stayed close, but one man stopped and glared at her.

"Witch," he spat at her feet before rushing past her up the stairs. She wiped the residue of her spell off her hands.

"How's that for a thank you?" She turned to Ember with a smile. Ember was watching the duel with fear.

"What about them?" she asked.

"Oh. Zyah can hold his own against Robert. They're old friends. Come on—the spell won't last long. He'll catch up."

Chapter 18

Campfire smoke pooled in the castle hallways, and the very stone walls crackled with magic. Ember hadn't believed Shep when he told her magic was in the air around them in Atlantis, but he'd been right. It filled her lungs like a deep breath that settled in her bones. Power. Love. She wished she hadn't left Shep behind, but how could she have known where this would lead? Their paths always seemed to divide. Different tasks. Different lessons. She followed Maryse's steady footfalls around the corridors and hoped that someday they might settle. Here, maybe. But there was so much of the world she wanted to see.

Tapestries lined the walls, but Ember couldn't tell if they were the same as in her time. They were brighter. Bolder. They told stories of magic—dragons, knights, and sorcerers. One reminded her so vividly of her mother's art that she stopped short: a man in a red cloak stood over a cliff. She'd seen him in a dream, only in the dream she was beside that man.

"It's the tale of Archos," Grace paused beside her. Somehow her jewelry and colorful skirts didn't seem out of place here. She shone. "Saved the city of Atlantis from an invasion or something."

"I remember it differently," Ember said. She tipped her head and brushed her fingers over the fabric. "The cliff was on the south side. The army to the west, and much greater in number than this. They had beasts greater than dragons." She searched the sky on the tapestry, but there were only two gold dragons embroidered there. She felt Grace's gaze.

"In my dreams," she explained, as if that explained anything.

Grace studied the tapestry. "There's much wisdom in dreams," she said. Sunlight streamed through the slitted windows and highlighted her dark hair. She turned to Ember. From below came the sounds of the merry city. "Though that usually depends on interpretation." She smiled. "Care to share?"

Ember didn't. The battle she saw in her sleep was long and dark. Some nights they won. Some nights they didn't. Some nights the man in the red cloak whisked her away before she could get hurt. Some nights he died.

"I don't think it's finished," Ember admitted.

"Hmm," Grace said. "Perhaps it's the future you're seeing, not the past?" Her face lit up as she thought about it. She opened her mouth to say more, but Aura called from the end of the hallway to hurry up.

"You are more than you seem, Ember Weathers," Grace took her arm.

"And sometimes even that is not enough," Ember said with a sigh. She tried to focus on the fact she was here, in Atlantis in its height. Something magical swept past the windows and disappeared in a poof of smoke. A child's laugh floated in from outside. The sound made her think of Shepherd.

"Make it enough." Grace squeezed her arm, then let go and ran to catch up with the others, her skirt billowing behind her.

Ember stepped to the windows. They had reached a stretch that overlooked the ocean and the stable, though from this height she could only see garden. The colors of the trees and flowers were like nothing she'd ever seen. The smell intoxicating.

"Careful." It was Alistair who came back for her this time.

Somehow, color had returned to his face in the short time since his release, as if he were a flower unfurling in the sun. She hadn't noticed the quiet strength of his gaze. He tipped his chin to the closest vine that wound its way into the window. A single small pink flower bloomed there. Alistair plucked it and tucked it behind Ember's ear.

"Even beautiful magic can have it's dark side," he said. "Just as roses have thorns."

Something tickled. Ember reached up to touch the flower. In her grasp, it became a small white bird. It chirped once, then fluttered to the windowsill.

"Why didn't you just break yourself out," Ember asked, "if you have such magic?" she watched the bird hop once on the sill, then take flight into the gardens.

"Timing is everything, Ember," he told her. "And sometimes the world demands suffering. A sacrifice."

Ember thought of all the suffering in her own life. The sacrifices. The choices. She'd never thought they'd made her stronger or better. They'd made her depressed, angry, and broke. But they had made her who she was. Her blood was part of it. Her heritage. But there was more than that. There was strength.

She shook her head. "Maybe." She moved down the hallway, peering into side chambers as she passed. "Or maybe that's what we tell ourselves when we're afraid."

She looked at him out of the corner of her eye. Even the rags on his frame looked less dingy.

He folded his hands together as if in prayer. "You might be on to something."

He seemed as if he had more to say. Lifetimes of conversations could be found in those very words, but they had little time to pull them apart. Sacrifice or no, they'd reached the kitchens, and it was time to find King Corin.

The kitchens were busy. Stoves burned hot. Food was spread across long tables. Servants darted in and out, casting barely a glance toward them, though Zyah kept them in the hall.

Aura's eyes teared up.

"Matilda," she said, glancing toward a young blonde girl. She turned to Ember. "She was left behind when we rose. I haven't seen her in so long…"

The girl kneaded bread without looking up, but Ember heard her humming a familiar song. Aura shook her head and looked away.

"The King would probably be in his study at this hour," Aura said. She swallowed. "And as for… me…" She hesitated, her tightening in her sleeves. "Outdoors, perhaps the gardens. In the library. There are so many places."

Maryse touched her arm, lightly. "From what I understand, you will not be in the same place as your former self. Magic will see to it we're redirected."

"Yes, well…" Aura ran a hand up her arm, where chills had raised fine bumps. "See that it does."

"It's really more of a theory," Maryse trailed off.

Zyah kept his hand on the hilt of his sword, but Ember didn't know who he meant to draw it for until a group of guards crossed the far end of the kitchens. His jaw tightened.

"Which is the fastest way to the study?" he asked.

Aura beamed. "I know the way."

She wove them between tables and servants, most stepping aside while other raised curious brows. Ember forced her face into calm. She tried to bury the fear and show no guilt. She was traveling back in time to convince a King not to become a monster. And if they failed, she didn't know what Zyah would become.

A red dragon swept past the window, so close it blurred the glass. Ember stopped abruptly.

Grace walked straight into her back.

"Arcturus," Ember breathed. She knew in her heart it was Shep's dragon. From the color he'd described to the feeling he projected.

Grace paused, then gave her a gentle push forward. They caught up to Alistair, who walked ahead, mumbling something that sounded like a chant.

Aura led them through a winding corridor deeper into the castle and toward a spiral staircase, which they ascended quickly.

"To the tower," Aura said.

Grace leaned close. "The King likes to hide out there," she said with a shrug. "So I've heard."

The higher they climbed, the darker it became. The windows were smaller, only slits that shone on paintings on the wall. No longer tapestries of victories, or peace. They were scenes of battle hastily scratched.

A chill crawled up Ember's arm when she saw a scene that looked too much like them. Six figures ascending the stairs. Herself, her dark hair falling to her shoulders. Grace in long skirts. Aura with worry drawn across her face. Alistair with his hands folded. Maryse and Zyah leading the way.

"What is this magic?" Ember whispered, but she was last and no one heard.

They'd reached the top of the staircase and opened the wide doors.

CHAPTER 19

King Corin was waiting for them inside the circular stone room.

Strange and unfamiliar scientific instruments crowded the space, but that wasn't what drew Ember's attention. Corin stood with his back to them, the same cloak she'd seen in her dreams. A red so deep it looked like blood. It ruffled as the breeze blew in through the windows. He clasped his hands behind his back.

Beyond him lay only puffy clouds and the ocean on the horizon. Even the sounds of Atlantis were far away, but magic? That she could feel, and it set her teeth on edge. It was as if magic were at war with itself here.

In the middle of the room, a miniature city floated inches over a table. It bobbed gently, as if it rode a wave. Ember marveled at the level of detail. The castle was there. The very turret they were in.

Below, in the tiny streets, miniature people moved about.

"It's in real time," Corin said without turning. Aura paled at his high, sharp voice. In many ways, he was the opposite his brother: skinny where Zyah was broad, blond to his brunette. A crown of gold with green jewels rested atop Corin's drab locks of hair.

He finally turned. "Everything happening now is reflected here. Were the tower open, you'd see us." He gaze swept the group, lingering on Alistair. "Of course I knew you were coming, and why. Thank you, Grace. You have done well."

Grace had the good sense to look sheepish, while the rest of them turned to her. Grace looked down.

"It's not what you think," she said, peering up through her lashes. "We all want the same thing."

Zyah tipped his head. His hand was on the hilt of his sword by his side, but he did not draw it. Not yet. "You were the one who told us about the portal," he told her.

"You set us up," Maryse finished.

Grace pursed her lips as Arcturus flew past the window. "My mother discovered the portal to return. She thought it was a sign—that things could be corrected. I stepped through and warned the King before I came to you."

Aura blanched. "Warned the King who then did nothing?" she spat. "All those years in the sky. The cost of it. Those left behind. The magicians you killed. Was it because they knew?"

"You are getting ahead of yourself, dear wife." Corin also had a sword by his side. He made no move for it but walked close enough to almost touch her. "None of that has happened yet. Though Grace has filled me in, as of now things will proceed as they were. We curse Atlantis to the sky. I live a long life, until I don't..."

He reached up to touch her face, stopping just short of her cheek. "You are still magnificent," he said. Something flashed in her eyes.

"Stay away from me," she told him. He let his hand fall.

"I suppose it is useless to apologize for things that have not yet happened." He nodded, as if deferring to her. "But I do. The mages tell me the decisions I make will poison my mind—" Aura huffed. "But I am not yet that man," he finished.

He reached out to take her hand, and she let him.

"I have seen you do things both great and terrible," she said. "I've seen the cost these decisions made on you. They destroyed you."

King Corin frowned. Somewhere inside, a soul remained. Madness had not yet taken root. "I cannot reverse those decisions," he said. "There is too much at stake. Things must unfold as they will, or the magicians warn me of an even greater disaster. But we must somehow mitigate your return."

He looked into her eyes. There was still love there. Respect. On his side, at least. Tears formed in the corner of Queen Aura's eyes. One slid down her cheek. How many years had it waited to fall?

"Corin..." she said, simply.

His voice was not much more than a whisper. "I gave everything to send Atlantis to the sky. I will give whatever left for her return. I fear it will not be enough."

Without warning, Zyah drew his sword. Aura gasped and stepped back, but it was too late. His blade was at Corin's throat.

Corin tipped his head up. There was no fear in his eyes. Perhaps he was mad, after all?

"This is all your fault," Zyah spat. "Tell me why I should not slit your throat right now?"

The door at the back of the room swung open.

Shepherd walked in.

He was not yet Shepherd. His face was unlined. His skin smooth. The same dark hair. The beginnings of a beard. Ember's legs went weak.

"Your highness?" He had his sword out in a heartbeat.

"It's all right, Casius," Corin said. "Stand down. My brother will do as he will. But if he were to strike, he should know that it would alter history enough that his companions would have no home to return to. The consequences could be... dire."

Cas looked from the King to the others, his gaze settling on Ember. Questioning.

"Your Highness?" he asked again.

"Stand down," Corin said, his eyes locked on Zyah as if in challenge.

Zyah cursed and lowered his sword. Cas lowered his.

"Thank you Casius, but I am all right," Corin said. "Stand guard outside, please."

"Shep," Ember whispered.

He narrowed his eyes, as if the name stirred recognition. She saw herself reflected in his dark irises. She saw their future—a future he did not yet know.

He hesitated, then sheathed his sword and walked back to the door, his gaze never leaving Ember's. The weight of his absence pressed down as the large door swung closed. Ember let out a breath and looked up to see Aura watching her with a quiet sadness.

Aura took her hand. "We will return to our time," she said. "I promise you."

"Return to what?" Ember asked, wiping the tear with her other hand. She had no time for such indulgences. Things were complicated enough. But emotions were what they were. Seeing Shep had shaken her to her core.

"Peace." Aura squeezed her hand before letting go.

"What your ideas, *Your Highness*?" Zyah spat the words, urgency in every syllable. "And hurry before the portal closes and they're trapped here."

"The portal closes?" Ember's eyes widened, but no one else seemed to notice.

"I have something in my possession that may help." Corin rounded the table, the miniature city of Atlantis on it. He headed to a container with wide drawers of all shapes and sizes. Ember swore they moved when you blink. Some were the size of her pinky fingernail, others as large as a watermelon. The King chose the one in the middle, laid his palm on it, and it clicked open. Inside rested a large, gray egg.

"Draco," Ember said. She felt the little dragon's pull. The King smiled.

"As I expected," he said. "I will leave this when we rise, to find you when the time is right."

She reached out, her fingers brushing the leathery surface, and their bond sealed instantly. She longed for home.

"She already has the dragon, brother," Zyah said, rubbing his chin. "It's not enough."

Alistair stepped between them, hands spreading to show he was harmless. "Perhaps I can offer a suggestion," he said.

"Speak, magician," Corin said, a hint of disdain in his voice. Alistair only stared him down. Whatever was happening between them was old, an argument that needed no words. Corin's cheeks turned pink, but Alistair did not buckle.

"You will need to bind the magic of the dragons to raise the city, but the others? Release them," Alistair said. His words were not a spell, but they had power just the same.

"You know I can't." Corin's voice wavered.

Aura watched them, piecing it together. Grace lingered by the door. Between them, Zyah and Maryse stood tense, waiting.

"Why did my husband put you in prison, Alistair?" Aura asked. "I was told it was treason. I... never saw you again."

Alistair didn't blanche at the revelation that he had spent his entire life in prison or faced death—but his gaze remained fixed on Corin as the silent battle played out on his face.

"I know not of raising the city—not yet, but this is not the only dragon's egg I know of," Corin admitted, his shoulder's slumping.

"He has been hoarding them," Alistair said. The red dragon flew past the window again, closer this time, as if he could hear every word. The smell of his smoke trailed in through the window. The city of Atlantis on the table went in shadow as a cloud moved over them.

"Why?" Aura asked, voice sharp.

"Power." Alistair's words rang as an accusation, but there was no malice behind it. Everyone knew who this King was, who he would become. What would he do of it now, though?

The far door burst open again. Shep stepped in, his gaze flicked to Aura with a question. "Your Highness," he interrupted. "The Queen... is on her way. I assumed you would want to know."

Aura took a breath in, and the rest shuffled uneasily. "The back staircase," she said, but made no move. "But what of the dragons?"

Corin leaned in and whispered something to Shep. The magic of their conversation carried in the energy around them. "They will be found when the time is right," the King said, straightening. He commanded Shepherd to stay with him, and Ember was glad. How would she ever explain this?

As they passed, he held out a hand and touched her arm.

"I know you," he said, the question simmering in those deep amber eyes she'd come to know so well.

"You will," she promised, surprised to find a tear in her eye. "But not for a long time." She risked a touch to his cheek, feeling his energy under the stubble on his chin. Here, he'd not yet turned. He'd not yet made choices that would condemn his soul. She could warn him—but then where would they be? No. The King was right. Things had to unfold as they would. They would have to return and find the dragons in their own time.

"Thank you," she said to both Shepherd and the King. Corin remained behind, shoulders slumped over the miniature city. Shep's gaze lingered on her, curious, knowing.

"I look forward to it," he said, and Aura led them off.

CHAPTER 20

In his heart, Hawk had always known something else was out there. He'd thought the voices he heard were those of the Atlantis' ancestors calling for help. That's why he rounded them all up on his ship before Zyah or whoever could destroy them. He protected them as best he could. But now that the city was on the ground, the call carried something more. He could feel it in his very bones. Bones that, at the moment, were hungry.

"Damn this curse." He slammed a fist onto the table in his study. Books and instruments rattled, sliding across the surface. He remembered the conversation he had with Shep here. Hawk had died in a battle with the hellhounds, and Shep revived him at a terrible cost. Shep had given a way to feed without taking life, but gnawing hunger persisted, always beneath the pull of magic. His eyes flashed red.

"Damn this curse!" he roared again, this time driving his fist through the desk, splintering the wood. His hand would heal—a benefit of that same curse—but what he would give to be free of it.

"What did that desk ever do to you?" Paine slipped in, and he immediately regretted his outburst. His hand may heal, but the ship would not. He ran his hand over the broken wood and sighed.

"Nothing," he admitted, forcing a smile that didn't reach his eyes.

Paine walked slowly, studying the instruments and books Hawk collected in his travels. Here was an ancient globe. There, a spy glass. Books on Atlantis lore. On magic and myths too far-fetched to be believed. What had he been searching for all these years? There were no gods coming to save them. There was no magic potion that could cure him.

Was he damned because of his curse? Was Atlantis damned because of their actions?

"Should we have..." he began.

"Shh." Paine cut him off. She'd reached his desk and put a finger on his lips. "We learned a long time ago that *coulds* and *shoulds* don't help. You're the one who said that."

She dropped her hand, and this time Hawk's smile was genuine.

"I've said a lot of things in my time, Paine." Her eyes were wide and trusting, as if he had the answers. He didn't.

His stomach grumbled.

"You taught me a lot, too." She hoisted herself onto his desk, legs dangling. "You have a way of doing that, you know?" She tipped her head. "Leading without ego. Showing people the right way. What do you think you've been doing all these years?" She gestured around to what Hawk thought was junk. "Do it again," she added. "Do it now."

Hawk laughed despite himself. He sat beside her on the desk, but his legs reached the ground. It had been over ten years since he rescued her from the streets when she was not much more than a child, and the last few years they'd had a flirtation he was still struggling to understand.

Still, it was natural to take her hand as they stared through the porthole windows at the blue sky beyond.

"Lead is a strong word," he said. "I was lucky enough to inherit this ship. Or perhaps it found me. But all I've ever done with it is run."

She squeezed his hand. "All you've done is keep us alive. For this."

He squinted out the window. Something drew them north, but where, and why?

"Do you know I wasn't the first to pilot this ship?" he said. "But my father kept her in the shadows."

Paine tipped her head and scooted closer. She'd heard the story. Some of it, anyway. How Hawk's grandfather had been in Atlantis. The magic for the ship had come through him, but he and Hawk's father both had used it to hide. Hawk had grown up on the ship, and when his parents died, he took it and ran. Maybe he'd needed that time to find the courage to stop hiding.

She rested her head on his shoulder. "We are not meant for the shadows," she whispered.

He slid an arm around her back. A gesture of friendship and a question for something more. "No," he agreed. "It's far too late for that."

Outside, Draco cut through the white clouds. They'd flown high and north to avoid discovery, but the altitude had turned the air brittle with cold. Frost webbed the pane. Paine shivered.

"What happens if we find them?" she asked softly.

Hawk was sure there were more dragons out there. But what then? War?

He rubbed a small circle on her back. "I know what it is you fear, Paine. I fear it too."

She tipped her head up, mischief in her eyes. "Oh?" she asked. "It's a long list."

He laughed. "Not that long. You are brave. Courageous." *Beautiful*, he thought but didn't add. "But you fear bringing war to the world. You fear that Atlantis's return will damn us all."

She sighed. "We all fear that, I think." She thought of her shipmates lost to the hellhounds, and how much hate and anger there could be in the world. "But that's not all I fear."

He stilled and let her speak. His stomach growled loud enough to take over the room, a reminder of who and what he was now. Was that what she feared? He heard the thrum of her pulse and turned his focus elsewhere. For now, he was strong enough to resist. Shep had provided him with blood from somewhere, but the pull of the hunt was growing stronger. His eyes flashed.

"I fear what will happen to you," she said. She inhaled sharply at the moment of vulnerability.

She was one of the first Hawk had rescued. They'd been many things to each other. Friends. Best friends. Confidants. They'd seen each other at their best and at their worst, but this? This curse had weighed him down in a way she'd never thought possible, and it frightened her.

"Paine." His sad smile undid her.

He brushed the orange curls from her face, his touch so careful it brought a tear to her eye. Would it be here? Now? The moment they crossed that line from friends to something more?

His dark eyes were unreadable as they searched her face. She remembered the first time she had seen him. She'd been in such a terrible place, and he saved her. But he always said he was no knight in shining armor.

"I would not wish for this curse, that's for sure. But you know as well as I do we don't always get to choose our paths. We can only walk them. Fly them." He smiled and gestured to the ship around them. She'd never stopped being amazed by it.

His hand lingered on her cheek. "And there's no one else I'd walk it with."

He leaned in. His lips brushed hers, soft and unsure. Then his stomach growled, loud and traitorous. A sharp rap struck the door.

He pulled back, his expression both exasperated and flush. "I would like to come back to this later," he said. His old humor returned.

She saw through it. She always had.

He opened a flask behind his desk and took a long swig as he walked to the door. Paine smelled the familiar copper scent of blood and her heartbeat picked up.

Sierra pushed her way in. "Sorry for the interruption." She looked from one to the other, a smile tugging the corner of her lip. "But the ship needs a direction. Which way do we steer, captain?"

Chapter 21

Shepherd watched the flashing lights wash over the sky, the sea, and the land beyond the wards that still held. Thank the gods. For how long, he did not know.

His daughter paced the room. Javiar stood by the door, staring out as the city slept.

"There must be something we can do," Aurelia said for what felt like the hundredth time.

She was like him when he was younger—impulsive, eager to act. He felt the same fire stirring his chest. But he'd since learned the value of stillness—and the cost of haste. If he'd not been so reckless in his youth, maybe he wouldn't have this curse to deal with. Or perhaps he'd be dead.

There was no use in what-ifs.

Things were as they were: Atlantis was on the ground, it was in danger, and its people were asleep.

"We must trust, for now," he said, forcing his voice into calm. He'd not been there for her childhood. But he could be steady for her now.

She rounded on him, eyes blazing with rage.

"We could go after them," she said.

"Where?" Javiar rubbed his eyes. The man looked older than he should, but perhaps he was tired. They all were. They hadn't fallen to the curse that had put the city asleep, but they needed sleep just the same.

"Anywhere!" She threw up her hands in frustration.

She favored her mother in looks: her long dark-blonde curls, the wideness of her eyes. Their color, though, was his.

He wondered what else she'd gotten from him and what she'd gotten from her mother. Was she patient? Kind? Brave? Intuitive? He'd known her mother only briefly, but cared for her all the same.

And then she'd died. There was no magic in Atlantis, or anywhere else, that could bring her back.

Aurelia caught him watching and he turned back to the window.

"The Queen will broker peace," he said. "Ember will see it." He watched Aurelia from the corner of his eye as she bit a fingernail.

"It's not just the Queen and Ember," she said softly.

"Yes, the child," he said, thinking of Grace.

Aurelia cut in quick. "She's not a child."

Shep cocked his head. "You know this girl?"

Aurelia lips pressed thin. "Yes," was all she said.

Shep pushed further. "How?"

She frowned. "I don't have to answer your questions."

"You do when our fate relies on the answer." His voice rose.

Javiar stepped between them. He spoke quietly to Aurelia, as if he'd been the father figure Shep never was, and it was a punch in the gut. Shep stepped back.

"I do not know everyone in Atlantis." Javiar said, looking between them. "I spent most of my time in the castle. Protecting the Queen. Protecting... everyone." He ran a hand over his beard. "But I have never seen this woman before. Aurelia, if you know something, please tell us. The Queen and the others went with her. We must know they are safe."

Aurelia's bottom lip stuck out. She waited a beat.

Shep fought the urge to yell the answers out of her, but his first attempt at being a father was to know that wouldn't work.

"Please," he added.

She exhaled slowly. The pout softened into sadness and worry. Shep felt it, too. Too much time had passed. Where had they gone?

Aurelia looked at her father with wide eyes, searching him for something. Forgiveness, perhaps? Understanding. He knew the look well. He'd worn it himself.

"It's all right," he said quietly, grateful to be helping in some way. "Whatever happened. Whoever she is. It's all right Aurelia. We'll figure it out."

"We just need the truth," Javiar added.

Aurelia turned her back to them. Her hair fluttered in the window breeze, but otherwise the city was unnaturally still.

"She came to me in a dream first," Aurelia said. "I know that sounds silly. And stupid. And crazy. But that's what happened. I saw her outside the city, which makes no sense because we were in the sky, but I saw it. I saw... this." She waved her hand around.

"The sleeping curse?" Javiar asked.

She shook her head. "No. I saw the city on the ground. I dreamt of it often." She met Shep's eyes. "I dreamed of a girl like Ember, though I only saw her from the back. And you. My dreams are complicated. Prophetic. I don't always understand them."

In that moment, she reminded him so much of her mother that it brought a tear to his eye.

"Your mother was a mystic," he said. "Curse that she was not here to guide you through these gifts."

Aurelia swallowed. "Grace came to me in this dream. She offered her hand to bring Atlantis back. And when I met her, it's like it was fate." A faint blush bloomed across her cheeks.

Javiar shot Shep a withering look.

"Or a curse," he said.

"She's not like that," Aurelia cut in quickly. "She's kind, and soft. Good." She met Shep's eyes, as if her passion alone could convince him. "She's a good person. She wanted Atlantis returned. Magic. And Love. Everything Atlantis was and stood for."

Shep smiled. She was convincing. He'd give her that.

"What else did she say?" he asked. "Who is she? Where did she come from?"

Aurelia shook her head. "Far away. She used some kind of magic, but it wasn't strong enough. But her mother knew some people..."

"I'll bet she did," Shep said.

"She can help," Aurelia said. "But we need to find her. We need to help her."

Javiar spread his arms. "In case you haven't noticed, we're trapped. I don't know where they went or what magic they used, but we have none of it. Not even a trail to follow."

Shep wasn't so sure.

They were of no use in the castle. Stuck. Hiding.

He thought of stone the witch had given him in the cottage, the one that would light the right path when he was ready. He disliked relying on something that felt like a wish and a prayer—and reliance on questionable magic, but Aurelia was right about one thing.

They couldn't stay here.

The castle felt like a tomb.

Chapter 22

Ember rushed down the castle's back stairway with Aura, Grace, Zyah, Maryse, and Alistair. They spiraled through dark levels of the castle she was only beginning to map. The kitchens. The throne room. Still, they made their way down.

She was wholly unsatisfied.

"We came all this way so he could hide dragon eggs sometime in the future?" she asked, winded. Alistair was the closest to her.

"Small things are often enough to change the course of time," he said. "You've heard of the butterfly effect?"

She rolled her eyes. The idea that a butterfly could flap its wings and change the weather across the world was ridiculous. But what if all you had were butterfly wings? Was releasing the dragon eggs enough? Would they save Atlantis when the time came, or be lost to time again? Or worse, change history?

"Where exactly is he going to put them?" she asked.

Aura stopped short and lifted her hand, halting them.

"Guards," she whispered. She looked back to Zyah. "Is there another way back to the portal?"

He frowned, but Grace cut in.

"My mother's magic is not exactly precise." She wrung her hands. "The way back is usually not the way forward." She gave them an apologetic smile. "She said it's a metaphor."

"A metaphor," Ember repeated. "Great."

"What way is forward?" The Queen asked, gripping Grace's shoulder.

Grace looked up. "If I know my mother, if we started below in the dungeons, then we'll end above in the tower. As above, so below. Or the other way around, I guess."

They all looked up but the only thing visible was the stone of the staircase winding over them. The guards had passed. They had a clear route to the dungeons.

"Are you sure?" Zyah asked, but it was his wife who answered.

Maryse nodded. "She's sure." She met Ember's gaze and winked.

The Queen blew a long strand of hair from her face. "That might have been helpful to know before we walked all this way down," she said with a degree of humor.

Grace answered with a tear in her eye. "I'm sorry. Her magic is unpredictable. I told you…" She shot a look at Zyah, who had the good grace to look away.

"You knew we might not get back?" Ember accused.

Zyah held his hands up to keep her voice down. "I knew her magic was complicated, but I have made sacrifices for it, too," he said.

Now it was Ember's turn to frown.

"It was the only way to change the future," he added. He stepped closer and put a hand on her shoulder. "I returned back. You will, too."

"And then what?" she asked. She looked to Grace and the Queen. "Then we find the dragons and what? Start a war?"

The Queen shook her head. "*Prevent* a war," she said. "We will have leverage. Power."

She looked back up the stairs.

"When the magic is freed, we will be free as well."

Ember shook her head. She missed Shep's counsel. He would tell her to think it through, but there was no time. She couldn't deny the dragons would be powerful allies.

"Come," the Queen said. "I believe we will find what we're looking for in the observatory."

She slipped through a back door into tall grass and led them on a worn path around the castle, where the very air felt different. There was the pull of magic, of course. This was in Atlantis after all, at the height of its power, grounded and awake. But there was more than magic. The heartbeat of Atlantis. Love. Acceptance.

A servant carrying a barrel screamed when she rounded the corner. She pointed to Zyah and stumbled back, eyes wide.

"You!"

"I should have probably mentioned," Zyah said, "that we are not exactly welcome at this time. The King has begun to spread rumors..."

It was too late. She had started the alarm.

The Queen rushed them through the beautiful gardens and across the fields. The observatory was attached to the castle grounds, but just. It stood alone, like an afterthought. Or perhaps it was there first, and the castle had grown around it.

The air changed as the guards hunted them. Ember felt it in the magic. Fear. Hesitation. She rubbed her hands along her arms as goosebumps rose.

"How do we get in?" she asked, staring at the base of the tower. There was no obvious entrance, and the only windows were at the top.

The Queen sighed. "Legend says you have to be invited."

Ember pressed her lips together. "Are you kidding me?" She turned back to the stone tower. It was beautiful. Gray and white stone fitting together seamlessly. Vines climbed the curved walls in lazy spirals, their leaves fluttering in the wind.

She placed a hand on the stone and felt it humming beneath her touch.

"It has a heartbeat. Don't you feel it?" Alistair asked. He placed his hand beside hers and she swore she could hear a deep thrumming. "Old. Older than the city, even."

"How do we get inside, Alistair?" she begged.

He shook his head. "I want. I want," he said. "You start by putting that aside. What you want is irrelevant. What does magic want? What does it ask of you?"

She bit her bottom lip as the others searched for a secret entrance. It felt a little like a sham, seeking her soul for the root of magic, but the others were having no luck either.

She went inward instead.

She remembered the place she'd go in meditation. The quiet. The connection. She tried to get there now. She reached for the tower and imagined it across ages. What it had witnessed. She offered it a glimpse of the future.

Help us get back, she whispered. *So we can set things right.*

The tower responded in images, the way Draco did when he was young. She had to reach for them. They were old and distant.

She saw the tower as it was being built, a long time ago. She felt the magic coiled inside it. The love. It was a source of protection for whatever was inside.

Years turned. Faces changed. Kings and queens passed through its shadow, rulers Ember didn't recognize. Atlantis was a good place then, with good rulers. Most of them, anyway. Their intentions brushed across her like warm wind.

But some were drawn away from the tower, from the city. Some were not worthy. Some had less noble intentions.

The images slowed.

King Corin knelt at the base of the stones, pleading. Begging to be let in. His advisor stood beside him, striking the tower with every kind of magic he possessed.

"He's never been inside," Ember said.

She turned to the others. "King Corin. He has no idea what's in here."

The Queen rounded the tower and shook her head. "He'd never spoken of it," she said. "The magic is old and powerful, but nothing I'd ever been able to explain or use. I'd heard of a door, though. Maybe it was through the woods?"

She disappeared into the nearby woods while Zyah and Maryse began knocking along the stone, searching for what history had hidden.

"Perhaps, just ask?" Alistair offered, a spark in his eye.

"Rarely is it that easy," Ember said, trying to match his lightness.

"Rarely are things as complicated as we make them," he replied. He bowed to the tower. "Please, may we have entrance."

Ember looked at the tower out of the corner of her eye. She felt the power in the stones. "Please," she repeated. "I'd like to go home. If you know the way…" She had felt sillier in her time. She did have an invisible dragon, after all. Speaking to a tower felt reasonable, but it wasn't just a tower. It was magic.

"Take me back to Shep," she whispered, because if magic understood anything, it was love.

The very ground rumbled under them.

The tower groaned.

Maryse's eyes widened. "What have you done?" she asked. It was already too late.

The tower did not open. The earth did. A set of stairs led down and around into the dark.

The Queen snapped her fingers. "That was it," she said. She had been pressing a nearby rock. Had that opened the door, or their pleas? "Not a door. A staircase."

She looked at the others.

"You have to go down to go up."

"A metaphor!" Alistair clapped his hands. Ember groaned. She'd done enough traipsing through tunnels. She'd paid her dues, but it seemed more were owed.

The Queen pursed her lips, surveying the group gathered around her. "Traditional magic won't work here. We'll have to go through the dark. Only an obsidian will glow—and I don't suppose anyone has one of those?"

Ember smiled, remembering her visit to Grace's mother. She shared a look with the girl. "In fact…" She rooted in her pocket for the dark stone. It shone with a soft, low light.

"You are most curious, Ember Weathers," Aura said. Alistair chuckled. Grace looked afraid. The sounds of the guards scrambling echoed from afar, but close enough to move them forward.

"I'm afraid this is where we leave you," Zyah said. "Thank you—for your bravery, your counsel. I pray you will find the dragons, and they will aid you in your quest to return the city to her majesty." He took both of Ember's hands in his. "Do not let magic die in their world. Do not let love die."

She offered a genuine smile. "I promise you, I won't," she said, and meant it. For she carried the love with her in her heart, and that would show the way home.

CHAPTER 23

Alistair hesitated at the top of the stairs until the Queen took his hand. "Come, brother," she said.

He shook his head. "But if I go to your time..."

She smiled sadly and glanced once more at the deep gardens surrounding the tower. "There is no chance of seeing yourself," she said. "I never saw you again. I believe you died in that cell, and quite soon."

Alistair pursed his lips. "I will go," he said. His blue eyes filled with tears for a moment when he looked back.

Ember knew what it was to stand on the edge of a moment. He was looking back at his own death, a future he'd escaped. And no one knew what waited ahead.

Ember patted him on the shoulder as she peered down the dark staircase. "Thank you," she said. She felt in her heart they needed him.

She beginning to understand that deep intuition was magic. She'd always felt it. She held the obsidian up. It lit the deep recess, showing a stone staircase.

"I suppose I should go first," she said, though her feet were moving before she had truly decided.

She wanted to go home, wherever that was now. It was no longer the island. No longer the bookstore. She'd heard it said that home was a feeling. A person. She had never wanted to put that kind of importance on someone else, no matter how many romantic stories she had read.

But family?

She sighed and righted herself when her foot slipped on a cool stone. Family was home. Not just Shep. Draco. Her sister. Hawk. Paine. All had become part of her now. She descended the depths to go home to them.

She felt the Queen's light steps behind her, then Alistair, then Grace, who had been quiet. Ember understood the responsibility she shouldered, though she wondered about the girl's motives.

Farther down, carvings emerged from the shadows. People. Civilizations. Dragons. Magic. All crudely hewn into the rock. Her obsidian flickered. The air smelled of mist, and moss grew on the stone.

"Careful," she called.

The stone lit up fear on the Queen's face. Grace remained resolute. Alistair was unreadable.

"How much farther, do you think?" Aura craned her neck. The light painted her blond hair blue, reminding Ember of death. She shook it off.

"I think I see something ahead." Ember's voice echoed. There was no telling how far they had descended. They no longer felt fresh air and the sunlight didn't reach this far. The stairway had narrowed until they could only move single file, and the magic shifted around them. Older. Primal.

She'd almost walked into the door before she saw it.

"Oof." She stumbled and reached out to stop her fall, feeling the cold under her hands.

"Iron," Aura marveled, eyes wide.

Grace shoved past her, eyes bright. "You don't suppose…"

Aura shook her head. "It's a myth."

Ember scanned the group. "Does anyone care to tell me what's going on?" She lifted the light to the door.

Carvings sprawled across the stone. Winged being. Flames. Some rode dragons and were human-sized. Some had fangs and red eyes. Others looked angelic. All were locked in a battle.

"Of course," Alistair breathed.

"Of course what?" Ember snapped. For a moment, she swore the pictures moved, but when she blinked, they were back in place.

"There is a legend…" Aura began.

"It's more than a legend." Grace's hand glided over the carvings. The door shuddered under her touch. "My people were hunted. Captured by the King's ancestors. They feared our power. They were imprisoned somewhere on this island. When it rose, we lost any chance to find them." She pressed her palm harder against the carvings. "They're here."

"Your people?" Ember asked at the same time the Queen spoke.

"You're part fairy?" Aura took a step back, and Grace narrowed her eyes.

"You should know better than anyone what prejudices produce," she said in a whisper. "The same thing happened with your people—so badly that your island had to be raised to escape. The fairies are just like you, only a little... wilder." Her eyes glinted for just a moment as she looked at Ember.

"I... wasn't expecting this," Ember admitted.

"You'll have to free them," Grace said. "The portal home is on the other side."

"You set us up." Aura's voice was low, but pointed.

Grace shrugged. "I had no idea where it was. Magic appears where magic appears. You know that. I'd be lying to say I haven't been searching. With Aurelia's help."

The Queen blanched. "Aurelia is involved in this?"

"Deeply," Grace said, her tone respectful this time. "But that is a conversation for another time."

Alistair chuckled, breaking the tension. "I've always wanted to see a fairy! It's a pleasure to make your acquaintance." He bowed. "Can you—"

"Not now," Aura interrupted. Even in the low light, she looked pale. Ember had never seen the Queen afraid. She glanced at Grace, who held her ground.

"I am willing to look past old prejudices, of course," Aura said, regaining some of her poise. Her eyes searching Ember's, seeking guidance. "But how do I know this isn't a trap? I want to go home, but at what cost? I will not unleash more damage to my city. Not now, not in the future."

Ember felt the weight of the question. Releasing the fairies could be the only way to go home. Could it be worth it?

Alistair stepped between them, leaving Grace in shadow. His hand traced the carvings, reverent. "This door will seal behind us," he said. He looked back at them, eyes sharp. "They will have to come through with us... or be trapped."

"Or we will be trapped here." Ember muttered, biting her fingernail. Home. Her friends. Draco. Shep. What was it worth to her?

Everything. It was worth everything.

She ran her hand along the door, feeling the magic beneath. What she didn't feel, however, was a handle or any other way to open it. "How does it open?"

Aura stepped back, her eyes widened with tears. "What have we done?" Her voice echoed through the tunnel. The obsidian flickered. Ember wasn't sure how long it would last.

Alistair laid a steadying hand on the Queen's shoulder. "It is done," he said softly. "Our fate has been sealed. The only way is forward."

Aura shook her head and regained some of her composure. "I wish it were so easy, brother," she said, patting his hand. "Though it is good to see you again after all these years." Her gaze lingered on him a moment before she turned to Grace, donning her mask once more. "How does it open?"

Grace shrugged, her voice quiet. "Legend says a drop of blood... from a fairy." All eyes went to her. She took a blade out of her boot and muttered. "Legend has been known to be wrong," she said as she pricked her finger. The small drop of blood shone. She pressed it to a carving of a stone table at the center of the door.

The blood seeped into the channels around the door, lighting it up from the inside. Gears whirled. The carvings moved. The outline of the door glowed, a lock clicked, and the radiance from inside outshone the stone. Ember tucked the obsidian away, letting the magic guide her.

"The way forward," she whispered, stepping through the door.

CHAPTER 24

The sun dipped low in the western sky as Shep returned, carrying the white stone the witch had given him. He looked for Draco in the dusty sky, but he hadn't seen the dragon since the attack. The horizon was lonely without him.

The first stars were overshadowed by the flashing lights not far away. They were surrounded on all sides. And the city slept on.

The white stone pulsed softly in his hand, like nothing Shep had ever seen. It shone from the inside and hummed lightly. "It's supposed to show us the right path," he explained to Javiar and

Aurelia. Shep believed in magic through and through. He was a child of Atlantis, after all—but what he didn't believe in was mumbo jumbo. Magic had its own rhythm, it's rules. The "right path" was not exactly linear. How could it know one way was better than another? The stone vibrated harder as if in response to his thoughts.

"This is from Grace's mother?" Aurelia reached out and took the stone from him. It quieted in response, and its light dimmed. She turned it over. "Hmm," she murmured, a smile tugged at her lips. "I feel her magic. Wild. Free. It would be just like her to put your essence with Ember's in here and tie them together." She handed it back. It hummed again, as if approving.

"Our essences?" Shep murmured, staring at the stone. He'd often thought about the concept of a soul. Was there such thing, and had the witch cursed his when she turned him?

Aurelia covered his hand with hers. "Love," she said simply.

"Perhaps there is no such thing," he muttered, but even he didn't believe it.

"Perhaps it's the most powerful force in the world." She smiled, and he felt himself swell with pride. He'd not been there for her childhood, but she'd grown into a good person all the same. A wise person.

"What do you know of love?" he asked.

Her smile thinned. "I love her," she said simply. He didn't have to ask who—he'd known from the minute Aurelia had started talking.

"Then let us find her."

Javiar watched the army press in from the window. "They inch closer," he said.

"I do not believe they will breach the city. Not yet," Shep said. "But..."

Javiar sighed, hand resting on the hilt of his sword. "One of us must stay back. I know." He put his hand on his sword. "I will protect the city. Just... bring them home."

Shep nodded. "We will," he promised, even though he had no idea where to start.

Aurelia held the stone up. "It shows your way back to each other," she said. "Look." The rock glowed on one side, leading them further in the castle.

"That's odd," she said.

"It's the only direction we have," he said. Ember and the others had walked out the front in order to broker peace, but he had no illusions that they'd simply sat down and came to a treaty. Something had happened. Something had intervened. The stone vibrated harder, pulling them forward.

They left Javiar to guard the castle. The hunch of his shoulders the only thing that might tell he was feeling the weight of it all. Shep knew staying in the shadows was the only way to protect sometimes. He'd spent years doing it—he'd given his soul. It was a lonely business, being a protector. Loving someone. But now, he was filled with fire. With purpose. He would find Ember and the others, and he would right the city's return.

A plume of smoke rose near the wall of the city, but whether it was Draco or the weapons they were using he couldn't tell.

"I wonder what they're saying on the other side," Aurelia asked. "The world, out there. What's it like?"

Shep ducked as he led her from the throne rooms and through sitting rooms and studies. "I imagine they're afraid," Shep answered. "They are people, just like us. With their own magic."

He thought of all the years he'd been alive and searching. All the years he'd waited for this very minute, not ever imagining it would happen like this. But things can't be predicted, and miracles come in all shapes and sizes. Atlantis was home.

The stone led them past the shadowy library, his favorite place in the castle and out the door to the gardens where the grass reached his knees. They followed the worn paths around the flowers the Queen had so lovingly grown. Their petals fluttered and let off a sweet smell.

"What type of magic do they have?" she asked, lifting her skirt to take a step.

"Long buried," he said. Then quieter, "But they still love, even when it's hard. They still believe in hope. They know what is right even though they do not always follow it."

He smiled and looked back at her and understood, in an instant, what love was, and what it meant.

"It is all so fragile," was all he could think to say. He'd seen so many people come and go in his time. Magic stretched lives, but only for so long. Even he would die someday. And then what remained?"Look." Aurelia pointed.

The stone flared brighter, pointing them past the gardens, to what was once the edge of the world.

"There's nothing out there," he said, but they followed the stone anyway, stepping through the clear night.

Sirens wailed somewhere distant. Wind blew through the trees. The clouds mingled with smoke as the city was assaulted. The smell of it carried on the breeze.

The city had fallen close to the ocean. He could see its reflection in the distance. Between them stood only the stone tower, the observatory no one had managed to breach in his time. It blended in with the scenery after all these years as if it were camouflaged here. Forgotten.

He'd forgotten it, too.

Shep laid a hand on the cool stone. The white light tingled in his palm and tugged downward. He kicked the dirt with the toe of his boot, but nothing was under but more dirt.

"This tower?" he asked Aurelia. He'd vaguely remembered that it stood, but not its purpose.

"The observatory." She stood with her hands on her hips. Her long hair blew in the breeze. For a breath, she looked so much like her mother that it took his breath away. She could be a mystic herself. She could be anything. "I always thought it was where the mages disappeared to," she said, brow furrowing. "But I've never seen anyone come or go."

His gaze lifted from the ground to the stone. "How do we get in?" he asked.

The stone pulled, so hard it shifted his hand.

"Legend says you need to be pure of heart and just ask." She shrugged. "If the observatory deems you worthy, it opens."

"Please let me in?" Shep said, half a joke, half a prayer.

He touched the stone. For a heartbeat he thought nothing would happen. Then he stumbled as he felt the stone touch back. The sensation crept up his arm. It felt him out. Judged him. Shepherd had never passed this test, not in this life and not in his former life as Casius of the King's Guard. He always fell short. Never enough.

But this time...

The earth split beneath the base of the tower. Stone groaned. A stone staircase uncoiled from the dark like a jaw ready to devour them.

Aurelia huffed out a breath. "That's not creepy at all."

"I'd hoped we were going up," Shep said. He suppressed a shiver from the feeling of the tower reading him. He eyed its height, then the staircase below. They had no other path. He took two steps then held up the stone. The air was chilly. Old. It wafted out from the depths.

"Not creepy at all," Shep tried to smile, but Aurelia didn't return it. She took a tentative step. Her boots were still clean enough to be shiny. Her dress reached to her ankles, trailing the ground.

"For Atlantis," she said. "Somebody has to wake them."

This time Shep did smile. He wanted to say he was proud of her, but the words died on his lips. Perhaps she wasn't ready to hear them. Or perhaps he wasn't ready to say them. He thought somehow she felt it, though, and that was enough.

"For Atlantis," he repeated. His words echoed down the staircase and caused a shiver. He gripped the stone tighter, and descended first.

CHAPTER 25

"We're following a *hunch*?" Paine leaned over the rail, squinting her eyes, trying to see whatever it was Hawk sensed. From her vantage point, it was nothing more than a feeling. Captain Shallow had let the ship "do its thing," which meant setting its course and letting it go. That course carried them over the ocean. The air had picked up a chill with the setting sun. Though they were too far up to feel sea spray, wind whipped up the water and blew stray curls off Paine's face. She tucked them back behind her ears.

"We've followed less than that before," Hawk said. He shrugged out of his jacket and put it over her shoulders. His shoulders were muscled. If he felt a chill, he didn't show it. She snuggled into the jacket and smelled his scent on it.

"That wasn't a matter of life and death," she countered. When they'd fled Atlantis, the city had been under attack by forces who didn't want magic restored. Or maybe it was fear. Fear did all kinds of crazy things to people. She knew that. She'd spent most of her life rescuing those who had magic from those who hunted them.

But never had they *run away*. Not until now.

He gripped the rails. His knuckles went white. "There is something out there. It calls to me. I do not know if it's my new… gift." He bit off the word as if it tasted wrong. Shep had saved his life, but at a high cost. Paine shifted her weight on the deck.

"But I feel it inside. And the ship feels it."

"What, exactly, is it?" she asked. They'd followed his hunches before, but they'd been more factually based. He'd rescued ancestors of Atlantis before they could be hunted. He helped them with their magic. In most cases, gave them a family they didn't have. Most of that crew was now asleep in Atlantis. Only she, Hawk, and Sierra had escaped.

"I've always had a strong pull to magic. You know that." His blue eyes searched the horizon. Whatever he saw, it was beyond the reach of ordinary sight. "There is something strong out there. Something new."

His stomach growled.

"Yeah. Atlantis," she said, pulling the coat tighter. His hunger made her nervous, though it fascinated her too. The only physical changes she'd seen were a slight paleness to his face and sharpened incisors if you looked closely.

"More than that." His mouth tightened. His lips thinned as he struggled with an explanation. She put a hand on his shoulder. He'd always been a good captain. He'd given their misfit crew purpose and kept the ship tidy and running. Kept them away from trouble and danger. She trusted him, and more than that, even.

"I believe you," she said. Her words misted in the cold air. "But how? What are we chasing?"

"I do not know." He balled his fists. His eyes found hers, opened and frightened. "It could all be nothing. A failure. Maybe we are just running away."

Paine's smiled softened the sting of his doubt. "I've never known you to shy from an adventure."

Something in his expression cracked, just enough to show the man beneath the uncertainty. "I do not know how to deal with this curse," he admitted. "And I am hungry..." His eyes flashed with a glint she didn't recognize, and fear stirred in her chest.

Before either of them could speak again, Sierra's footsteps pounded across the deck.

"I found something!" she called, waving a small black book as she ran toward them.

"*The History of Devil's Island*?" Hawk pulled his gaze from Paine and took the book from Sierra's hand. "I've read this a million times. Magic has protected this island, yes, but there's nothing useful in it. At least not from this book."

A lone seagull flew below them, calling out. Where he was flying from or to, Paine didn't know. But she knew that lost feeling all too well.

"Me too," Sierra said. Her hair was loose around her shoulders, blown by the wind. The ship was in the best of shape, but the decks had begun to show signs of wear. Sierra pointed to the book. "But look. There's something new."

Hawk flipped through the pages, disbelief knitting his brows. Paine leaned in. "How could there be something new?" Hawk asked. "This book was published years ago."

"Magic is magic," Paine mumbled. She'd flipped through the book when she went through Hawk's library, but research had never been her strength. Cooking for the crew, keeping them fed and calm—those were her talents. Hawk, though, knew every line of this book. If something inside had changed, he'd know.

And something *had* changed. The look on his face said so.

Sierra pointed to a folded page. "Here," she said, hopping from foot to foot.

He opened it to a chapter on the mansions. She tapped the page.

"Several relics were found when they cleared the land for the new developments," he read aloud. He looked up. "Where your house was?"

She nodded. He continued. "The relics indicate a civilization on the island decades ago. They were removed for study at the Delaney Institute."

"That wasn't there before. I'd have known it." She cut him off.

Hawk flipped the book over to study the cover. A photo of the main street looked down at the dock. Ember's bookstore wasn't even visible, but he felt its presence. The author was listed as George Delaney. He flipped to the back to read the bio: "Delaney was a part-time resident of Devil's Island, an amateur historian, and generational owner of Delaney Institute. He summered on the bluffs and published a series of mystery books, but the history of the island was his passion. He spends most of his time at the Institute, waiting for magic to come back."

"Hmm," Hawk continued. "Sounds like something is there?"

"I searched your books for the Institute they referenced. All I can find are coordinates to an island," Sierra said, her eyes twinkling.

He smiled. "We have a direction after all?"

She nodded. "There is something else there. Something that changed recently. I know it."

Hawk rubbed his chest, feeling the pull of hunger gnawing at him even as he rationed the blood bottles Shep had given him. *How long before he ran out?* He didn't dare think past that. He swallowed. "Set our course," he said, voice low but certain. He'd figure it out. He had to.

CHAPTER 26

Ember's eyes adjusted to the low light as she stepped through the doorway at the end of the dark staircase. She wasn't sure what to expect, but a long stone hallway that glowed faintly wasn't it. She hesitated.

"I thought you said they trapped fairies in here?" she asked without turning. Far ahead, lights flickered and danced across the wall.

"I said that was the rumor," Grace replied, pushing past her. The hallway was big enough for both to pass, with some height. *How tall were fairies?* Ember hadn't read enough about the magical world of Atlantis. She thought they were tiny—but then side-eyed Grace, who was taller than her.

"Can you tell me what I'm getting into?" Ember asked, brushing her hand over a glowing stone on the wall. A hum of old magic ran through her fingers, stirring something deep in her blood. Something that sounded like an old, lost song—full of joy and danger.

Grace smiled as Aura and Alistair followed them. They took hesitant steps as Grace piled her long hair back into a bun, tying it with a ribbon. "I suppose I feel fairy magic the way you felt Atlantis magic," she said. Far off music echoed, but they couldn't hear the rhythm. "It's been generations," she added, voice low. The air grew cooler, and Ember stepped over a puddle.

"But it's a calling," Grace continued. "Their magic? It's wild. They were banished from Atlantis for breaking its rules—they couldn't keep their magic to love and light. Sometimes magic is dark. Sometimes it has to be. They crossed the wrong person, I suppose." She shrugged.

"Does there have to be dark?" Ember wondered. There was no answer to that and never had been. She'd always honored the balance in the world. Either side seemed stronger when attention was on it, that's why she never watched the news or followed social media. For some reason the spotlight always finds the worst of things. Maybe there's a middle ground. Maybe it lived here, in the fairies?

The music ahead grew louder, and the lights in the tunnel brightened. The tempo rose, light and quick. A peal of laughter called out. Ember looked back at Aura. She was not laughing.

Alistair offered a small, sad smile. "Fairy folk are good and evil, as humans are." He folded his hands before him, leaving his face in shadow. "I know not who will greet us, but let us hope it's one of the good ones."

Ember swallowed. The tunnel twisted, then opened into a wide entryway. It was carved of simple stone, but the symbols on the doorway glowed brighter as they approached. The music slowed, then stopped. Flashes of light flickered in the air. Colors shimmered. Voices whispered. And wings rustled in the quiet.

"What do they mean?" Ember asked, looking at the intricately carved symbols.

Grace shrugged as if none of it bothered her, though her face had gone pale. "The old language has been lost," she said. She raised her hand as if to touch one but let it fall. She forced a smile. "Maybe they say *welcome*?"

Alistair tittered. He was the only one.

A bright and curious little face peeked through the doorway. Blond hair. Pointed ears. It quickly vanished and was replaced by another. Laughter. Shouts.

Aura stopped short before crossing the threshold. "Let me do the talking," she said. No one argued. They fell in line behind her, half hiding, half bracing.

The Queen turned to them, her voice low. "Do not make any deals. Do not take any gifts. Above all, do not eat or drink anything." She looked to them all in turn.

Ember nodded. Only then did she realize she was hungry.

The Queen stepped through the doorway and was surrounded by light. Grace went after her. Alistair followed.

Ember lingered at the threshold. She glanced behind her. The way back was only darkness. The low stone light had nothing on the light in front of them. She drew a breath, turned forward, and stepped inside.

The fairy home was like nothing she'd seen before. It was as if they'd recreated the forest from the stone. It had been carved from ceiling to floor to mimic a home in the trees. If she didn't know better, Ember would have thought she was above instead of below. Light shone from the very stone itself. Here and there vine carvings twisted down, and between all of them were beautiful, winged beings of all sizes.

The stories had been true. Some were as tiny as a pencil and flew around them, laughing. Some were the same size as humans with folded wings behind them. The room stretched so far that Ember couldn't see where it ended.

Most of the fairy kept their distance, watching from the safety of carved shadows. A few were brave enough to come close. Their faces reflected curiosity mostly, but Ember felt anger as well.

She held her breath.

"Are you from above?"

A child-sized fairy tugged at Grace's skirt. She a long sundress with a cutout for her wings, and long dark hair trailed behind her, full of twigs and flowers. Aura touched Grace's shoulder, signaling that she would answer.

"Yes," Aura said.

The child laughed. Someone pulled her away before she could ask more, though her blue wings flared once in the light.

Aura straightened to her full height. "I am the Queen of Atlantis," she said. It wasn't exactly a lie. "I seek your leaders."

A fairy in a deep blue dress stepped into the circle that had formed around them. Ember saw a mosaic beneath her feet that reflected the light. Everything down here glowed. Even the floor. The colors were so vivid her temples began to throb.

"There is not exactly a leader," the fairy replied. She spoke with an air of authority. Her hair was tied back with a simple flower. Her cerulean eyes matched her dress, and her wings were of the most delicate ivory. "More of a council."

Aura nodded. "I would speak with your counsel, then."

The woman looked behind them. "The doorway is open, then?" she asked.

A hush fell over the fairy.

Aura shook her head. "I do not believe so," she answered. Her voice was deeper than the fairies'. "But there is another way. We seek your help. In return, we will help you."

"Help us?"

A male fairy stepped forward. He wore a fitted black suit, and his hair—bound in a braid—had gone silver at the temples, matching the wide wings on his back. "Now you wish to help us? After centuries of imprisonment!" His wings flapped with impertinence.

The murmurs rose. Wings beat in agitated bursts. Aura held a hand up to quell them.

"Not me."

She shook her head and the crowd quieted. Ember studied them. Hundreds lined the floor and flew overhead. Others lined the terraced hallways that went farther up than she could see. Light spilled from tiny apertures high up the walls. A nearby fairy caught Ember's gaze and winked, though his wings fluttered with tension.

"Not us," Aura continued. "We have only just returned Atlantis to the ground. We are trying to right old wrongs."

"Excuse me." The male fairy cut her off. His wings beat sharply, though he didn't rise. "Did you say Atlantis was *not* on the ground?"

Aura took a deep breath. "It's a long story. May I speak to your council?"

Ember stepped beside her. For someone who prided herself on reading people, she struggled here. There were too many mixed emotions. Anger. Relief. Fear—so much fear. And beneath it all, hope.

"We want to help," Ember echoed.

"Smooth," Grace muttered. Ember shot her a half smile.

The two fairies who seemed to hold authority murmured to one another. More stepped from the crowd until there was a group of around ten gathered. Most were older, though two looked almost as young as Ember. The youngest was a dark-skinned fairy in a deep red dress with matching wings. She gave Ember a small wave. Ember recognized her as the one who'd winked.

"Our chances of survival are fifty-fifty," Alistair said, sounding entirely unbothered. "Oh look! Mushroom!" He crouched to examine something sprouting between the cracks in the mosaic tiles.

Ember followed his gaze. The mosaic depicted the castle spires, their blue flag fading with age. There was the same symbol she'd seen on her mother's paintings. Yet, this version was new to her.

"I don't like those odds," Grace said.

The gathered fairies shifted, agitation rippling through them. Their wings flared. For a heartbeat Ember thought they might turn on them.

Grace stepped forward.

"There are some who survived," she blurted, the words tumbling out one long breath. The group turned to her. She took a deep breath. "We have no wings, but we have your blood. And we have been searching a very long time. You were never forgotten. Not by any of us. Let us fix this. Come back to the light."

"Smooth," Ember whispered as the fairy in blue approached, her boots barely brushing the ground as her wings carried her.

"Fairy?" she asked Grace, who only nodded. "Interesting." She looked to the others. "We are intrigued by your story. Retire with us to chambers and we will hear your requests."

She turned sharply and the fairies shifted, parting to reveal a path.

Alistair stood, brushing dust off his robe. "Our chances have increased," he said, pocketing whatever he found in his robe.

"To what?" Ember asked.

"Sixty percent!" He chapped his hands. "Goody!"

Grace groaned under her breath. "Maybe we should have left him back."

Aura only tipped her chin up and followed the council into the glowing passage. The others fell in behind her as the fairies led them toward the chambers and whatever fate waited there.

CHAPTER 27

The hair on the back of Ember's neck stood as they wove through hallways that seemed like honeycombs. A sickly yellow light pulsed from the walls. It wasn't quite sunlight, not really. She felt the whispers of the fairies—distrusting and hopeful, though some were downright mean and vindictive. Some wanted to burn them at the stake as a sacrifice, but then they would never get out. Evil could be self-destructive like that. Not today.

Five fairies led the way and five followed behind. Their wings beat in slow rhythm, yet their feet stayed firmly on the ground echoing with each step. Ember walked alongside Grace, who kept a cool face. Aura moved with the same unbending control she always did, while Alistair stopped here and there to peer in rooms or to make comments about how delightful everything was.

"Delightful. Right," Ember muttered. The image of the pyre still clung to her thoughts. Ropes biting her wrists. Nowhere to run. Heat crawling up her legs...

"The council chambers aren't as scary as they sound." The dark-skinned fairy skipped up alongside them. Ember watched the way her red wings opened and closed lazily. There was just enough room for the three of them alongside.

"I have so many questions," Grace blurted. Ember stood between them, and she had the feeling Grace would have touched the fairies' wings if given the chance.

"They call me Starling," the fairy said, with a bright smile. "All of us here were born after the banishment." Her smile faded. "But there are stories. Is the sun real? Is it as warm as they say?" She ran her hands up her arms.

"It is." Ember smiled, hoping she would again see it. "And rain."

"Rain..." Starling echoed with amazement. "What does it feel like?"

"When it's light, it tickles." Grace maneuvered her way between them. "But sometimes it comes down so hard it's like little needles. And the wind..."

The fairy in black looked behind him and frowned. Grace and Starling exchanged conspiratorial looks and smothered their laughter.

"I would like to breathe the outside air," Starling said. "I never thought I would."

Ember understood that all too well. She'd never thought about a lot of things, like returning a magical floating city, but here they were. They reached the council chambers before anyone could say more, and Starling was wrong. It *was* intimidating. The room looked like a court chamber, with terraced seats surrounding an empty section in the middle. Ember and her friends weren't even given chairs as the fairy took their seats in a circle around them, slightly looking down. Starling grabbed Ember's hand and squeezed before she left to sit, but it did nothing to make her feel better.

Two fairies sat directly in front in judgement. The fairy in the blue dress regarded them with cool amusement, while the male fairy in black scowled. Ember did not like their odds. She hoped Alistair wasn't calculating them.

"The council will hear your argument," the woman said, her tone softening slightly. "They call me Twilight, and this is Grim. We will be running your hearing." The fairies shuffled in their seats.

"A hearing?" Aura raised an eyebrow. "I thought we were in conversation?"

"We are. Just... formally." Twilight leaned forward. "None of us here were alive for the banishing. We've been down here for generations. Tell us of the above. How it happened."

Ember looked to Starling, but she wouldn't meet her eye. The rest of the council were a mix of ages and sexes. She felt curiosity. Hostility. Fear. The ceiling was impossibly high above and let down pin tips of light that looked they were underwater.

"I do not know," Aura said. "The lore has been lost."

Grace touched her shoulder lightly. "Not all has been lost. The stories remain, carried by our people. Stories of great magic, great gifts. I can see now they're true beyond our wildest dreams." She took a breath. "The stories say you were banished by an evil king. I promise it was not one in our lifetime or those just before. He tried to erase your story, to keep your prison hidden. But we have been searching for it all this time."

Alistair stepped forward. "Atlantis has been through its troubles in that time, too." He looked sadly at Aura. "We have paid our penance. I'm sorry for what happened here. But it is time to correct it. We will free you—if you will help us."

Ember wondered what would happen if the fairies returned to the future. Were the stories correct? Would they run rampant, destroying everything in their path? As she watched Starling, who was in conversation with a young fairy next to her, she thought that some might. But the same could be said of those without magic. Humans also had a great capacity to cause pain.

The male fairy slammed a palm onto the table. "Why should we trust you? The last people from above sentenced us here. We have made a life—a good one..."

Twilight touched his arm gently. "A vote, Grim. They deserve a choice." She turned to the others. "We will confer. In the meantime, you may enjoy our hospitality in the hall. Would someone take them back?"

Starling stood. "I will." She jumped and flew down from the benches. Her red wings fluttered, turning the light around them a deep maroon. She couldn't hide her smile. She leaned toward Ember and Grace. "I have so many questions," she said.

"Thank you," Aura said, inkling her head to the council. "But please know this: we are on a tight timeline. Atlantis hangs in the balance. They need us."

Twilight met her gaze. "Let the others go, and you may stay to discuss this," she said.

"Thank you," Aura said. She turned to the others. "Go. I've got this. You should rest. I don't know what we'll return to."

Return. Though she loved their adventure, the word had a special hum. Everyone they'd left behind. Everything they'd lost. What would it look like when they went back—with dragons found and fairies freed? Maybe nothing would change. Maybe everything would?

Starling skipped ahead with Grace. "Is it true dragons fly free in the skies? Is it true magic floats through the streets?"

"That was a long time ago." Grace laughed as they walked out the way they'd come. "And I'm not even sure about *then*. Atlantis was... is... the same as everywhere. Good and evil. Peaceful and contentious. Filled with people—and you know how people can be."

"I don't," Starling said, delighted. "Tell me."

"A lot like fairies, it seems," Ember said.

They walked back down the honeycombed corridors with Alistair on their heels. Ember noticed details she had missed before. The way the doorways were intricately carved, as if they held names on them in a language she couldn't read. Residence, maybe? Did fairies sleep? She had some questions of her own.

Grace and Starling carried on. Ember let herself fall a few steps behind.

"Enjoy their company, but be cautious," Alistair whispered. "Avoid any food or drink I do not counterspell. Have fun." He gave her an encouraging smile.

"Fun?" She snorted. She'd been on adventures on a flying pirate ship. In dreams. Above the world in a magic city. *Had they been fun?* She guessed so, even when her life was in peril. But she desperately missed her friends.

Alistair read her mind. "They will be there upon our return. Which will be marvelous!"

"Marvelous?" Ember's attention pulled forward as the hall came into view ahead. Grace walked arm and arm with Starling. "I'd settle for peaceful."

She wasn't only worried about Atlantis. She worried about home, and the people there, who were surely confused at a city dropping from the sky.

"Peaceful?" Alistair tilted his head. "Perhaps. But everything has a degree of chaos. It moves things along. Fuels change. Yes, as peaceful as can be. But exciting too." He winked.

"Valhalla?" Ember breathed. The hall stretched before them, cut to mimic a forest and alive with fairies of all sizes and shapes. Music called out, something with fiddles and drums.

"Perfection?" Alistair asked. "No. There is no such thing." He took her hand and guided her toward where the upbeat music played. "But we can enjoy the madness for a time."

CHAPTER 28

Hawk had all but grown up aboard the flying ship. It had been piloted by his father, and his father before him. Hawk had expanded the operation to rescue the survivors of Atlantis and bring them together. Though the ship could fly itself, it had always had a crew of more than three. Hawk found himself walking the empty decks and missing his shipmates. He walked past empty bunks, past the kitchens where Paine and the others were usually hard at work, past the decks they used to gather. The ship was so empty he could hear the air whistling by and the dragon's sad rumble as it circled them.

"There you are."

Paine's voice carried down the stairwell a moment before she appeared, out of breath, on the lowest level where the storage was. He sat on a barrel, flask in hand, sipping what Shep had provided him from the stores. She bent over and held her knees, gulping in air.

"Ship is big," she huffed. "We're almost to the island. Why are you hiding down here?"

Hawk looked into her green eyes. Freckles dusted her nose, and her orange hair was, as usual, tied back. He tucked a strand behind her ear. They had become close in the time since Atlantis returned, but he couldn't curse her with what happened to him. He didn't even know the ramifications of it himself.

Sometimes, he wished Shep had just let him die.

"Hungry." He barely broke a smile as he held up the flask. The faint scent of copper filled the room. Blood.

"Oh." She looked from the flask to his face. He wondered if any clung to his lips. He ran his tongue over his teeth. No fangs. They only showed when he was angry or ravished and he was learning to control it. Slowly and painfully.

"It's not your fault, you know," she said, hopping up onto the barrel beside him. She was so tiny her feet didn't touch the floor. "It doesn't make you evil. Or damned."

"You think?" He tipped the flask back and drained it. Once the taste would have sickened him. Now it was the only thing that settled the burn. Perhaps he was trying to repulse her? To scare her away. He'd done it before. To others. To her, even. Yet she had stayed. As a friend. As something more. He wiped the side of his lip with his thumb, and it came off with blood.

"I think there is a cure," she said, softly. Her chin dipped, then she raised her gaze to him. He hadn't expected the shine of tears. "I think we'll find it." She pushed up and off the barrel, so she stood in front of him. "Even if it takes forever."

Her hope tugged a smile from him. He drew her into a hug. "I pray that you're right," he said. His stomach growled. Even now he could feel her pulse—strong and steady.

"I always am," she murmured against his chest.

He ran his hand through her hair. "I know. My only regrets are the times I didn't listen." He carefully kissed the top of her head. She held him tighter, then tipped her face up. Her eyes were wide but no longer full of tears.

"Listen to me now, then," she said, teasing.

"Oh? And what are you saying?"

She had to stand on her tiptoes to even reach his chin, but he bent his head so their lips met. He feared she'd recoil at the thought of the blood he'd just consumed, but she kissed him with the fire that had smoldered between them for years. It consumed them both. He wrapped his arms around her, holding her tight, wondering if he'd have any of this without her—and it didn't matter. Nothing mattered but her.

"Ahem."

Sierra cleared her throat from the top of the stairway. Her exaggerated footfalls began to echo as she descended. "I am coming down to search the storage spaces for you. Here I come."

Paine pulled away with a shy smile, and only then did Hawk notice the bucking of the ship.

He held Paine's hand as they met Sierra at the bottom of the stairs. "What's happening?" he asked. His feet slipped along the floor as if they were in a storm, which was impossible. It had been a cool, clear night when he'd come down.

"A complication." Sierra bit her bottom lip, a twinkle in her eye. "We've reached the coordinates where the author is from," she said. "There's an island chain full of mountains. Big ones."

"An island chain?" Hawk let go of Paine's hand to smooth his hair back. As far as he could guess, they were over the mid-Atlantic. "What island chain?"

"That's the thing," she answered. "It doesn't exist."

CHAPTER 29

As soon as they entered the fairy's hall, Alistair managed to get himself lost. Ember couldn't find him in the shifting crowd. Everyone wanted to see them and touch them. Fairies of all shapes and sizes. Color and music swirled in the chambers. It was upbeat, joyful. She was offered a drink, which Grace tactfully took and set aside.

Ember reached the far wall where benches were inlaid and sat on a smooth stone. Grace and Starling sat on either side of her. Starling perched at the end of the bench, fluttering her red wings in rhythm with the beat. Her presence kept away all but the bravest. A cloud of small, glowing yellow fairies buzzed above their heads, humming gently. Ember could barely hear them over the music.

"They're harmless," Starling said, with a laugh, shooing them. "They thank you and wish you well." Together they made a cloud and imitated a bow.

"Well thank you," Ember said, "But we haven't done anything."

"Yet," Grace added.

"You've given them hope," Starling said, leaning back against the sandstone walls. Her slim, dark frame stood out. The red feathers on her wings reminded her of Draco's feathers—soft and tough. A pang of homesickness struck her. For a moment, she missed that quiet life she'd known—just Draco and the bookstore, a quiet afternoon by the fireplace...

Here and there, fairies offered them little gifts. Many were food or drink. Ember set each one on the bench beside her. Even Starling avoided them. Magic hung in the air—powerful, and chaotic, pent up for too long.

"If we get out of here..." Ember began.

"When," Grace corrected.

"When," Ember echoed. "What will happen to them?"

Starling watched the merriment around them. Fairies danced and feasted, their glances flicking toward the humans as if they couldn't help themselves. "They've been here their whole lives," she said. "Some will be happy. Some will be angry. No two are the same."

"Will they be vengeful?" Ember asked. The question felt heavier than she'd expected, though she wasn't sure if it would keep her from returning home.

Starling pursed her lips. "Not all," she answered.

"What have we done?" Ember whispered. Grace took her hand before the question could spiral.

"We did what was right," she said. "They don't deserve to be trapped here any more than Atlantis deserved to be lifted into the sky. Someone, somewhere decided to punish those who were powerful. Magical. It had to be righted."

Ember bit her bottom lip. Perhaps Grace was right, but it felt too much like playing God.

They spied Alistair by the front. For someone who'd warned her to cautious, he'd shown none if it now. He'd somehow found a long, white robe, and it looked like it belonged on him. He laughed and Ember heard the echo of it across the hall, but that wasn't what took her attention.

Aura stepped inside, Twilight at her heels with a pinched expression. Aura searched the hall, found Ember and Grace, and began weaving through the clusters of fairies, small and big.

Ember rose. "Your Highness?"

Aura offered a tired smile.

"We are past that now," she said, "but I'm afraid I bring bad news. The fairies won't help us with the portal. They fear our motives and have invited us to stay and live here with them."

"Forever?" Grace paled. "Like prisoners?"

"No more than we made of them." Ember pressed her fingers to her temple. Fairies drifted closer in tight circles, some bold enough to hover inches from their faces.

Alistair pushed his way through the crowd, eating what looked like a cupcake.

"Their mood is changing," he said, around a mouthful. Crumbs dropped down his robe.

"I thought you told us not to eat anything," Ember said. Her stomach growled at the smell.

He stared at the cupcake as if surprised it was in his hand, then shrugged. "Counter hex," he said. He stuffed the rest in his mouth. "Fairly sure it works."

The music climbed in pitch and tempo, becoming a chaos of sounds. The lights flickered as fairies flew in front of them. Ember lost sight of Starling, but here but every so often, the crowd broke, and she saw the fairy Grim, his arms folded and his wings wide. The look he gave her held no warmth. He smiled, and she spotted a fang.

"What now?" Ember yelled over the music.

"We enjoy their hospitality?" Grace suggested, though she edged closer to the others. Their small circle shrank by the moment. Ember craned her neck. Starling had vanished.

"Hospitality?" Ember asked, but the music swallowed her voice. Color flashed around her. She blinked—fairies streamed between her and the others. Hands pulled her one way, then another. Wings brushed her face. She tried to push her way toward the door, but she didn't know where it was. Something sharp scraped her arm. Blood welled up, warm and wet. Her heart hammered. She fought through the crowd of bodies, searching for her friends. *How had this happened, she asked herself. What could they have done differently? Perhaps nothing. Perhaps everything.* The smallest decisions sometimes change the course of the world, and now here she was, surrounded by angry fairies. Someone grabbed her arm and pulled.

"Here!"

This tug was different. Starling pulled her to the side and pressed something into her cuts.

"The others..." Ember tried to pull away, but Starling showed her the frenzy was dying down. The fairies were fighting each other now instead of them. Grim had Aura by the arm, shouting that the outsiders were a threat that had to be neutralized, but other fairies were trying to help her. The music had quieted. Now it was only the sounds of cries and shouts. Buzzing.

Ember looked around the hall—fairies everywhere. *Where would they find the portal here? What if they were stuck?* A tear escaped. She wiped it quickly. *There was always a way out.*

Grace fought her way through the crowd and took her hand. She, too, had blood on her face. The fairies shirked away as if ashamed. "What now?" Grace's eyes filled with tears. She didn't bother wiping them.

What now, indeed?

Now they could only watch what played out at the front. Aura was between them. She'd pulled away from Grim and kept her chin tilted high, but his rage kept climbing. He blamed their expulsion on her. He blamed everything on her. He told the fairies that she knew the way out, that she'd always known and kept them prisoner. That she was the enemy. That she would free them only to hurt them.

"What is he doing?" Grace asked. She took a step toward them, but Starling caught her arm.

"He is inciting hate," she said simply. "I only hope enough of us are smarter." She scanned the room. The crowd was quieting under the weight of Grim's rising rhetoric. "Though I do not know."

"Kill her!" someone shouted. A bolt of magic shot out. Aura ducked just as the bolt missed her. A fight broke out in the crowd. Aura held her hands out to calm them and tried to speak, but no one listened to her. No one listened to Grim anymore, either. He'd already achieved what he wanted. He'd created chaos. Fear.

"Why couldn't we have worked together?" Ember whispered. The Queen used the confusion to slip to the side.

Starling shook her head. "It has been a long time." She drew a steadying breath. "Come. Perhaps I can hide you in the tunnels."

It wasn't an escape Ember relished, but she relished even less the thought of being torn apart by fairies.

Grace grabbed her arms. "I'm claustrophobic," she said.

"Me too," Ember admitted. "But we have to get there first."

They pushed through, pressing toward Aura at the front. Some fairies split to help them, hands steady, wings fluttering like gentle banners. Others circled, sharp eyes glinting, wings buzzing in staccato rhythms that cut through the noise. Some hovered silently, observing.

Starling took Aura's hand—but she was a second too late. Grim's fingers closed around her wrist. "Traitor!" he barked.

The accusation hit the room like a lightning bolt. Fairies erupted in argument and accusation, voices overlapping, wings slapping, magic sparking uncontrollable bursts. Ember felt the heat of the crowd, the sting of brushes against her skin, the bite of panic creeping up her spine. The noise swelled into a wave, only broken as a ripple of chaos surged from the back, knocking bodies and spells alike into disarray.

And then the hall seemed to swallow itself, leaving only the chaos to pulse and roar, carrying them forward into whatever came next.

Chapter 30

With every step down the stone staircase, Shep regretted that he didn't go with them from the start. He'd dragged Ember into this—he'd promised to protect her. Protect the Queen. Protect Grace, even. She was important to his daughter. And yet. He couldn't shake the feeling he had failed.

The stone in his hand glowed faintly. It cast just enough light to reveal slick moss underfoot. The bottom of the staircase remained hidden in shadow. Damp air clung to him, cold and musty, and his boots slipped on moss.

"Oof." Aurelia stumbled and fell to her knee. He turned quickly and helped her upright. She wiped blood off her knee but was otherwise unharmed. Her long skirt and corset had been fine in Atlantis but here they looked out of place. He'd had time to get used to changing styles—modern styles. How would the people of Atlantis ever adjust? If they even woke.

He tried to ignore her pounding heartbeat, a symptom of his condition he hated. He fed when necessary, but only reluctantly.

"It's fine." She dabbed at the cut with her skirt. He wished he had advised her to be more practical. How could she run if they needed to? She solved that problem herself, tearing the bottom of her skirt free. The fabric tore easily.

"There." She smiled. "A little easier."

"I'm surprised so little has changed on Atlantis in so many years," he said. He'd seen the world shift so much—sometimes for the better, sometimes... not so much. But change, indeed.

"I suppose we were less than motivated," she said. She pocketed the ripped parts of her dress. At least her outfit afforded her pockets. "Why bother?"

He wished he could explain to her why bother. Why creativity, newness, and forward movement mattered. How do you explain passion? It was something they would have to find for themselves.

"I think I see the bottom." She peered over his shoulder. Her blonde hair shone in the light of the stone. He could no longer see where they'd stepped in. It felt like they'd been descending for ages. He'd been in worse places—more desperate and dangerous—but never when those he loved were at risk. Now he understood just how much he had to lose. He pinched the stone between his thumb and finger, feeling its cool, steady weight.

"Come. Let's go," he said. She was right. The steps led to an iron, barred door. Dirt shifted as he nudged it with the toe of his boot. The door had been opened recently.

"They came this way," he said. He tugged on the door, but it didn't budge.

Aurelia ran her hand over the markings. "Fairy," she whispered, almost in wonder.

Shep grunted. He'd heard whispers of fairies being wild and unpredictable, and though he knew better than to believe in such tales, the stories were not encouraging. "They're dangerous," he said. The marks meant nothing to him, but she seemed to be able to understand them.

Aurelia frowned. "I thought you would know better than listen to rumors." She turned back to the door. "It says something about being kept away until the time when balance was restored to the world. See the scales?"

He tipped his head to look at her in the low light. "How do you know?"

She flushed. "Grace has been teaching me. She's... smart." The pink in her cheeks deepened.

"Can you read it?" he asked, tactfully avoiding her embarrassment. "Does it say how to get in?"

She leaned in to look at the markings. "It says you need a drop of fairy blood, or..." she paused. "It loosely translates as *love*."

"You speak the language?" he asked.

She didn't answer. Instead, she smudged the blood from her knee onto the carved lines and touched the door. No rumble. No magic flare. Just a soft click. The door opened inward an inch, revealing nothing but more darkness.

He pushed the door a little. "Fairy blood?" he asked.

"Something like that." She bit her cheek. "I should also mention it says something about going forward. As in... we won't be able to leave the same way we came."

He smiled. "I suspected as much."

She narrowed her eyes. "They're in there?"

"I think so, yes."

She squared her shoulders. "Then let's go."

He held the door open but paused. "This woman, Grace. She's important to you?"

Aurelia met his eyes this time. "Yes," she said quietly. "As Ember is to you."

Perhaps this was family. The thing he'd been missing all these years. The quiet recognition between them was more than pride. He wished there was a moment he could hug her, tell her how proud he was, and apologize for all the times he hadn't been there. All the times he'd failed.

"Then we will go get her," he said.

Aurelia scoffed and stepped through the doorway. "For all we know, they need no rescuing."

He held the stone up high. "You're probably right. Let's just try not to mess things up." Behind him, he kicked a rock under the door and wedged it there. *Just in case.*

They walked the dark halls, the air heavy and thick. He thought about what he'd heard about the fairy, and their riddles. *The way out was not the way in.* They couldn't go back the way they'd come. It felt like a trap.

Aurelia spoke in a hushed whisper. "Grace told me they were expelled long ago. Long before Atlantis rose. Her family hid because of it."

He thought of Grace's mother and the curse she'd given him and stayed silent.

"Because they couldn't be controlled," Aurelia continued. "The King called them chaotic, but chaos is a choice, too." Her voice climbed with her passion.

Shep held his hand up to stop her. He heard something ahead that sounded like chaos, but took a moment to turn to her.

"I know not if it was the right or wrong decision," he said. "But in my experience, there is a little chaos in everything. It's more about balance than control."

She nodded, though he wasn't sure if she agreed or if she finally heard the yells and shouts echoing ahead of them. The sound bounced through the tunnel in strange ways. He couldn't tell if it were miles away or just around the corner, only that it carried no warmth. A knot formed in his stomach. If Ember was there, she was in trouble.

In the low light of the stone, he watched the carvings on the tunnel walls sharpened into shapes that looked angrier. More violent. Bloodthirsty.

Do not make any deals," he said. "Do not accept food or drink..."

"I know the rules," Aurelia whispered. The tunnel widened, enough for them both to pass, and a light appeared far off. "I know what can calm them," she said, though her voice trailed off.

"Now would be a good time to tell me," he said.

"There is a song." She hesitated. "But..."

He stopped. They were close enough to hear cackles. Screams. "What, Aurelia?"

She met his eyes. Her eyes were wide, trusting, a tear gathered at the corner. "It could put them to sleep."

He pressed his lips together. "Aurelia..." His voice didn't carry the anger he felt, but the tremor in his hand betrayed him. "You know the curse that fell on Atlantis?"

"I know of the magic." She looked down.

"I do not want to know any more right now," he said. He forced his gaze forward, toward the chaos waiting for them. The mission, and only the mission. Ember. The Queen. Grace, though he had some questions for her later. "Be ready."

But what was ready? Had his daughter really conspired to put all of Atlantis to sleep? For her lover? He glanced at her from the corner of his eye. She held her head high, but she was afraid.

Was she in love with Grace? Love can cause you to do great and terrible things—this he knew. He would stand by her, even through her mistakes. He put a hand on her shoulder.

"We will fix this," he said.

A scream cut them off and he wasn't so sure.

"I'm sorry," she whispered. And she was—he felt it in her. But sometimes *sorry* wasn't enough. He wondered if she understood the weight of what she'd done. With every step, he felt it more.

They reached the entryway and stepped inside.

Chapter 31

Hawk, Paine, and Sierra stood at the ship's rail and watched the mountains rise out of islands that shouldn't exist. Their peaks should have been visible even from the mainland, which they weren't far from. Any tourist with a camera could have seen them. Any fishing boat. Any passing plane. Yet the islands had appeared only for them.

"It's the coordinates," Hawk said. He'd seen magic before. Strong magic, even. But this... this bent the world in ways he couldn't begin to comprehend.

"Or because of Atlantis?" Sierra asked. Draco cut through the clear sky toward the mountain and back, breathing fire. None of them could hear his thoughts the way Ember could. All they felt from the dragon was frustration.

Sierra turned to Hawk. His usually pristine ship was tarnished from the last few days. "Maybe it's because magic returned? Do you think other people can see it?"

"I doubt it," Paine said. No boats in the vicinity. No planes in the nearly cloudless sky. The sun had peaked and was headed down, though night and day meant little now. "Maybe it's both. Atlantis returning and the correct coordinates. Like a lock and a key."

Hawk had stilled the ship as best he could, though wind gusts still shoved at the hull in uneven bursts. He guessed the peaks at four thousand feet. And he guessed they somehow had to reach there. Normally, he welcomed adventure. He lived for it, but he worried for his crew. He worried for Atlantis. And he was hungry.

The blood Shep had left him was nearly gone. He needed to figure out how to feed on his own. If he didn't... he wasn't sure what would happen, and he didn't want to find out. His fingers tightened around the rail.

"There." Paine pointed. "There's a ledge. Or something close to one."

His eyesight was better, a side effect of his new enhancement. There was indeed a ledge in the middle of the mountain. He raised his eyes to the sky.

"And the dragon?" he asked. "Does he come?"

Arriving with a dragon brought clear, unmistakable advantages, but it also came with challenges that were hard to balance.

"I think Ember would want that." Sierra smiled. The dragon had taken to her. She spent time on the deck stroking its fur, but if it had told her anything, she was silent on it.

"A hidden island," Paine said, a sparkle in her eye. "What do you think is there? Treasure?"

Hawk smiled despite himself. He'd been rescuing people from Zyah for so long—and dealing with hellhounds—he'd forgotten what a true adventure was. "And what would we do with such treasure?"

Paine shook her head. "The important things don't cost money." Her gaze drifted away before she turned back. "But I've always wanted to go to Greece."

Sierra laughed. It reminded him of Ember, and he said a silent prayer for her and the city. He was still angry at Shep for turning him, but what was the alternative? He would have died. He prayed every day for a cure—perhaps that could be found in these mountains.

He heard Paine's heartbeat, steady and strong, and put a hand on his temple, trying to drown out the noise.

"Forward, but slow," he said. He retreated to the bow to steer her, though she could do it on her own. He needed the time to think. Paine followed quietly, her soft steps carrying across the deck.

"Is there anything you'd want to do with a treasure?" she asked, pushing herself up to sit on a barrel.

"That barrel is full of explosives," he warned, but quickly smiled. "Just kidding. It's full of rum."

She looked down. "In that case, we may have a celebration later?" She smiled. "I mean it. What would *you* do? With time and money and freedom?"

He steered with one hand. Once, he might have answered flippantly. Once he might have even known. But life had become so complicated. All he wanted was his friends. His family. Her.

But he couldn't meet her eyes. "There is only one thing I want," he said, softly. He did meet her eyes this time. She was the only one besides Shep who knew how hard he struggled. She got up to walk to him.

"I do not know if I can control it still." He ran his tongue over the sharp incisors just beginning to poke through.

She didn't slow. "Then do not." She moved the braid off her shoulder, and he could see her pulse. He stepped back.

"Please don't do that," he said. He raised his gaze to hers. "Please. I don't know if it will hurt you."

Paine stopped. "It's just blood, Hawk," she said.

His eyes teared up, but his vision stayed clear. Everything was sharper than usual. Eyes. Ears. Nose. His nostrils flared, and red-hot blood filled almost all of his perception. Almost. He stepped back, hand gripping the wheel. "There's something there."

Paine turned, and Hawk let out a slow breath. "I don't see anything," she said. The top of the mountain was shrouded in fog, but there was a cave on the ledge. He pointed it out.

She hesitated. "I trust you," she said. "But what are we getting into?"

Sierra joined them on the deck, her gaze scanning the peaks, but Draco held back. Even the dragon seemed to sense the danger they were sailing into.

CHAPTER 32

The energy in the fairy hall shifted with a single note.

Someone sang, and slowly, the fairies lessened their angry shouts. And just in time. Ember, Aura, and Grace had been dragged up to the front. Alistair was nowhere in sight. What they were to do there, Ember didn't know.

Their eyes had glowed red, their voices sharp and bloodthirsty—but the song calmed them. The language was unfamiliar, but its energy spoke of softness and light. Ember allowed herself a breath.

Around them, fairies paused in mid-flight, turning to watch. Even Grace got a dreamy look and a wide smile.

"I know that voice," she said, and Ember didn't have time to ask.

She assessed their exits. Back the way they'd come— but that's where the music was coming from. Or forward into the fairy tunnels. She looked up. The light she thought was coming from the surface was just an illusion. Could they tunnel up? She doubted it.

She turned to Aura.

"We need to get out of here," she said with desperation, but Aura had turned to the music, too. Everyone had lost their minds.

"I agree." Aura faced her, and something in her expression made Ember pause. Her blue eyes widened, and for a moment, hope reflected in them.

The singing grew louder. Someone walked toward them in a halo of light. The fairies slowed, hovering as if mesmerized, circling lazily. Ember watched from the corner of her eye.

"So let's go," Ember said, seizing on the Queen's hope. She took her hand and tugged gently. That was all she could think of. There was an escape here somewhere.

Grace let out a sob, and Ember didn't turn. Not until two people approached and the room stilled.

"What magic is this?" she asked Grace.

"It's an old song," Grace said, tears in her eyes. "One my grandmother taught me. And I only taught one other person. Ember... look."

Her notes carried in the hall as if by magic—and magic it was. The fairies had stopped. Even Starling, who'd been trying to help them. Even Grim, who had been rallying the fairies against them looked half asleep.

As the crowd parted, Ember saw a girl with long hair singing, moving slowly toward them. And beside her... a vision she never expected. Her heart skipped in her chest.

Shep.

How long had it been? It seemed like days and years wrapped into one. His gaze was trained on her, ignoring the fairies and the danger, though his daughter beside him seemed to have that under control. Ember's hands shook. "Is this real?" she whispered. The spell of the music seemed to take over her senses as well.

Grace stepped down to meet Aurelia when her singing tapered off. Aurelia pulled Grace into a hug, but Ember's eyes remained on Shep as he stepped toward her. How much they'd been through since he'd walked into her bookshop. How much they'd grown.

Physically, he was the same: cords of muscle, and curly hair that needed trimming. But inside they'd both become stronger. Closer. She wanted to ask about home. About Atlantis. About her sister. But the words died on her tongue.

"You," she said, a smile tugging at her lips.

"I couldn't let you have all the fun," he said. Then he kissed her—long, hard, as if to make up for every lost moment. For a heartbeat, she was home. He tucked her hair back off her face and held her to his chest for only a moment.

"How long will they be quiet?" she asked, her voice muffled against his shirt.

He cleared his throat, a subtle sign he had no idea and was winging it. "That was actually Aurelia's idea." Already the fairies were moving, waking up from the spell. "Probably not long enough to escape," he said, looking back at the entry.

"We can't go that way," Aura interrupted. "It's barred."

Shep smiled. "Did you prop the door?" he asked, mischief on his expression.

Ember matched his smile. "Prop the door?"

"A rock," he said.

Aura frowned. "There's supposed to be a portal here somewhere... back home."

Aurelia turned to her. "Would you like to search for it, or would you like to go home?"

The fairies stirred, but their movements were slow, lazy. They'd lost the fire they had before. Grim approached, Twilight at his heels.

"I apologize for our frenzy," he said, running a hand through his hair. His wings beat lazily behind him. "Our incarceration has taken a toll." He turned to Aurelia. "How did you know that song?" he asked. "It was from our ancestors. I'd forgotten it. Our use of magic is quite limited here. It has been so long..."

Grace spoke up. "Your kin are still on the surface, waiting for you to return. They will teach you. Remind you..."

Ember held her breath. For a moment, she remembered what it had been like. Would the fairies have torn them apart? Would they have escaped? She turned to Shep and took his hand. He'd arrived just in time.

"Remind us. Yes..." Grim looked to the tunnel Shep and Aurelia had come in by, as if he'd known it all along. "Freedom," he said.

Starling stepped beside him, her wings fluttering in quick, bright pulses. "Show us the way," she said.

A ruckus interrupted the crowd. Alistair pushed through, fresh with iridescent green wings that had broken through his robe. He flapped them as if he was proud.

"Don't drink the green concoction." He hiccupped.

Starling leaned toward Ember. "They will disappear by dawn," she whispered. "Sadly. They'd beautiful."

Dawn. Ember's jaw cracked with a yawn she couldn't stop. How long had it been they were gone? Hours? Days? There was no sky, no sun, no sense of anything but caves and crisis.

Shep tugged her hand. "Let's go home."

"And then what?" Ember asked. The fairies were flying around them now, waiting. Twilight had given the word. They were free. Some cried. Some cheered. Some flew in circles.

Shep pulled her into a hug. "Then, I suppose, we save Atlantis," he said. "Again."

She felt his strong arms around her, and though she loved adventure, thought it might be nice to just sleep in.

"How much saving does this city need?" she asked.

It was Alistair who answered, another green drink in his hand. "You'd be surprised," he said. He offered her a sip.

She looked to Starling. The fairy only shrugged mischief in her eyes. "It will just give you wings for a day," she said.

Ember met Shep's gaze. "Like an upgrade," she teased.

"Ember, I don't think—" but she'd already put it aside, though she was filled with thoughts of what she could do back home with those wings. And flying—she'd always wanted to fly.

Those adventures were for another day.

He rubbed his forehead. Aura was already halfway across the room.

They were going home.

CHAPTER 33

Hawk hovered the ship off a ledge carved into the mountain. It looked wide enough for the dragon and the ship to both land on, if he trusted it—which he didn't.

Draco roared loud enough to bring out whoever was inside the cave. Nothing or no one stirred except the wind in the trees that grew along the side. Scrappy pines covered with a dusting of snow held on to the land with roots like claws.

"We have to go in," Sierra said. Her eyes gleamed with a little too much excitement. Though Hawk had always been one for adventure, something held him back. Perhaps that something was everything they had gone through. The shipmates lost to the hellhounds. Atlantis was in peril.

Perhaps it was that he simply felt responsible for Sierra and Paine. Perhaps, he even felt love. He rubbed the part on his chest where his heart once beat. A gift he'd been given, but a curse, too. He watched Paine marvel at the island and confer with Sierra what to do.

What did he have to offer her now? A lifetime of chasing down blood? A mess they'd made of Atlantis? It wasn't like Hawk to wallow, but death will to that to you. He shook it off as best he could.

An adventure was an adventure, after all.

He hopped up on the rail. "Only one way to find out." He gave them his most dashing smile and jumped. It was only a few feet, and he landed lightly. The ship responded by sinking lower for the others.

"Traitor," he murmured, touching the bow with affection. That ship had saved so many. It had seen him through difficult time—and fun ones, too. He'd been lucky with his inheritance. And maybe that's what life was, a series of good things and bad things strung together.

"Okay, hold on." Paine climbed down next. Her braid bounced as she landed with sure-footed grace beside him. The sun brought out the orange in her hair and green in her eyes, and he wanted to tell her she was beautiful, but Sierra jumped down right in between them.

"Right." She stumbled, then brushed dirt off her pants. "What now?"

They all faced the cave. They'd seen worse dangers. They'd even faced hellhounds. But there was something different about walking inside the unknown. Anything could be in there.

"This is like a game show," Sierra commented.

"What kind of game show?" Hawk asked, keeping his eyes trained on the entrance. A cold breeze blew out and ruffled Sierra's long hair.

"There's one where you pick a door and either win big or lose big," she responded.

"How do you know which?" Hawk asked.

"You don't." She flashed a grin at them. "You take a risk."

Paine raised an eyebrow. "I once knew a guy who loved risks," she challenged.

"Door number one." Sierra took a step toward the cave.

Hawk looked back at his ship. It hovered where he left it, faithful as ever. He had no fear it would leave. They were tethered, like Ember and her dragon. Draco circled the mountain and roared. Hawk wished he could read the dragon like Ember did, but he suspected the dragon would push him on. And despite his cautions, he wanted to go forward.

He spared a last look at the ocean. No land in sight. Only clear blue skies with lazy clouds. Where they were in the world, he couldn't guess.

He reached for Paine's hand.

"Door number one?" Paine asked. She waited for him to follow Sierra.

"It could be filled with trolls," Hawk said.

"Or gold," she countered.

He froze for a moment, caught off guard by the sudden rush in his chest. Love. He'd felt it before. For his family. His shipmates. But this was different. It took his breath away.

"Maybe you should stay on the ship," he suggested.

She broke out in a wide grin. "Right," she said, and tugged his hand. "Let's go, Captain."

Sierra had already entered the dark, her silhouette swallowed by the cave. Paine and Hawk followed.

Behind them, the ledge shuttered. The light blocked out. Draco was pushing his way inside. His body filled the cave as he waddled forward.

"I sure hope he doesn't breathe fire right now," Paine murmured.

Sierra shook her head. It was hard to see in the low light. "He won't," she promised.

But the light was coming from in front of them now. They followed it deeper inside, down and around the mountain. The cave walls were filled with scratches in the rock they chose to ignore. A muffled sound came echoed.

"Was that a roar?" Paine whispered.

Hawk had dropped her hand to take up his sword. "You sound entirely too excited about that," he said. He risked looking at her out of the corner of her eye. He could just see her profile and her red hair. "Trolls, Paine. Remember?"

She had a sword of her own and was quite adept at using it. She pulled it out. "Trolls," she said with no less excitement.

But it was not trolls.

The tunnel opened into a massive chamber. Sierra tried to enter, but she was pushed back. "It's protected," she said, holding out a cautious hand.

Paine pushed her face up to the barrier. "You're not going to believe this," she whispered.

Hawk had let his sword arm drop. Inside the cave—if you could call it that—were hundreds of dragons. The space was larger than it looked on the outside. As far and wide as the eye could see. Dragons of every size and color flew and slept. The dragons hadn't spotted them... yet.

"How do we get in?" Paine asked.

"Do we want to get in?" Hawk kept his grip tight on his sword.

"I think I know," Sierra said. Her eyes widened. "Run!"

Draco's chest swelled. That was all the warning they got. He gave them enough time to run around him far enough so when he let loose his flames, they barely singed. But singe they did. When Draco let out a roar, it echoed long and loud and Hawk swore the beast turned around and *smiled* before flying into the mountain. The noises and smells were overwhelming now, but the three stayed as they were.

Hawk let out a breath. "Well," he said. "I guess that's one way to get in."

Sierra and Paine leaned around the corner. "There's hundreds," Sierra breathed. Draco had disappeared in their midst, and one by one, the dragons began to fly past them. Paine lost count at thirty.

Draco flew past and stopped, with a red dragon next to him. The beast was smaller than him, but his golden eye twinkled. It dipped its head to them.

"I think he wants us to ride him," Sierra said.

She took a step forward, but Paine grabbed her arm. "Are you sure?"

Sierra smiled. "I'm sure. I can hear her." She pressed a hand to her chest. "In my heart."

Hawk knew the feeling. "Thank you, but I already have a ride. Paine?" he asked. He was capable of flying the ship on his own, and he'd never begrudge her the opportunity, but he felt the weight of her decision, too.

"I'm with you," she said. "Not quite ready for a dragon yet,"

Sierra climbed on the ruby red dragon as if she'd known her all her life. She patted the soft fur beneath her scales and the dragon let off what can only be called a purr. Paine laughed.

"How about just a ride to your ship!" Sierra called out.

"She's got a point," Paine said. "We could be crushed leaving here." She sheathed her sword.

"I would not want to be crushed," Hawk said. He followed her to the red dragon, who dipped its head to meet them. Paine leaned in and spoke in low tones to her. Hawk took care not to listen.

Paine turned back beaming. "Come on."

She climbed on behind Sierra with the kind of ease that made it look natural. Hawk climbed a little slower and clumsier. His feet were made for a ship's deck—not a dragon's back.

He sat behind her and held on. She patted his leg. "It's an adventure." He tried not to feel sick.

He tried to breathe through it. "If you say so."

He attempted humor, but his stomach did a flip when the dragon took off at a run. She was young. He could feel the power in her. She made the tunnel in only seconds and took off into the blue skies.

Hawk spared a glance for his ship as they passed it. Relief hit it first. Awe came second.

Then the dragon flipped.

"Oh no," he said, right before his stomach dropped.

Paine let out a whoop of pure joy. The dragon answered with another roll, sharp and playful.

Hawk just held on.

CHAPTER 34

Ember and the others stayed to the side as the fairies rushed out of the tunnel, tentatively at first, but slowly more and more braved the freedom. They came in a whoosh of color and air, a blur of wings and laughter that brushed past like a living wind. Starling stayed next to Ember, her gaze fixed on the exodus with sad eyes.

"What will they do?" Ember asked, her voice quiet.

Starling looked at a green fairy as she twirled and laughed. "Live, I suppose," she said. Her voice was soft, reflective. "Some will stay. This is their home." She twirled a lock of her dark hair. "Not many, though."

"And you?" Ember asked.

Starling's deep purple eyes sparkled. "Of course not."

Aura's gaze darted from fairy to fairy, wide and uncertain. "What have we done?" she whispered.

"We've returned magic," Shep said, putting an arm around Ember's shoulder. His voice carried both reassurance and awe. "For better or worse. We've returned it to the way it was."

Ember shared the Queen's concerns. Returning magic to the world was one thing. Dropping a magic city out of nowhere and releasing a bunch of fairies was another entirely. Sometimes the world changed gradually, and sometimes all at once. It seemed this was an all at once moment.

She looked up at him. "Are you sure you propped the door to the right time?" she asked, only half kidding.

"I actually have no idea how that works," he admitted. "I hope so."

Grace laughed, taking Aurelia's hand. They only stopped looking at each other long enough for her to say, "We'll figure it out." She didn't meet Shep's eye, but Aurelia did.

"Yes," he agreed, touching his daughter's arm gently. "We will."

The stream of fairies slowed enough for them to risk venturing out. Grim had stayed back, along with Twilight. Ember saw them in the doorway, arms raised, trying to hold the other fairies back. Twilight caught her gaze and pressed her lips together, whispering to Grim.

"I thought freedom was what they wanted?" Ember commented as she turned away.

"Control is what they want," Shep said, not sparing them a glance.

Grace and Aurelia headed out the tunnel first into the light of the world. Ember held her breath. Would they arrive at the right time? She stifled a yawn. Whatever time it was, she'd have to rest.

The tower stood against the low moon, with silver light spilling over the horizon. Waves crashed in the ocean nearby. Fairies danced all around them. Some scattered, but the small ones buzzed around the tower. Ember waved one away.

Aura rushed out past her, helping Alistair. Ember had never been so happy to see the reflection of blue light on the water, or the low drone of a helicopter in the distance.

"We're home," she said, brushing her bangs off her face. She felt for Draco, but he was miles away. Their connection was intact, but the distance made it difficult. She turned to Shep. "But where is everyone? Have we helped by bringing them back?"

"Only time will tell that," he said, scanning the horizon with a frown. Ember couldn't tell if it were dusk or dawn. She hoped for dusk. She finally let out that yawn.

Aurelia rushed back to them as if she didn't share the same exhaustion. "The fairies will help broker peace," she said, looking back at Grace. "I know it."

"Perhaps," Shep said. He looked at Ember who was aware of the bags under her eyes. "In the meantime..." His gaze lingered on her. "I suggest we retreat to the palace. Look for our friends. Plan how to approach the world."

Aurelia huffed. "Less planning and more doing. I'll go..."

Aura's smile was thin. "Patience." She placed a hand on Aurelia's shoulder. "I have taught you that much about leadership, have I not?"

A look passed between Aura and Shep. So much was said without words. That Aurelia was still a child, despite her years. That she was impetuous. That Aura was deeply sorry for the time lost. Ember felt all it and stepped closer to Shep.

Aurelia let out a breath that misted in the cool air. It had gotten chillier since they'd been out. Dusk, then. Ember let out a sigh.

"The castle," Aurelia said, scanning the skies, but this time her thoughts were her own. She met Aura's eyes. "But we must do something."

"Yes," Aura agreed, watching Alistair crouch to pick mushrooms and put them in the pocket of his robe. "Perhaps morning will give us more insight."

Many of the fairies followed as they went to the castle. Starling stayed close to Aurelia and Grace, peppering them with questions about the modern world. Some were laughable, and some Ember flinched.

Her body felt heavier with each step through the gardens and around the path. Thankfully, they weren't far from the back gates. They circled around and returned to the hall where Javiar waited, surrounded by tiny fairies that arrived ahead of them.

"We released the fairies!" Aurelia called, laughing as she stepped forward.

"I see that," Javiar said. He sheathed his sword that he had use to bat them away. "And this is a good thing?"

Aura approached him slowly, fatigue wearing on her. "Righting a wrong is always a good thing," she said, allowing a rare display of emotion and letting him hug her. "But if it is the right thing *right now*, I do not know."

Javiar touched her shoulder lightly and tipped her chin to look in both her eyes. Fatigue was evident even to Ember, though the Queen bore it gracefully. "Perhaps," he said, his voice soft, as if he wanted to hold her again but restraining himself. "But for now, you all need rest."

Shep cleared his throat, poised to argue, but Javiar cut him off. "The wards are holding..."

"...but the fairies?" Aurelia asked, staying close to Grace, who pressed her lips in a line.

"I believe if the warding keeps the others out, it should keep them inside." Grace shrugged, a trace of uncertainty in her expression. "The science is imprecise. I want to talk to them, though. There's so much to learn."

"There are hours until daylight," the Queen said, acquiescing. "We will reconvene at dawn." She tipped her head toward Starling. "Do your kind need rest?" she asked. "The legends are..." She spared a smile. "...imprecise."

Twilight fluffed her wings. "It would help, yes, though I think the others are too excited."

Aura looked out the window. "Will they hurt my people?" she asked. "They are defenseless."

Shep's arm tensed, but it was Javiar who spoke. "I believe the curse that slumbers them also protects them." Ember let out a slow breath.

Aura nodded. "Very well, then," she said. "You all know where the rooms are? I'll show Alistair and Starling to theirs. Be back at dawn."

Dawn, Ember thought. There was so much time until then. Time to work out where her sister and Hawk were. Time to cross examine the fairies. Follow them. Understand their motivations and their ways. But not tonight.

"Come," Shep said, a twinkle in his eye. "I'll see if my old rooms are open."

Aurelia and Grace followed them through the castle. While Shep's old room was not available, there was a place where they could rest their heads. His daughter stayed nearby, the moon shone high and bright. Ember rested her head but she did not sleep, not right away. She propped her had on her arm and watched Shep disarm.

Wind blew in through the window, and she shivered, tugging a large blanket around her. The fireplace across the room stood cold and empty.

"What is she like?" she asked carefully.

He tipped his head. "Aurelia?" he asked. She nodded. "She is... more than I'd dreamed. Smart. Funny. Resourceful. Adventurous." He sank onto the bed, burying his head in his hands. His stomach grumbled. She forgot what a burden he carried. Did he need to feed?

"And I missed it all," he added quietly.

She touched his arm. "Not by choice."

He stood and bounced on his heels, stretching his neck. "By enough choice."

"How?" she asked softly. "How do you feed?"

"Ember..." He shot her a warning look. "We've talked about this. It's not something I share."

She sat up, letting the edge of her shirt slip from her shoulder. "Maybe it's time you did."

CHAPTER 35

She was his undoing.

He'd shared his story before—parts of it. To women he'd left in the morning. To men at bars who wouldn't remember his name by sunrise. Transients. People who wouldn't judge. People who understood what it meant to hurt. There were so many of them. There were even some, he'd heard, like him. But none he'd ever met. Not until Hawk.

No, there were no other monsters, not like him. And though he'd shared parts of his story in order to return Atlantis, he'd never shared his pain. No one had ever asked. This world, what it had turned into, treated pain as entertainment or turned a blind eye. But she was different. She always had been, in every lifetime.

A noise escaped his lips. A moan. A release. A plea—silent, unspoken—not to ask this of him. How could he open up after all this time? How could he reveal the darkest parts of himself to someone so light? So forgiving.

She looked up from the bed, tired but wide eyed. The sheet tangled around her. And in that moment, his body betrayed him, revealing the depths of his hunger.

His shoulders hunched. "I am a monster," he said.

"Shep..."

"No." He looked up, meeting her eyes—so trusting. He'd done that. He'd asked her to trust him when he was filled with darkness. "There is no changing that fact, Ember. I must feed." He turned to look at the door. What choice did he have? Animals could suffice in a pinch, yes, but he needed human blood.

She shifted, moving the shirt further off her shoulder, making her neck accessible. "Take me."

He closed his eyes. "No." When he opened them, her gaze was fixed on him, wide and trusting. He stepped back, hearing her heartbeat. "It's too dangerous."

She rolled her eyes, and he couldn't help but smile. "Oh please," she said. "Like you'll hurt me?"

He took another step back and bumped against the door. "I may not be able to help it," he admitted. "It can be a frenzy. It can take over."

She didn't move an inch. "I trust you," she said.

He shifted, slightly, toward her. Her shirt dipped below her collarbone, and for a moment it wasn't blood he thought of. "You may get lightheaded."

"That's what they say in the books," she replied, her eyes twinkling. "And some other things..."

"Some other things, hm?" He edged closer, letting his magic spark a fire in the hearth. Flames flickered, casting dancing shadows across the room. "I can't be sure about that, Ember." He perched on the edge of the bed, careful not to touch her. "Mostly how I've fed has been destructive. I've never done it like this."

She sat up and put a hand on his shoulder. "But it can be done?"

He nodded, curt. "I have fed and not killed," he said. "But I have killed. Over and over."

Ember drew in a sharp breath. She'd known, of course she had, but never like this. Never so raw. Still, she kept her hand on his shoulder. "There is a cure somewhere," she said. "I feel it."

He grit his teeth, fighting to keep the long fangs from emerging. "That fact does not change the past, nor does it help me right now." He made to get up, but she held her hand firm on his shoulder.

He thought he knew love before. He hadn't known Aurelia's mother long, and held strong feelings for her. But those feelings had been a love born of youth. Innocence. He didn't know if it would have lasted had she lived. Such thoughts were useless now. The love he felt for the woman before him was encompassing. She sat with the side of her shirt falling off her shoulder, and her heartbeat strong and steady. Did she know what she was asking?

This time he rose, brushing her hand away, pacing to quell the steady need growing in his gut. He looked at her sadly. "I will return," he said, but what his choices were, he did not know. Her expression fell to one he was used to: disappointment. "I will return," he promised again. She looked away.

"I know," she said. Her words were honest, yet the disappointment didn't leave her expression. He turned and left the room, feeling every bit of the monster he believed himself to be. Where would he go? How would he feed?

It was a compulsion, this illness, but a necessary one. He wouldn't die if he didn't feed, but he would become something from a nightmare. At least now he still had control.

Atlantis still slumbered under the moonlight, and it looked almost peaceful. Until you saw the lights in the distance, or the fairies darting about in a frenzy. It was the small fairies who scrambled—pixies, he remembered. Where Twilight or Starling had gone, he did not know, and he hoped to not run into them. Hunger ran hot in his gut as he descended the castle steps and into the dark city, the moon as his guide.

His eyesight was excellent—a benefit of this curse, but he needed to get as far away from his loved ones as possible. The thought of hurting them... he'd sooner burn Atlantis to the ground.

He walked areas he once knew, residences and storefronts and taverns—all darkened. The residents hunched over sleeping were breathing steady but slower. They were losing their souls. They had to break this curse.

He considered crossing the boundary to feed on the mainland. The thought gnawed at him until he saw a light in one of the taverns he used to frequent. He paused. It wasn't one light, but many. *Fairies.* They were gathering there. He clenched his jaw and headed that way.

The streets of Atlantis were crushed stone, so fine they felt like walking on sand. Abandoned carts lined the shadowed road, and here and there someone slumbered next to them. Their pallor had become pale, but Shep didn't doubt they could stay like this for a long time if the spell held.

Another round of attacks hit the defenses and petered out.

The tavern door was as rusted on its hinges as he remembered, and it almost cost him a smile. He'd had good times here in his youth, pretending to be older. Back when he knew not what the world would turn him into. He waited for that moment to pass, but it stayed with him—the hope of youth. The optimism. Ember had brought that back. Despite the curse. Despite the darkness.

You wouldn't know there was darkness inside. The fairies had lit every corner with their magic. He didn't kid himself that they were all in here, but many were. And they were happy. It wasn't that the ale flowed, but that they were free.

Starling clapped his shoulder as he stepped inside. The tip of her wing brushing his cheek. "I'd have thought you'd be out exploring the world," he said softly.

She smiled. "The world doesn't seem like much right now, does it?" She tipped her chin toward the alarms and the lights and the attacks.

"We have a bit of a problem right now, yes," he admitted.

Footsteps tapped behind her. Twilight approached, with Grim on her heels. Shep stiffened. He remembered how they'd treated him, and again his hunger stirred. He had to make this quick before his instinct took the reins.

"Shepherd." She nodded her head and raised her voice over the music that had begun playing in a corner. "We owe you an apology."

"Accepted," he said. His eyes had already marked the nearest exit. He needed distance. Control. Before the monster in him answered instead.

Grim stepped forward. "We'd hoped you'd join us for a drink."

Shep shook his head. "I must—"

Twilight grabbed his arm before he could make his escape. Her grip was light, but it stopped him cold. "It's a *special* drink," she said.

Grim's silver wings shifted as he opened his coat. A flask glinted from an inner pocket. Shep sniffed and gave her a questioning look.

"You know?" he asked.

She gave him a smile that broke his heart. How long had it been since he'd told someone and they'd accepted him. They'd smiled?

"It's not hard to tell. We're fairies, remember?" She fluffed her wings. The bar had become so crowded her wings brushed another fairy in the face. "Perhaps we can talk in the back."

Shep knew the back room. He'd played many games of cards back there, under the owner's nose. A small, circular space where deals were made.

"Perhaps we can," he offered her a smile back, but his was guarded. Starling took his wrist and led him through the crowd.

CHAPTER 36

The small, windowless room contained a circular wooden table in the middle with a desk in the corner, overflowing with papers and dust. Floating candles flickered and puttered as if even magic weren't enough to illuminate the room's darkest shadows.

So many shelves had been added since his youth he couldn't even tell the color of the walls, each burdened with various jars and bottles which carried over to the table. Twilight swept them aside and offered Shep a seat which he reluctantly took. She remained standing while Grim squeezed through the doorway followed by Starling. Shep flexed a fist.

"Be still, Shepherd. Grim will cause no harm." Twilight gave him a stern look then took her own chair, squeezing her wings in behind her.

Shep looked quickly at the papers on the desk. Formulas covered the scattered papers. Diagrams. Maps. Notes in hurried hand. They, too, had been trying to get Atlantis home. Different methods. Same desperation.

Grim removed the flask from his pocket and set it on the table with a deliberate motion.

Shep recoiled. He knew the smell, but it was different. Intoxicating, but wrong, somehow.

He shook his head.

"We took great pains to get this to you." Grim slammed his palm on the table. "A little appreciation is warranted."

"Grim…" Twilight's voice cut through the tension, a single warning threaded through the word.

"What is this?" Shepherd rasped.

Starling took the seat beside him. "It's the blood of fairies," she said. She placed a hand over his. "And it contains great magic."

His breath caught. "A cure?" The question left in a whisper.

"No." She shook her head. "I'm afraid that is much more complicated, but a temporary aid. Hope," she added.

Shep shook his head, but he could sorely use hope. The blood called to him in a way human blood did not. It sang an old song. He took the flask in his hand but did not open it.

"How?" he asked.

Grim shared a look with Twilight. Their wings lit up the dingy room.

"With reluctance," he said.

Starling placed a hand over his. "Not from all of us," she said.

Grim continued. "We've agreed to help you. Not trust. Not yet. And not all of us. But you have freed us. We owe you a debt."

Shepherd held the flask up, aware how his pale hand shook. "And this is payment?"

"It is the beginning of such," Twilight said. She took in a breath. "There is a rumor of a cure among my people..."

Shep sat forward. "A cure?"

Twilight pursed her lips. "Perhaps." She paused. "I would not give you false hope." There was a twinkle in her eye as she said it.

Shep smiled. "I would take any hope, false or no."

He unscrewed the cap. The scent was intoxicating. He downed the whole flask before it could even register a taste. The scent was hard to get over in the beginning, and the taste of it the hardest hurdle. It still curled his stomach at times, and he saw how Hawk struggled.

He wiped his lips with the back of his hand, leaving only a trail. A faint scent, one only someone of his kind could tell. The fairy blood was a different sensation. Senses were always heightened for him—a side effect of his curse—but now there was a whole array he hadn't known before. Colors. Sounds. Smells. It had been overwhelming in the beginning, so many years ago. But now...

He looked around and could see the minutest detail of the wooden table they sat at. A tiny imperfection in Twilight's skin. The words on the back of a piece of paper tucked in a corner. And... *thoughts?* He cocked his head.

Grim smiled, a gesture that looked out of place on his face. *It will fade*, his voice murmured into Shep's mind.

Shep sat back and tried to clear his thoughts. Meditation was something he'd learned long ago. He'd also learned that clearing your head wasn't as easy as it sounded. The candles in the room flickered. Starling giggled.

Twilight moved to his side. Her wings filtered the light. "There is a responsibility to the process of reading one's thoughts." She covered his hand in hers. "And practice. Much practice." Her wings shifted, scattering another ripple of light. "It's one reason my people guard our blood so fiercely. You are open to our secrets now, Shepherd. That comes with a great deal of trust."

A quiet pulse brushed against his mind again, softer this time, carrying her unspoken words.

And responsibility.

"I understand." He swallowed hard. He'd never been so full, so satiated, since the beginning of this curse. "This will lead to a cure?" His gaze drifted from face to face, searching for the slightest confirmation.

Starling looked away. Grim held his gaze.

The first thing is to settle Atlantis, he said, holding Shep with a stare that lived up to his name. Shep nodded.

"Of course," he said out loud, but risked looking up. "But then?"

"There is a rumor," Twilight's hand was still on his. She squeezed it tightly. "The path to the cure is difficult, but our people will help you if you convince them they're safe. You must make this place safe, for all of us."

"No small task," Grim said. He took the flask back and Shep found himself missing it. With all this power, what could he do? What kind of peace could he broker? He wanted to reach back for it, but instead balled his fists.

"What path?" he asked through clenched teeth. "Where?"

Twilight only gave him a sad smile, keeping her wings close. With the fairy blood he could see each individual feather, felt them bristle. "When the time is right, it will appear."

"I've heard that before," Shep said before he could stop himself, sharper than intended. He pushed his chair back. His countenance softened. "I ... apologize," he said. "You have just been freed, and this world is in chaos."

He found himself looking at Grim, who only shook his head.

"Dear child, this world is always in chaos. We may still it for a heartbeat or we may dance with it." He flapped his wings and brushed papers off a nearby shelf.

Shep returned his smile. "It has been a long time since someone has called me child," he admitted. "The blood... how long will its effects last?"

Starling grasped his arm. "Longer than usual but not forever," she said.

Twilight cut in. "There can be no more," she warned. "Its effects can be intoxicating. Maddening."

Starling bit her bottom lip and looked away.

Maddening, he wondered. More maddening than drinking blood? Than turning into a monster? Under his palm, he felt the wood of the table, the grain of it. The thoughts of the people who'd sat there before. Their frustration. Despair. Even love. Ember had a gift such as this, and he understood why it was overwhelming sometimes.

Ember.

He had to get back to her. He pushed back from the table.

"Thank you," he said. The room was hot, the noise in it taking over. The flutter of the fairies' wings. Their heartbeats—fast and feathery. And the colors. He closed his eyes and ran a hand over his chin.

Starling put a hand over his. "It will subside," she whispered. "Or so I've heard."

He opened his eyes to see the shadow of a smile on her face, the others watching with quiet concern. "Thank you," he said, rising to his feet. "I would like to welcome Atlantis home, but I have no idea where to start."

Grim stood as well. It was the first time he'd seen empathy on the fairy's face. His wings were held back, but instead he opened his arms, offering a hug. "Forgiveness, I suppose," he said. "It is always a good place to start."

Shep returned it, a one-armed hug that quickly became full. *Fairies,* he remembered, *were known for their affection as well as emotion.* "Thank you." He patted Grim on the back and pushed away.

"Tomorrow," Grim promised, while Starling mouthed "*Go!*"

With renewed hope, Shep left the tavern to return home. The streets seemed brighter, even the stone under his feet shone with the paths of thousands of souls. With their hopes and dreams and fears. He flexed his fists, feeling the new power in his body, watching the fairies sail past while taking in their new world. He passed the street he'd met Grace, the closed shop barely registering in his mind.

He tipped his head up. The stars were the same. Their light filtered through low clouds. A breeze wafted by carrying more than just a chill. It wasn't a smell, exactly, but energy. Something had changed. Something more than his power.

Shep froze. He felt, more than heard, the flap of wings in the distance, so close to his heart he stopped and felt his chest. It conjured a feeling that hadn't stirred in a long time, long before Atlantis was cursed to the skies. He looked up again, but the skies were clear. It was more than just Draco. He felt the pulse of their wings, their determination and emotion.

The dragons were coming home.

He set off to the town square in a run.

CHAPTER 37

She heard the sound of her dragon in her heart.

His call was distant, lonesome, but Ember felt a spark ignite in her chest. She'd sent Draco off with Hawk, Paine, and Sierra when the city was attacked, but their connection never severed. It was faint at first, but steady, and growing stronger. Her dragon was returning, but what would he be returning with?

Ember rose from the bed she hadn't slept in, stretching out the stiffness in her muscles. She moved to the window and looked down at the courtyard bathed in moonlight. The palace wasn't her home, she doubted it ever would be. In her heart she still thought of the little apartment over the bookshop in that first moment when she opened her eyes.

She remembered wondering if she'd had some grand dream and she'd wake to the leaks and breaks of everyday life. The seasonal customers. The bestsellers and the amazing stories downstairs. And a little dragon only she could see.

Home shifted all your life, she supposed, swinging her legs out of bed and stepping on the cool floor. Moonlight shone in along with the faint sound of the attack to their defenses. Slower, now, but a steady barrage. She rubbed her face. They were really determined, she thought. Someone had to talk to them.

By her reckoning, the darkest part of night had passed. She dressed quickly in whatever she could find. It was the most acceptable of Atlantis clothes—loose tan pants and a long shirt. It would have been a stark contrast to her black hair, but the coloring had grown out to a dark auburn.

If she could look in the mirror, she'd wonder at how the lack of makeup softened her. *Soft.* It had never been a word she used to describe herself. Funny she reached for it now in these circumstances.

She debated seeking Shep, but he had his own demons to face. She missed him, though. How he'd marvel when Draco returned. She felt his pride. His love in her. His belief. It touched parts of herself she didn't know existed. Confident parts.

She missed him, but she knew he'd be back. She felt it as she felt her heartbeat.

She creaked her door open and froze. Aurelia leaned against the hallway, arms crossed. "Took you long enough," the girl said, blowing a curl off her face.

Ember smiled. "Was I that loud?" She looked back to her room.

Grace appeared around a corner, dark to Aurelia's light, but still content. She took Aurelia's hand. "We feel them, too," she said, the smallest squeeze to Aurelia's hand.

"Them?" Ember asked. She closed the door behind her. Best Javir think they were all asleep. They walked at a quick clip down the hall. Grace led the way toward the kitchens.

Grace raised an eyebrow. "You would only feel your own, I suppose," she said, trotting downstairs with only moonlight to light the way. Perhaps her fairy side helped her navigate, but Ember, having no such gifts, was slower and clumsier. She struggled to keep up.

"Draco?" Ember called louder than she wanted to. Grace and Aurelia seemed to sense she was behind and slowed.

"The dragons," Aurelia breathed. "More than just Draco. They're coming home."

Ember's stomach dropped. A wonderous thing, indeed, but... she looked out the slit of a window. At this height she could barely see over the tops of Atlantis's residences in the moonlit dark, and then— to the world that waited beyond. A world of flashing lights and attacks and danger. "What are they returning to?" she asked, a tear in her eye.

Grace took her hand. "Peace."

Ember only offered a half smile and squeezed her hand in return. Peace, indeed.

She lingered by the window, watching the light of the fairy's bob through the streets. Lights shone in taverns. The fairies seemed to be getting their bearings, she supposed. *Is that where Shep was? Getting his bearings. Could he feel the dragons?*

Grace slid her hand out and turned toward Aurelia, already halfway down the staircase. Shep's daughter bore so many of his traits. Strong. Stubborn. Curious. She had his height and build, but so much of her was foreign, too. Her light hair to his dark.

Her fair skin to his tan. But the tilt of her head. The way she held her shoulders. Her confidence—those were his.

Ember took the stairs lightly. It was one thing to reunite the city, quite another to reunite a family.

The thought of Draco pushed away any doubt, though. She followed Aurelia and Grace quickly through the quiet castle. Occasionally, she sensed a fairy presence, but many were out exploring the city, she hoped. A quiet wind blew through the empty halls, lonely without the souls of Atlantis' people inside. They emerged onto the steps, and Ember dodged the sleeping Atlantians to step to the middle of the square where Grace and Aurelia looked up expectantly.

"The last time I stood here..." Ember began, unexpectedly choked up. She faltered, memories surfaced unbidden. It had been the night the world attacked the city. Hawk had flown his ship away with Paine and Sierra on board. She wondered where they'd gone to, though knowing them as she did, she suspected they were trying to help. And help they were.

Aurelia gasped, breaking her reverie. Ember followed her gaze. The horde moved through the night sky like a shadow, and the ship—usually cloaked—was on full display. A pinprick at first, growing larger and larger. Ember's knees wobbled at the familiar sight.

"They're back," Ember cried, her voice breaking. The words carried through the square, catching on the still night air, both relief and awe trembling in her tone.

"With friends," Grace added.

The flap of wings in the night felt like a caress, even more so when she spied Shep running toward them. He slowed when he saw Aurelia, suddenly shy.

"The dragons," he said, not even winded.

"I know." Ember replied, pointing. They could now see the various colors and streaks of light approaching. But then her stomach dropped.

The attack came before she could blink. The weapons on the mainland were sharp, and they were quick. The missiles were just launched before they reached the dragons, who easily dodged them, but the ship... Hawk's ship was slower and more cumbersome to move.

The missiles sailed through the sky. Some landed on Atlantis' defenses and fizzling out, but one hit its mark on the side on Hawk's ship. Ember screamed, or maybe someone else did. The noise carried through the empty streets.

There was nothing they could do as the ship began to list sideways. Shep put an arm around Ember, steadying her, and she tried not to imagine her friends falling gracelessly into the night. Then a shadow flew under the ship and propped the side up, lifting it just in time. The dragon beat its wings, so hard Ember heard them slap with each beat, and Shep froze.

Perhaps it was the scarlet red of its scales, shining as it came closer. Perhaps it was Shep's reaction. Or perhaps just a knowing.

This was Arcturus, Shep's dragon. Home.

"How?" he breathed.

"There is indeed magic in the air," Aurelia said, her hand on his shoulder. Arcturus maneuvered the ship toward the landing. Toward them, in fact. Ember marveled at his bronze eyes, but she tore her gaze to the ship. It was too far away to see if anyone was on board, but behind she felt Draco's familiar presence.

She pulled free of Shep's embrace, a tear sliding down her cheek. Arcturus maneuvered the ship close enough that they scrambled for purchase. It hit the ground roughly, avoiding the sleeping townsfolk. The dragon pushed it off its shoulder and swept around for his reunion. Ember only briefly saw her friends scramble off the side as Draco landed beside Arcturus.

She barely registered stepping away from Shep. Her feet took her toward her dragon at the same time Draco dipped his head. His golden eyes shone, fixed on her, but in them she could see the reflection other dragons, landing with careful precision around them.

He padded his front paw lightly, the nails scraping on the foundation. As she got closer, memories rose unbidden: the first time she'd seen him, a little puff of purple. She remembered trying to hide him, then realizing no one else could see. Except maybe her mother, who'd been trying to protect them for so long.

She threw her arms around Draco's long neck, fingers tangling in the soft, downy feathers beneath the hard outer plumage. Purple with flecks of white, they yielded beneath her touch. One floated free as she pulled back, and she laughed as it flew to the ground.

Stars still covered the night sky, but morning was not far off.

"You've been busy," she told the dragon, giving him a knowing look.

He dipped his head. A tiny fairy darted between them, trailing dust. She sneezed as Grace jogged up, followed by the fairy Starling. Draco raised an eyelid and huffed smoke.

Starling's dark eyes were wide, her red wings tight to her body. "Dragons hold great magic," she said. Her breath clouded in the morning chill. "We have not seen one in..." she trailed off and looked around. There were dozens, maybe a hundred. Ember couldn't help but smile.

Grace touched her arm gently. "Perhaps if we harness the power of the dragons, we can break the spell?"

"And then what?" Ember asked, but her heart skipped a beat as Sierra and Paine joined them. Sierra enveloped her in a giant hug. It was a strange sensation, after thinking her sister was dead for so long. She pulled back slightly to look at her. Sierra still smelled like flowers and looked like sunlight. She wondered how her sister always pulled that off, when she herself was in desperate need of a shower.

"Fairies, hmm?" Sierra said, letting go and nudging Ember with a shoulder. She turned to Starling. "I'm Sierra."

Starling bowed, her eyes wide, a hint of a smile tugging at her lips. "They call me Starling," she said.

The rest of their group gathered, welcoming Draco and the other dragons, even the Queen and Javiar. As Hawk returned, he offered them a smile. "As far as I can tell, we break this sleeping sickness, find Maryse so she can do no further harm, and broker peace." He hugged Ember briefly. "No big deal."

"No big deal," Aurelia laughed.

Ember peeled away from the others, her gaze seeking Shep and his dragon at the corner of the square. She approached slowly, careful not to startle them. Arcturus had scars on his massive back, and feathers missing in places.

"I'm surprised you're not in the air," she said softly. Shep's hand rested gently on the dragon's flank, grounding both of them.

"It's been hard for them, trapped inside," he said, turning his gaze to her. His eyes were red—exhaustion etched into his face.

She knelt next to him. Arcturus leveled his head with them. She could see the strain in the dragon's eyes. In the huff of his breath. He was tired. Perhaps they did not have as much magic as Grace guessed, as Ember hoped.

But they were alive.

CHAPTER 38

Hawk slipped away as the others made their way to castle. Atlantis was more than he'd ever dreamed—overwhelming on even a good day, and this was far from one.

He caught the eye of the closest dragon—a wide, white creature who'd once had kind eyes, but not for Hawk. The beast narrowed its eyes and huffed smoke. He was an enemy now. A monster.

He caught the details of the city while stepping over its inhabitants. The glittery cobblestones that wound around the main square and down the streets. The carts that sold wares and food so magical it hadn't spoiled even yet. He yearned to taste the berries on the closest cart, but it was not berries his body craved.

And the smell hit him all at once—an overwhelming mix of human and magic, of earth and animals, of smoke. He crouched in the shadow of a close shop and covered his eyes, for all the good it would do. It was not his eyes that were the problem. His stomach grumbled.

He sensed Shepherd before he saw him, and his anger bubbled to the surface. It was insane and irrational, too. Shep had saved his life, but what a life it was.

"Does it get easier?" Hawk asked, eyes still closed.

Shep lowered himself beside him on the damp cobblestones. The clouds had parted, revealing the sliver of a moon. And still the city slept on.

"No," Shep answered. "Not really." He pulled up a sleeve and offered his arm. "It will not help much but it will quench the thirst. It's been enhanced by fairy blood, for whatever that's worth."

Hawk opened his eyes startled again by the new reality around him. The sharp colors, even in the dark. This man, a monster beside him.

"You should have let me die," he murmured.

"Perhaps." Shep didn't lower his arm. "But your friends would disagree. Paine would disagree."

Paine. Hawk sighed, his body trembling as her face filled his mind. Her face when she saw the dragons. Her smile. Her joy. She still believed in a cure, in the city's salvation.

"Is there a cure?" Hawk asked, gripping Shep's arm and hating himself for it. Shep closed his eyes and offered Hawk this moment.

"I have to believe there is," Shep said.

Hawk paused. Shepherd wasn't a monster. Perhaps there was hope for him too.

"The others wait for us," Shep added gently, a quiet prod. Hawk needed no such thing. His hunger took over, and as he sank his fangs into the soft flesh of Shep's wrist, a tear appeared on the corner of his eye that he quickly blinked away.

This was survival—for now. And Hawk would survive.

CHAPTER 39

Magic pulsed again through Atlantis, and the city was home, yet it was not the happy ending Ember had hoped for.

She couldn't see her home island, but she could feel it—a complicated pull of longing, homesickness, and sadness. Good memories and bad. Old ones. Memories from before the accident. Holidays with her sister. Stories by the fire. The house. The bookshop. She turned away and brushed a drop from her eye. Not tears, it was raining softly, muting the colors of the emergency vehicles.

"We can use the dragon's magic to wake the town," Grace said. They remained in the square in the chill. Shep had returned to his dragon's side. Arcturus looked at her curiously, but Draco saddled up next to him and nestled the new dragon with his nose. In the air, fairies darted through the air. Some stopped to try to help the sleeping townsfolk, but it was no use. Their magic wasn't enough.

Ember brushed a wet strand of hair off her cheek and suppressed a shiver. "How?"

It was the Queen who answered, but her voice was sad. "We need to work together. All of us." Javiar put a hand on her shoulder.

"All our magic," Grace added. She held Aurelia's hand, eyes bright with hope. "Directed at one place and one time." She turned to Shep. "It's so powerful. It can work."

Shep frowned. Whether it was at the display of his daughter's affection or the possible magic, she didn't know. Ember reached out and gently took his hand. It was cold.

"Perhaps," he said, and she understood. She knew he wanted to wake Atlantis, that he wanted peace—but not just for the city. For himself. For Hawk. Ember watched him out of the corner of her eye. He was pale, his lips red. He nodded, a small gesture to show he was okay. But was he?

"If I may," Sierra said, stepping forward. She eyed the dragons with a smile. "Could we take this indoors? Where there is a fire? And maybe some food? It's been a long journey."

Aura took command, a sense of calm and capable leadership. She directed them all to the castle, which was still sound despite the attack. In the back was a garden that was open on one side. The dragons could perch there next to the roaring firepit.

Javiar and Sierra set off to gather supplies and food. Grace and Aurelia quickly followed. Ember stayed back, noticing the three fairies who joined them. She nodded to Twilight, Grim, and Starling.

Shep took a protective stance, but Ember waved him off.

"I am sorry for my assumptions," Grim said. Raindrops clung to his opalescent folded wings, glittering faintly in the dim light. "We have heard stories for many generations..."

Ember smiled. "Please... join us." She gestured to the castle as Shep tensed.

"We do not speak for all the fairy," Twilight cut in.

Shep shook his head. "Nor do we speak for Atlantians, though at the moment..." He looked around. "There are few other voices."

Starling fluttered her wings. "We only wish to return to the world," she said, light in her eyes as she looked around.

Paine slipped an arm through Ember's. "If only it were that easy," she said, but she was grinning.

"Maybe it can be." Ember squeezed her arm. "Come with us," she told the fairies. "Let's figure it out."

The castle cut an imposing figure, especially in the misty moonlight as if it were meant to shine at such a moment. Its white walls gleamed, casting shadows on those sleeping below. It was as if the raindrops never hit them, they slept on protected and entranced.

Ember was the first inside, spying Shep and Hawk across the plaza. The dragons had settled. Hawk's ship was moored for the night. The world held its breath as Atlantis decided how to fight back.

Moonlight streamed through the windows of the great hall, only gently tinted with far away sirens. Candles lit up the entrance to the gardens, giving just enough light to see the grim look on their faces.

Aura spoke as the dragons flew in and lit the fire, which quickly took. "We have to approach them," she said.

The others perched on chairs arranged in a circle, as if they were at a book club and not deciding the fate of the world. Shep placed one down for Ember and she took his hand lightly.

"Maryse has weaseled her way into power," Sierra said, looking out and past the windows. To her home, perhaps. The one on the island she may never see again.

"I'd hoped our little adventure has changed that," Aura said smoothly, taking control. "But the Maryse of here isn't the Maryse of old. The loss of her husband poisoned her, and she does not act alone."

"She is strong," Shep said quietly.

"But not all powerful," Hawk countered, his tone steady.

The fairies stayed silent. Aurelia held Grace's hand, which trembled slightly. Grim leaned back and crossed his arms. Next to him, Starling and Twilight leaned forward. Sierra looked cautiously at Hawk, who had picked up color. Javiar waited on the Queen.

"We have the might of the fairies," Sierra said, "and the dragons." She raised an eyebrow at Grim, who nodded once.

"Our goal is to come back in peace. To let go of old grievances. At least..." he rubbed his chin, thinking. "...I believe that is most of our goals. Some may have left the confines of the city already."

Aura shook her head. "The wards keep us in as they keep them out." At the moment, they seemed to be keeping everyone out of the castle, too. "We need to open a discussion. See what she wants. See if we can get around her."

"How?" Shep asked. Ember took his hand.

Ember wondered how it was all playing out. There was panic in the world always. Surely this didn't help. They needed to reach the people directly, let them know they weren't a threat. If it wasn't too late.

"I have an idea," she said. "Does anyone have a phone?"

They were going directly to the people—if they could. Paine had an old device hidden on the ship. The fairies marveled over it, even though the technology was clearly outdated.

"You can reach every person?" Starling said, twisting the phone all around.

Ember took it carefully. "Sort of," she said. "Only people who have devices…"

"Which is everyone," Sierra said. She'd set Aura up in her throne and improvised what looked like a stand for the camera. It amounted to a chair with books to prop the device.

"Does it work?" Shep whispered, rubbing circles on her back with his thumb.

Ember yawned. "It turns on," she said, "but what to say?"

Daylight had started to stream in the room in shades of pink and orange. A sailor's warning, Hawk had said. She hoped not.

"I find these things are best approached with honesty," Aura said. She gestured Ember next to her. "And naturally."

She smiled. It was a rare sight on the Queen, at least as long as Ember had known her. Ember wondered if she'd smiled more often in her youth—when Atlantis was still on the ground. When she'd loved her husband. So often, she found people had history and trauma beneath the surface that affected their choices and moods. Aura's had turned her into a leader, but Ember suspected it made her sad, too.

"I agree," Ember said. "Or at least it doesn't give us time to be nervous."

"We're ready." Sierra bit her bottom lip. "I think, anyway."

Their friends formed a circle behind them. Starling and the other fairies might become friends in time, but the others…

Hawk leaned casually, his cavalier attitude punctuated by a wink at her. Paine smiled and waved. Sierra fussed with the camera. Javiar's eyes were only on Aura, steady and attentive. Aurelia and Grace leaned on each other as if they were meant to be with each other.

And Shep. He stood apart, a solid form on his own, arms crossed, his eyes flickering to the doors and windows for danger, as he always did. But the danger was closer than he realized. If they messed it up...

"Ready," Aura said. She cut an imposing figure. Her white dress gleamed, the red cloak falling perfectly over her shoulders. Behind them, the tapestries of the hall told the story of Atlantis, one of magic and love woven with gold thread on maroon tapestries.

Ember stood beside her in scavenged clothes. She wasn't as regal as the Queen—she never would be. But she was comfortable with herself. Sierra had pulled the sides of her hair back and dusted her face. Confidence wasn't a word she'd ever used to describe herself, but she knew in her bones this was the place she belonged.

She reached out to Draco, who sent love and safety and return. That's what magic was, after all—something you couldn't define, something that moved the world and made it better.

Ember smiled back at Shep. "Ready," she said. And she was.

CHAPTER 40

The technology was old, but it still worked. No one had bothered to delete Sierra's old social media pages. Her friends' well wishes had dwindled over the years, a trail of fading concern. She lingered a little too long on her ex's page, now updated with his new life.

Sierra sighed so low Ember doubted anyone could hear. She looked up and blinked a tear away. "Ready when you guys are." Sierra forced a smile, but her eyes twinkled. This was what it felt like to change the world.

"Ember, Shepherd," Aura called. Javiar had found her crown in the King's dusty quarters and placed it on her head. A line of fine silver with turquoise jewels. It matched the colors of the flag, and changed her, somehow. It shifted her presence, as if the crown remembered who she was supposed to be and reminded her of it.

"With me," she said, then paused. "And Grim, or one of the fairies, please."

The fairies fell in conference as Ember and Shep stepped up the dais. She fussed with her hair and her shirt, as she wondered if she looked pale or gaunt. The last few weeks had changed her in ways she didn't expect, both mentally and physically.

Shep took her hand and tugged her close. "You are amazing," he said. He paused while Twilight stepped forward. Her wings shielded them as he tucked a piece of her hair behind her ear. "I have searched through lifetimes for you, and still... you're more than I ever dreamed."

He kissed her forehead and left her with that.

Once, her mouth would have fallen open. Once she would have listed every reason she was just an ordinary girl and unworthy of some great proclamations of love. Once, she would have said it was just luck.

She looked around at her friends. Sierra, showing Hawk and Paine the device. Aurelia and Grace in a corner. The fairies deciding who their spokesperson would be. And Javiar ever at Aura's side.

Yes, she was lucky. But she was more than that. She was smart, adventurous, and brave. She was worthy. And she finally knew that.

Aura offered a smile. "Let's begin," she said.

Ember and Shep stepped into place, his hand on her back off sight of the camera. Javiar stood on the other, with Twilight beside him, her red wings spread out just enough. Sierra gave a thumbs up. She'd alerted local media, whatever that meant, and assured them they'd have an audience. A big audience.

Ember's stomach flip flopped.

"I've never been a fan of social media," she admitted under her breath. Shep rubbed slow circles along her back.

"This is different," he whispered in her ear, brushing a quick kiss against her ear. It *was* different. The stakes were higher. Magic itself hung in the balance. Yet, a strange stillness found its way over her. She looked at the phone, pointed their way, and she was ready.

Aura cleared her throat. With both hands gripping the sides of her throne in a gesture of nerves Ember could understand, she began.

"My name is Aura, and I am the Queen of Atlantis, the city that has returned from the sky. I'm told you still read stories of us." A faint smile crossed her face. "I am glad our legend lived on, but the versions I've heard are exaggerated of fact, or plain falsehoods. The truth of it is much simpler. Ages ago, before your time could record, our city was cursed to the sky. We have waited there, patiently, for the time to come to return love and magic to the world."

Her tone became sad, and her gaze shifted to Ember.

"With the help of our friends, we have returned. But whether the time is right is up to you. There are those who don't welcome our magic. One has already cursed our inhabitants to a deep sleep. We need your help, the dragons, the fairies, and all of you. Welcome us back home. Return the love that we carried with us to the sky. Show us that magic is indeed real and wanted. Help us to live in peace."

She took a deep breath and looked directly at the camera. "We need your energy to break that spell. Your thoughts. Your kind wishes. Magic still lives within you. Release it. Welcome us home." A tear had formed in the corner of her eye. "But in order to do that, we must lower our wards. We must trust that you will not attack. We return in peace, and we offer love. Please, welcome my people home. The ceremony will begin at sunset. When my people wake, I will open our gates and meet with your representatives. Until then, we offer only peace."

She nodded, and Sierra cut the feed.

Silence filled the hall. Only the faint buzz of a small fairy across the room and the huff of a dragon outside.

Paine stepped forward first. "That was amazing," she said, looking toward Ember.

"I didn't say anything." Ember laughed, but her hands were shaking.

"You're getting responses already." Sierra swiped through the phone, her eyes widening. "It's all over the internet, and the news picked it up."

Aura stood and smoothed down her dress. "And?"

Sierra bit her bottom lip. "Mostly good," she said, but her expression said otherwise.

"Let me see." Ember took the phone and looked at the streaming comments rushing down the screen faster than she could read.

Bunch of fakes. Kill them all.
Magic? They want us to believe in magic, you guys?
F*** them
This is it, you guys! The age of Atlantis!
Are you good with Jesus?
And on and on.

Sierra east the phone from Ember's hands. "Maybe this wasn't a great idea," she said back. She wondered how regular people were taking the news. Her neighbors on the island. The people she once went to college with. They were scared, probably. Confused. Trying to decide if they believed any of it.

"Let me see it," she said.

Before anyone could object, she turned the camera on her and hit *live*.

The frame was shaky. She held it with one hand, and the angle was all wrong. The light didn't help. The background was the castle walls and the others, talking low. Fear reflected on their faces. Ember took a breath.

"My name is Ember Weathers, and before this all happened, I was a regular person." She smiled at that. "As regular as anyone, I guess. After my parents died, I ran their bookstore on a small island in Maine. I didn't think I fit in."

The others started to realize what she was doing, but no one stopped her. She pulled up one of the chairs and perched on it.

"I was afraid of things like making the rent payment and getting people to like me. Politics. Snowstorms. Falling in love." Her gaze flitted to Shep. He gave her a warm smile and the courage to continue.

"I wasn't nobody, but I wasn't important. At least I didn't think I was. It's a long, complicated story, but this got kind of thrown on my lap. I think most of you would have done the same thing. I found out this island, with an amazing, beautiful history, was cursed to the sky. And I helped bring them home."

She paused. Her gaze didn't settle on any one person, yet she felt Draco move behind her, a familiar thrum in her chest.

"Their magic is..." Her voice thinned, then steadied. "It's love. We have it too, but we've lost it somewhere along the way. It's the most powerful force in the world. I can't promise they're here to change the world or anything, but they're here to make it right. To bring things back where they belong. They deserve to be home."

She swallowed, then leaned closer to the camera.

"Please, welcome them. Please, use your own magic to help us break this spell. We need you. Umm..." A flush crept up her cheek when she realized what she'd just done.

"Thank you."

She squeaked and cut the feed.

She tossed the device over to Sierra. "I don't ever want to see that again," she said.

"Good," Sierra laughed. "It's almost out of battery." Sierra enveloped her in a big hug, warm and fierce. "I'm proud of you," she whispered. She pulled away, a hint of that characteristic pink on her cheeks. "You've come so far from playing hide and seek in the house."

Ember smiled. "I always hid," she said. And they both knew she wasn't talking about the game.

Sierra pushed a lock of her hair out of her face. "You did," she murmured. "But not anymore."

"No." Ember's gaze drifted to Shep. He stood at the castle doors, watching the quiet city with the posture of a man ready to shield it from the world. A protector by nature. By choice. Maybe by fate.

She turned back to Sierra. "It's too late for that."

CHAPTER 41

As far as Ember could tell, sunset was still a couple hours away. The rain had let up, and light filtered in and out of the low clouds. Only a fine mist lay over the city, but somehow, its inhabitants stayed dry. Aura retreated inside the castle walls with Javiar, but the others followed each other through the city. Sierra and Aurelia knew it best, but they all followed the cobbled paths toward the market where the smell of cooking wafted through the air.

"Fairies." Starling shrugged. "They have to eat, too. Mostly what we could grow, but..." she sniffed. "Smells delicious."

Ember's stomach growled at the hint of cinnamon and spices. Everything was better on a full stomach and a night of sleep, though it was unlikely she would get either. Aurelia held Grace's hand and gave them a running commentary of where they were and who lived here. Shep walked close by, lips pressed into a hard line, a look of sadness on his face.

"And this place..." Aurelia tugged Grace toward a small corner bakery. "Best almond croissants. Remember?" She asked Grace, who smiled.

Sierra sighed. "I could smell them, but I couldn't eat them."

The pastries still sat in the window. Kept good by their magic, though damp and melting in the middle.

"So, you were here?" Hawk asked Grace. He raised an eyebrow in the way only he could. "And... there? How? Were you the only one who could travel between?"

Grace smiled sheepishly. "Astral project, actually." She turned toward Sierra. "I couldn't actually eat the croissants, either, but oh the smell made up for it!"

"Astral project." Shep turned it over in his mind, but as for what he was thinking Ember didn't know. He'd retreated behind his walls. "I am sorry for all the years you were stuck," he said to her.

Aurelia shook her head. She took her hand from Grace's and put it on her father's arm as they casually walked through a market, past shops of clothes and housewares and jewels. She touched his arm casually.

"Thank you," she said quietly. "For never giving up."

It had the effect of a hush over the street. Paine exhaled, a sound of contentment. For they had, indeed, freed the city. And if anyone had been wondering if it was the right thing, they knew now. They knew it had to be done, and somehow, they'd done it.

Shep patted her hand. There was nothing forced or stilted—only love. "You're welcome, but..." he looked around. "We still have some work to do."

Ember followed Shep's eyes to a group of dragons that sat on the far side of the square, waiting patiently. She squeezed Shep's arm. So much had changed so quickly for all of them. "I have an idea to kill some time," she said, her smile met with his.

She hadn't had time to train on her dragon—not properly. Draco had been a baby for most of the time she'd known him, invisible to others except those who could see magic. Was that everyone now, she wondered, stepping over the slick cobblestone. The others followed, Twilight and the other fairies taking light steps and flight. It was charming to witness.

Ember paused before Arcturus and gave a small bow. "Welcome home, friend," she said. Her warm smile disarmed him. He dipped his head and allowed her to pat the soft fur under his magenta scales. Older than Draco, by many, many years, his magic was settled—but it felt the same. It felt like home.

She turned to Shep, smiling. "We can't go far," she said, gesturing to the mainland, where the streets lined with police and military.

"Far enough," he said, reaching for her hand and tugging her close. She rested her head on his shoulder briefly. This was home, too.

The others had fanned out. The fairies had no need of dragons. Hawk paled at the sight of them. "I'll stick with the ship," he muttered, and Paine laughed. Aurelia and Grace had already befriended a smaller dragon. Shep pressed his lips together, silent, knowing the danger—but also the life it promised. And they deserved to live it.

Ember retreated to Draco. "What an adventure you've been on," she murmured, patting his coat and remembering how he used to burn her little store. She wondered how that store was doing now. Was it all boarded up? "Let's fly," she said. The wind picked up and blew her hair off her face. She tipped her chin to the chill. The sun had begun its descent. The evening would be cloudy and cold.

Draco dipped his head, inviting her to climb on. She relished in the feeling of freedom it gave her. Could they fly away if they wished, back where the dragons had come from? Perhaps, she thought, settling in, but she was done running. It was time to make their stand. But first, she tapped Draco's hide, ready.

He wasn't saddled but they could feel each other. He'd follow her commands, even if they only came from her heart. *Up, Draco.* They were the first. Draco took a step, then hopped into the sky and beat his great wings. Her stomach still flipped. *Maybe it always would.* It wasn't like starting her Camry on a cold morning. It was freedom—plain and simple. She leaned in.

Stay away from the flashing lights, she thought, but she knew those lights stretched above them, too. They had some time, and they had some space. They also had friends in the other dragons circling around. She wasn't naive enough to think they wouldn't be hunted, but for the moment, they were safe.

Draco took her high enough to stay with the pack. He dipped and rolled, and she caught glimpses of Shep, a look of pure exhilaration on his face. To be reunited with his dragon and bring Atlantis home... his emotions must have been deep. She focused on her own. She poured love into Draco—appreciation, trust, and warmth—and in return, felt his deep well of magic. Magic that could, perhaps, awaken the city and return it home peacefully.

But this feeling couldn't last forever. She patted Draco, and he instinctually angled down. The sun was setting over the ocean, and it would be a beautiful one, filled with oranges and pinks. Ember could just pick up the magic of the wards, keeping their enemies out. Perhaps they weren't enemies at all, but they'd fallen for Maryse's dark magic. Maybe this spell could break them all out.

Or perhaps they'd die. Trust was the hardest risk of all, but it was one they had to take. To trust the world to do the right thing. Trust the Queen. Her friends. Shep.

She glanced at him. He'd followed her lead, guiding his dragon back to the square with a careful, almost reverent motion. She didn't need to step closer to know he was crying. She felt his gratitude, his quiet overwhelm, radiating from him like heat. He'd returned his daughter, and his dragon. Could they broker peace? Was love, truly, greater than hate?

She avoided the square, landing, instead in the gardens in the back of the castle. The scent of late-blooming flowers hung in the air, mingling with the faint warmth of the setting sun. Her gaze found two figures on a bench, silhouetted against the fiery sky, and she felt herself drawn to them.

Aurelia rested her head on Grace's shoulder, eyes fixed on the dragons as they descended. Tiny shivers ran through her, and Ember realized she was crying, too. She couldn't name the emotion exactly, but it tugged at her chest, echoing the months of changes she lived through. Scary, overwhelming, but real. Each trial she'd endured had felt impossible in the moment, yet now it all seemed to fit together, as if the path had always been meant for her.

This path had brought her sister home. It had brought friends she couldn't imagine living without. And it had brought Shep. She recognized the love in her heart mirrored on Grace's and Aurelia's face as they got up to meet the dragons.

Aurelia squeezed Grace's hand and discretely wiped a tear from her cheek. "It's almost time," she said, then turned her attention to Shep as he landed and led his dragon away. He gave Arcturus a soft pat before facing them, a soft, weary smile tugging at his lips.

"But we have a problem," Aurelia continued, her voice steady despite the unease Ember felt radiating from her.

Shep's shoulders slumped, but he didn't lose his good nature. "We're familiar with those," he said, forcing a smile. His relationship with his daughter was new, but strong.

It was Grace who answered. "Your friends," she said, her voice quiet but edged with urgency. "They're missing."

CHAPTER 42

"Our friends?" Ember asked at the same time as Shep said "They're missing?"

Grace looked over her shoulder, a smile on her face as she tightened her hold on Aurelia's hand. "I don't think they're far." She tugged Aurelia's hand. "Come on."

Ember watched them go. Shep's daughter disappearing into the gardens with the girl she loved sent a soft warmth through Ember's chest. *Yes,* she thought. *Everyone deserves to be loved.*

The citizens of Atlantis had not deserved to be cursed to the sky, nor did they deserve this sleeping sickness. Ember paused by a woman sleeping next to her child on the square. Some magic had kept them dry through the mist, and their cheeks were pink and healthy. Ember moved a strand of hair off the woman's face.

"I promise you we'll break this," she said.

A gentle touch at her back. Shep.

She stood and turned to him. The square stretched behind him like a field of fallen stars, every citizen dreaming beneath the same quiet curse. Her breath caught. "And then what?" she asked. "We wake them up, only for Maryse to curse them again. Or someone else. When does it end, Shep?"

He put an arm around her. "Maybe never."

She raised an eyebrow.

"Maybe we'll always have to fight," he said. "But we'll fight together."

He started toward Aurelia and Grace who had reached the edge of the square and headed toward the gates. "For years, I fought alone," he said. "I made terrible choices. I paid for them. I'm still paying."

He quickened his stride while the sun dropped lower, stretching the city in long streaks of gold. Dragons circled overhead. Here and there they'd pass a fairy, both full size and small. They moved with curious purpose, fluttering through open windows or drifting close to storefronts as if studying the town. Ember scanned every face she could, but she hadn't seen her friends.

Shadows had begun to fall as Grace led them through the city streets. Ember still didn't know her way around, but she suspected this was a market, and a busy one at that. Their wares were still out in the windows, items magical and mundane. Fabrics. Jewels. Fruits. The streets were cobbled beneath their feet. A brisk wind blew, carrying the smell of the sea. Ember could almost forget the danger they were in.

"Many of the fairies have found the taverns," Grace waved down a side street where music was playing.

"But that's not where we're going?" Shep asked.

Aurelia shook her head. "Your friend Hawk had an idea." She exchanged a glance with Grace.

"It's best if you see it for yourself," Grace said.

They moved past the cobbled streets and shuttered storefronts, past quiet homes with lanterns burning in empty windows. Sleeping Atlantians lay wherever the curse had caught them. Ember wanted to stop and help everyone. Each body pulled at her, a soft ache in her chest, but Shep kept her moving with a gentle tug.

They entered a part of the city she hadn't been in before, turning a corner to an old brick church with spires.

"The cathedral?" Shep rubbed is chin and looked at Aurelia, baffled. "Why here?"

She took both his hands. "Hawk thinks the fairies have the cure there," she said, walking backwards and tugging him. Time was short. Shadows had grown long in the city. If they were going to direct their energy, it had to be soon.

"Shep," Ember warned, but the look on his face broke her heart. A cure was everything he'd dreamed of. "Quickly," she said. "The fairies will still be here after."

Grace shook her head. "Not all of them, and perhaps not the ones we need." She looked at Aurelia, worry threading through her voice. "They want to leave the city. Once the wards are down..." She hesitated, then pressed. "This might be our last chance to learn what they know about the blood sickness."

Shep hurried up the cathedral steps. Ember followed, breath catching as she finally took in the structure. How had she not seen it before? The building was magnificent. It was not the tallest building on the street, not even close, but it held a quiet authority. The cathedral was nestled in, like it had existed forever and everything grew around it. Its red stained glass cast shadows on the steps.

Shep pulled the great doors opened and chuckled.

"The blood sickness?" He arched an eyebrow, stepping aside so Ember could enter first. "First time I've heard it called that."

Aurelia and Grace filed into the nave before he closed the door behind them.

"I've heard it called that." Grace shivered and hugged herself. The cathedral was old, and had a great entryway, beyond which were doors that low light spilled out of, as well as the sound of merry voices.

"Our people had stories." She turned to Shep. "But I thought they were just that. Stories." She looked to the doors, but Ember saw fear cast on her face. Not the kind that made you freeze, but the kind that came from recognizing something you had hoped wasn't real.

"Perhaps they were true," Grace whispered. "Just…" She swallowed, then faced Shep fully. The color had drained from her face. "It will not be easy. Purging this sickness. It's… painful. And not only on the body." Her voice dipped, almost reverent. "To purge yourself of this, you must purge what you carry. All of it."

Now it was Ember's turn to raise an eyebrow, but Grace had Shep's full attention. Ember could tell he recognized the stories. Something in his posture tightened, like a man bracing for a weight he had carried once before.

"I will do what I must," he said. His gaze drifted to the inner doors, where the voices on the other side grew louder, closer. "I only wish I need not bring Hawk with me."

Ember touched his shoulder, softly. "You saved him."

His reply came so quietly, she almost missed it. "I've damned him."

Before she could answer, the doors swung open and Hawk stepped through, flushed and full of joy. Or maybe that glow was from the flask in his hand.

"You've arrived!" Hawk put an arm around Ember, pulling her into his warmth. "And just in time. The fairies have been sharing all sorts of things about this blood sickness. Right here. In these hallowed halls."

He brought her into the heart of the church.

Ember's eyes widened at the statues and stained glass. She didn't recognize any of the things they worshiped or the scenes they depicted, but the images were intricate and colorful. Paine caught up with him and took the flask.

"I'm sorry," she said with a flush. "But after what they've told us, well..." She looked at Hawk. "A little drink didn't seem like the worst idea."

She turned to Shep. "Did you know?" she asked. "That it had to be here. And why?"

Shep nodded. "I'd heard whispers." The area was filled with fairies who flew here and there, lighting up dark corners. "I thought it was only a rumor."

His voice dropped. "Hawk doesn't have to go through with it," he said, almost pleading. "Not if there's another way."

"He doesn't have to go through with what?" Ember asked.

They'd arrived at the front, where Sierra stood waiting with Twilight, Starling, and Grim. Grim's expression lived up to his name. The others didn't look much brighter.

"He doesn't have to what?" Ember repeated. Her voice carried across the vaulted space. The fairies spoke in hushed tones.

Twilight drifted closer and touched her shoulder. "Confront the darkness in himself," she answered. "Only then can the sickness be lifted."

Ember's pulse sputtered. Twilight shifted to gaze toward Shep, who stood a few paces away with Hawk, their heads bent in tense conversation.

"It is not for the faint of heart," Twilight continued. "He carries much from his years. His soul is burdened. Heavy. He has seen so much. Done so much. In the name of love, yes. Perhaps that will see him thought. Perhaps..." she paused, "it won't. This is a lengthy and risky process, Ember. Only he can decide."

Ember turned toward the stained-glass windows. *Almost time*. A cold urgency washed over her.

"We don't have time for a lengthy process," she said.

Twilight gave her a sad smile. "Lengthy for him. Time on the other side does not pass as ours does."

"The other side?"

Twilight took a breath. "Hell," she answered. "Shepherd must travel to Hell to release its bind, and he must purge all that is dark within him to be there."

Chapter 43

"Hell," Ember repeated. The word felt heavier inside the cathedral. Light from the red-paned windows slanted between the pews, painting the aisle in streaks of dark wine. She turned to Shep. "Now?"

Shep took a deep breath, but this time he didn't reach for humor. "I'd heard rumors," he said.

Twilight stepped between them, wings flickering with a muted pulse. "Together the fairies can open a portal." She turned to Ember. "But only for a short time. Time passes slower there. I think thirty seconds of our time should do it."

Shep did the calculations, but Hawk beat him to it.

"Twelve hours. Give or take." He went to take a sip from his flask, but it was empty. Ember noted his red eyes, but she didn't think it was from the drink. He was afraid, and who wouldn't be?

"You don't have to," Ember said. "You could just..."

"Live like this?" Shep finished. He spoke softly. "No. I owe it to Hawkins to try. I owe it to myself. To us."

Around them, the fairies tittered softly. They were eager to be on their way, out in Atlantis or into the world. They were doing Shep a great favor. He couldn't waste it.

She nodded. "Then I go with you," she said, taking a step toward him.

He shook his head. "You wouldn't survive it, Ember. We have to go alone. But thank you." He took her hand and kissed it. "For being willing."

She swallowed and looked around the chapel. Sierra and Paine waited with Hawk. Aurelia and Grace stayed by Shep. *Friends.* They were surrounded by friends, even here on the edge of something terrifying.

"Thirty seconds?"

"Thirty seconds for *you*," Hawk said pointedly. "A little longer for us. Let's get this over with."

To everyone's surprise, Paine pulled Hawkins aside and full on kissed him in the nave of the church.

"About time," Sierra said with a laugh, though she turned her face away, giving them a sliver of privacy.

Ember's heart swelled. *About time* didn't even begin to cover it. She'd known for so long. From Hawk. From Paine. Paine pulled away, flush. "Come back," she said. "Don't do anything stupid."

"Stupid is what I'm known for," he said, but he said it softly and held her hand.

Now it was Ember's turn to look away.

The fairies gathered then, wings glinting in the crimson light. They turned as one to create their portal, and of course they did by singing. Grim began the melody, a low and unsettling rumble. The others joined, weaving harmony through the cavernous space.

Sierra put an arm around Ember as the song deepened. The very walls of the cathedral shivered, and the hair on the back of Ember's neck stood. Hell was not a place to sing about, never mind go.

"They'll be okay," Sierra whispered.

Ember wasn't convinced. She watched Shep and Hawk speak in low voices near the front, heads together as if they could plan their way through the gates of hell. *What sort of plan would achieve that?* Steal their souls back and walk out again?

"I wish I could do it for him," Ember said. Her voice cracked. "He's done so much for so long for so many people."

Sierra brushed her hair off her shoulder and rested her head. A soft, steady comfort. "Oh Ember, you always have been a solver," she said. "But you can't solve everything. Sometimes people have to fight their own battles. Shepherd chose this. Just because his intentions were true doesn't mean it was right. He chose it, and he has to be the one to fix it."

Ember took a breath in. "He chose it for me," she said. "For all of us."

Sierra forced Ember to look at her. Into her blue eyes, steady and unyielding. "And that's why he'll come back. He'll fix it for the same reasons." She threaded her fingers through Ember's. "Love."

Ember let out a small laugh, the tension in her chest easing just a little. "When did you get so wise?" she asked.

The church tower rang the hour. They would soon have to get to the square. The fairies' song swelled, filling the cathedral with weight and sorrow. It was in a language she couldn't understand, but low and sad. A shimmering circle appeared near the altar.

Shep came back and pulled Ember into a hug. "I'll be right back." He kissed her head.

She looked up into his dark eyes, the mirror opposite of Sierra's blue, but both fill of love and intensity. She kissed him in front of everyone, wiping a tear as she did. "Come back to me," she said. This seemed more dangerous than all they'd done. Saving Atlantis. Fighting Maryse. She remembered the hellhounds, and shivered.

"I will," he promised, giving her shoulder a squeeze and heading to the portal with Hawk. They didn't turn back or hesitate. Shep nodded once to his friend, and they stepped into the portal together.

All Ember could do was wait.

CHAPTER 44

Shepherd had no hesitations for what he was about to do, but fear? He had plenty of that.

He'd once been known as Casius, though over the years that man had died a thousand deaths. None were of his own hand, yet many by his choices. By his failures. By the deep, gnawing weight of loss. By surrendering when he should have held on.

He recognized the parallel to the fallen angels—the endless damnation, the inevitability of consequence. An angel he was not. But this curse... it had damned him for so long.

Had he started his life, once, as a good man? He supposed so. He took a measured step toward the portal and waited for Hawk to follow. Years had eroded the man he once was, but had he lived a normal lifetime, then yes, maybe he could have called himself good.

Doubt crept in when his wife died. It grew when he saw what Atlantis was becoming. And the years since? The years spent searching for the one called to return the city home? Well, they'd been worse and worse.

He'd killed, yes, and not just for this curse.

Was it worth it—to bring home the city, to meet Ember?

He stole a glance back, and only one. He couldn't let his resolve waver. *Yes. A thousand times, in a thousand lifetimes, yes.*

Hawk gave him a nod. That was all he needed.

He'd stepped through portals before. The effect was immediate and jarring. The world tilted, vision blinding him. For a heartbeat, he was neither here nor there. He wondered if it were possible to get stuck in such a place. There were times in his past he'd have welcomed it. Then a wave of heat slammed into him, and he was through.

Hell.

It was hot. Ridiculously, brutally hot. He had thought that was just a rumor.

Then he heard the bray of a hellhound. He opened his eyes. Fire and brimstone and all that.

"Huh," Hawn commented, shaking the effects of the portal out of his head. "I'd expected more... pizzazz."

He was right. The landscapes was bleak—dull, scorched land as far as they could see. The sky was a smokey brown. Heat from the land under them burned, and so did the air. Shep was already sweating. He crinkled his nose. The smell of sulfur, blood, and death was thick and suffocating. Yes, this was Hell all right. But now what?

"Who do we seek?" Hawk asked.

Shep studied the skyline. It was miles in all directions. "He who is in charge, I suppose." But he had no idea what direction in which to walk.

"They could have dropped us off a little closer," Hawk grumbled.

Shep looked around, gaging direction and grateful time was slowed on the other side. He pointed toward the mountains in the distance, miles and miles away. "I see a faint smoke rising," he said. "That might be our only clue."

Hawk sighed and took a step forward. All other directions were sand and desert. "Good of a direction as any. Erm..." he looked back. The portal was faint. "How do we get back? This thing is in the middle of the desert."

Shep forced a smile. "It emits a faint energy," he said, though he didn't actually believe it. "We'll know the way."

"If you say so," Hawk said, but he started walking. Shep knew Hawk wanted this curse gone as much as Shepherd did. Neither relished the idea of returning to the world a monster again—at least the physical kind.

Shep's eyes lingered on Hawk's pale profile in the yellow light. The whiskers on his face had picked up the sand blowing around, and his face turned pink from the heat. Hawk had lived a long life, too. He'd fought. Run. Saved people. Fell in love, too—perhaps more than once. Had he done the things Shepherd did to survive? He didn't know.

His friend was a good person. Shep wished he could say that about himself.

Part of this journey was internal, he knew, but he wished they'd thought to bring water. Could he say the same, was he a good man? Would he make the same choices? Would he hurt other people again, to save those he loved—or even for the *possibility* of it? What if they were terrible people, people who would have gone on to hurt others?

Shep sighed. It was complicated.

"Tell me about growing up on Atlantis," Hawk said. They trudged across the scorched plain, but the mountains seemed no closer. The wind picked up and blew sand around them.

"My childhood?" Shep managed a dry laugh. "Why?"

Hawk gestured in front of them. "We have time," he said with a hint of humor. "And if part of this is—" He made air quotes with his fingers. "—to confront the darkness in ourselves, let's get on with it. Tell me about your parents."

Shep laughed, then quickly shut his mouth as grains of sand blew in. "My parents." He wiped the sweat from his brow.

Hawk had become flush also, his breathing labored. Shep noticed all the little details this curse revealed—the tension in muscles, the shallow breaths. And Hawk was hungry. He'd learned to deal with it, but the need never fully disappeared. Shep looked over the barren landscape. There would be nothing to feed on—not that he would. But there were times the need could overtake.

"I grew up with Corin, you know," Shep said, side-eyeing Hawk to see his response. "And his brother. The Queen kept his brother well hidden. If anyone has childhood trauma, it's Zyah."

"And Zyah came through in the end," Hawk said with more enthusiasm than deserved.

Shep gave a noncommittal *hmph*. There were no heroes in this story, both Zyah and Corin had made their mistakes. Corin had helped them the ability to get the dragons back, but that did little to make up for his crimes.

"Were there signs that Corin was a bad seed?" Hawk asked softly. Far off, a bird cawed. The wind roared like a lion. A small tree attempted to grow under their feet, gnarled and bent over.

"Not when we were children. Corin was boastful. Entitled. Charming, even." Shep smiled despite himself. "But he was the heir to the crown. It was only as he aged that the darkness gathered. His brother saw it. He fought it." Shep let his voice trail off. The path that led Corin to madness was not something he relished revisiting. And he didn't even get the worst of it. No—that was reserved for those he left behind.

"And you?" Hawk asked, the hint of a mischievous smile on his face. It seemed out of place in such a desolate area, but that was Hawkins—always teasing, even in the face of danger.

Shep glanced at his friend, gratitude tightening his chest. For Hawk, for all he'd done, for every life he had saved—the ancestors of Atlantis and those he would never meet.

"Me?" he asked. He looked down at the cracked sand beneath their feet. A millipede scuttered across the fissures, disappearing into the shadows. "I was just a man. Raised to be in the guard. Strong. Quiet. Troublemaker."

Hawk laughed. "Sounds about right."

"Then I met a woman. A healer. Quiet and mysterious. I was enamored with her. Not as I love Ember—but enough. Enough I could have built a life with her on Atlantis. But then the darkness gathered. She gave her life to save Aurelia. And I had to choose: stay and raise her or leave and help bring Atlantis home. I don't know even now if I chose correctly."

A lump had formed in his chest, just as it always did when he thought about such things—mistakes, forgiveness, lives altered by his decisions. "And I did everything I could to bring the city back. I chased Ember's magic across ages. I made terrible choices. I've dragged you into them, my friend, and I'm sorry."

He took a long breath. It had been a long time since he'd visited such dark corners of his mind, and longer still since he'd voiced them. He felt a flush and not from the heat.

Hawk clapped his shoulder. "I suspect, in a lifetime, everyone must make such hard choices. No path is exactly correct. You walked your conscience, my friend. No one can ask more than that."

Shepherd sighed. "They can," he said. Was it his imagination or was there a dark cloud on the horizon. "They can ask for goodness, and kindness."

"Both you have in spades."

"I haven't always," he admitted. His voice thinned in the burning air. "The darkness that must be absolved to leave here? It's still in there, Hawk. I can feel it sometimes. Stirring. I am capable of terrible things. I am a creature of nightmares."

Hawk narrowed his eyes at the gathering dark. "Perhaps," he said. "And perhaps we all must conquer such thoughts. My own..." He trailed off and shielded his eyes. The hazy light bled from nowhere. No sun. No source, but it blinded all the same.

"Are those wings?" he asked.

Shep followed his gaze. The cloud moved. It rippled. And indeed, coming toward them was a horde of animals in flight, the type of which he couldn't tell.

And there was nowhere to run.

CHAPTER 45

Shep didn't bother with an answer. He squinted into the glare but couldn't see what type of creatures barreled toward them. Only that they were huge. He imagined they had fangs and claws. He'd seen what hellhounds could do, after all. His heartbeat quickened and he looked for an escape route, of which there were none.

"We could tunnel?" Hawk suggested, halfheartedly kicking the scrabbled sand under the toe of his boot.

Shep turned around. He couldn't see the portal anymore. "We could run," he suggested, though even he didn't believe in the suggestion.

"No, my friend." Hawk turned toward them, the black mass growing by the second and the sound of their beating wings like drums. "We make our stand."

Hawk tried to smile but found he was out of humor. Hawk wasn't sure that he and Shep would be killed in this place, but there were things worse than death on this plane. They could be hurt, and hurt gravely.

There were no weapons. No blades. Not even a rock. They hadn't time to take them, and what use would one weapon be?

As the creatures flew closer, they started to take shape. Not buzzards. Not winged hellhounds.

"They're human," Hawk marveled.

"I wouldn't be too quick to say that," Shep muttered.

The group surrounded them, their beating wings silencing as they took to the ground. The air stilled as their wings folded into long black capes that whispered against the scorched ground. Men and women, all in obsidian fabric, their skin pale as bone despite the blistering heat.

The woman closest stepped forward. She could have stepped right out of a movie with her long, dark hair and bloodred lips. She looked Shep up and down and smiled, revealing a fanged tooth.

"Welcome home," she purred, reaching out to touch Shep's arm. He pulled it back and the group around her growled and bristled.

"This is not my home," he growled back.

She tittered, and the sound was soft yet sharp enough to cut. One raised hand quieted the others behind her. She was clearly in charge. She moved her gaze to Hawk, then to the mountains to their side.

"You may want to reconsider," she said. "He doesn't know you're here yet. If you fly with us, you will be safe." Her smile was both beautiful and awful. "You are one of us, are you not? You both? Though you smell different. You smell of the world still..."

She stepped toward him and inhaled, closing her eyes. "It has been a long time since we've felt the winds of the earth."

She opened her eyes. "It takes some time, but most of our kind find their way here. It's not so bad. We have ways to survive." Those behind her snickered. Shep noticed one edge closer. He was large and dark eyed, and had not offered a speck of humor.

"Forgive me," the woman said, "I have been known as many names over the years. The most current is Lilith. You can call me Lily. Or mother." She grinned, and this time the one behind her grinned as well, but it was not a welcoming sight.

Shep stepped back on instinct and bumped right into another waiting vampire. "We have come here to break this curse," he said.

"The fairy opened a portal for us to come here," Hawk added. "But we are going back."

She raised her eyebrows. "The fairy, you say? Is Twilight still around?"

Shep blinked. "Twilight?" He struggled to imagine that the fairy he knew could be tied to a creature as ancient as the woman before them. "She is," he said, cautious.

Lily twirled a strand of her hair. "One of my ancestors. I keep track, you know." She winked, the gesture both playful and predatory. "Though if she sent you here to break the curse..." She shared a look with her kin. "She either believes you are very brave or very foolhardy."

Her gaze swept down their bodies, assessing, weighing. "And I believe it is foolhardy. There is no cure, except for the cave itself. And in there..." She shivered as if remembering a nightmare she still carried in her bones. "You will see things you I would not wish on anyone."

"We are ready." Hawk blustered, and again, Shepherd felt the weight of the curse on him, and he was sorry.

"Are you?" Lily asked. "Foolhardy indeed. But perhaps one can be brave at the same time." A small smile tugged at her lips. "No one's attempted it. No one has ever wanted to. Why would they?" she asked. "Why give up this power? This lifetime?"

Shep did not hesitate. The answer rose from him like the very air he breathed. "For love."

"Aah." She took a breath. "It's always for love. You could turn her, you know?" She spared a glance at the man behind her, who crossed his arms.

"Respectfully, I would not," Shep answered.

Lily's attention turned to Hawk, sharp as a blade. "And you?"

He dipped into an exaggerated bow, his hand sweeping the air with theatrical grace. "The same, my lady."

She pressed her lips together. "The world is getting softer."

"Perhaps," Shep added, "but perhaps softness and strength can exist together. Like foolhardiness and bravery. But what do I know?"

Something in Lily shifted then. A flicker behind her eyes. Perhaps it was regret, but Shepherd had not spoken falsely. He knew next to nothing of this curse, of this place, of the woman standing in front of him. But if she were human once, she had regrets.

The man behind her shifted and spoke in her ear. She considered.

"The others wish me to kill you right now," she said. "You set a bad example. But I am, or was once, a romantic. I'll take you to the cave, but there we will leave you." She stepped in close enough that only Shep could hear. "Perhaps this is brave. Perhaps it is foolish. Perhaps I will lose all my followers when they see you succeed. Or perhaps they will watch you die. I will admit, it has been so long since I have played such games." Her voice dropped, with a bit of humor. "You have earned our escort to the passage, Shepherd, but it does come at a cost." "And what cost is that?" he asked.

She drifted nearer, close enough that her breath brushed his cheek. It carried a sickly sweetness that turned sour at the edge, as if fruit had rotted under heat. The skin along her jaw cracked in places and there was a hint of green underneath. "Your soul," she breathed.

He rolled his eyes.

"Just kidding," she said, smiling with those same sharp canines. She might be undead, but he was sure she could still cause a lot of pain.

"What is your cost?" he repeated, louder this time and stripped of any attempt at civility.

Her gathered kin shifted. Darker clouds moved in, giving the landscape a bloodred tint. A strong gust blew sand up and around them.

Lily looked back to her group as if seeking confirmation. The closest of her kin nodded.

"The cure." She turned back to him. "If you find it, I want access to it, too." She squared her shoulders and tipped her chin up, expecting a fight. A fight he would lose. He had no idea what direction to go or who to face. Before he could form a reply, Hawk spoke.

"You've got a deal," Hawk said, then shot Shep an apologetic look. "We've got limited time, mate," he said. "Let's go."

"Go where, exactly?" Shep asked. The sky had darkened even further, shadows thickening until the world felt smaller. Lily noticed it, too.

"The dark cave," she answered. "And quickly. You don't want to be here after nightfall. There are worst things than vampires in the dark."

As if summoned, a howl cut across the plains, and another answered. The hair on the back on Shep's neck stood.

"Hellhounds," he said.

"And worse," Lily agreed. She shook out her wings. Some unholy magic allowed her to fly, and he was not looking forward to it. "Come close, brother." She smiled. "I will take you under your arms. And you." She tipped her chin to Hawk, "will go with Ivan."

Ivan grunted.

"Goody," Hawk replied, though his eyes sparked. They were one step closer to a cure. One step closer to going home.

And for Shep, that was all he ever wanted.

CHAPTER 46

As the sun dipped lower, Ember waited. Only minutes had passed, but they were long minutes. Longer than she thought they would be.

"Any time now." Starling tapped her foot, which was difficult since it hovered an inch over the floor. The portal flickered, offering a glimpse at the other side. The dark landscape of Hell itself. She wished they hadn't gone, but he couldn't live with the weight of the curse on him forever. He shouldn't have to.

She opened her mouth to say so, but Aurelia's hand found her shoulder.

"He'll be okay," she said.

Ember managed a smile. "Thank you." It didn't surprise her to see Shep's daughter possessed a quiet, steady wisdom.

"Grace told me once that facing yourself is the hardest thing a person can do," Aurelia said. The portal dimmed again, as if some unseen cloud passed over whatever light Hell claimed. "I think she was right. Don't you?" Ember considered. "I'd say it's right up there." She hadn't had to walk through her own demons. She'd been too busy fighting actual ones. Beneath her practiced confidence, what waited? Shame, probably. Fear. A mess of things she hadn't had the luxury of naming. She wondered if even walking through Hell would burn that away. If it could have, she'd try. But this was Shep's task. Hawk's too.

Paine paced at the front of the altar, shoulders tight, steps sharp. Ember didn't dare approach her.

Ember bit her fingernail. "How long did you say it was going to be?" she asked.

Grim frowned, his wings giving a betraying tremor. "It takes as long as it takes."

"What he means," Twilight said gently, sliding in before Grim could bristle, "is *soon*. Very soon." She turned to him, but he didn't acknowledge her. "Time passes much slower there. Another minute more, perhaps..." She trailed off as if she weren't sure.

They watched the portal in silence. Aurelia walked up next to Ember. Their relationship was tentative— how could it be otherwise?

"I didn't know much about my father. Who he was," she said. The portal shimmered, and the cathedral's stained glass splashed colors across the floor in shifting patterns.

"I was raised by the Queen," Aurelia continued, her voice soft, "who was always trying to keep me from the King's eyes." She pressed her lips together. "But the townsfolk... they would tell me things, here and there. In the square, at the tavern. The Queen forbade me to speak of him because his betrayal stung the King so deeply, but the people—they whispered anyway."

Ember pulled her eyes from the portal to look at Aurelia. Despite being older than Ember in years, her maturity carried the fragility of someone still very young, and still very scared.

"And what did they say?" Ember asked, reaching out to take Aurelia's hand.

"They said he was a good man." She swallowed, a tear forming in her eye. "Is he, Ember? Is he a good man? I could never forgive him for leaving, but I know he had his reasons."

Ember took a deep breath. "Sometimes the right decisions are also the hardest. The most painful. If not for Shepherd, the city never would have returned home."

Aurelia turned her gaze to Grace, who whispered with Twilight, both of them tense, shoulders tight. "That doesn't make them easier to swallow."

"No," Ember agreed softly. "It doesn't. But perhaps it could make them forgivable?" She squeezed Aurelia's hand, feeling warmth and hesitation beneath the surface.

Aurelia smiled, a genuine gesture that lit up her face. "And perhaps that is the way forward for all of us?"

Ember felt the weight of her own forgiveness waiting to be offered. Some resentment she held was for things beyond anyone's control. Some for choices others would never regret. And some of it was for her own choices, right or wrong. Letting it go would be a feat unto itself.

"We'll do it together," she said. Aurelia swept her hair off her shoulder.

"Agreed," she said.

And again, they waited.

CHAPTER 47

Shepherd had flown on a magical ship. He'd ridden through the wind on the back of a dragon. This experience was nothing like that.

"It's like being a package out for delivery!" Hawk yelled, but there was something off in his voice, as if the wind itself refused to carry it.

The demon's hands grasped them tightly under their arms as they flapped their wings through the sky. The horizon itself darkened, a trick of the light or perhaps it was getting later.

Time was short. How much had passed back home? Was his quest really worth this?

And he smelled their blood. It was different from humans who pumped so energetically. This was a slow, steady drum that smelled of power. If he chose, he could stay here and lord his own domain. Never be hungry. Afraid. It was not a choice he would make, but the temptation was there. It was always there.

His friend had acclimated to this curse as best he could. Making jokes—that's was Hawkins's way—but Shep knew the weight beneath the humor. Even without extra senses, he felt it: shame, fear of losing control, of hurting someone he care for. Shepherd wouldn't let him do that. No, this was the right thing for them, no matter where it led.

The mountains came up swiftly, scraggly and bare. They were made of stone, and the demons perched them on the lip of a cave halfway up. Shep felt a wave of nausea as they landed. Motion sickness, he told himself, but the truth was fear. This place was wrong. And he simply wanted to go home. Back to Ember.

"Here we leave you," Lily said. She paused as the others readied to take flight. Even the demons were afraid of this place. She lowered her voice. "I wish you luck, Shepherd. I've not seen anyone confront this and come back." She took a step toward him. She'd been beautiful once, but now there were cracks in her façade. "And if you do come back, you owe me a debt. Don't forget."

For a moment, a look of pain flashed across her features, and Shep understood. This curse was power, but it was also a terrible burden. How long had she lived, he wondered. Did she yearn for death? For whatever was next? For simply ceasing?

"I will not forget," he promised.

An eerie noise echoed out the cave, a moan or perhaps a low growl, or something between the two.

"Umm, what exactly is in there?" Hawk asked, his voice half curiosity, half apprehension.

Lily smiled and stepped toward the cliff. "No one knows," she said. "Legends say it's yourself you have to face on the way out. Good luck with that." She pressed off the ledge and took flight into the gathering dark, the others behind her.

For a moment the rhythm of their wings was almost calming, until it faded leaving only Shep, Hawk, and the cavern. The wind whistled low past the mountain, tugging at his resolve. Shep pushed down his fear. It had never served him well. Some things were just made to get through.

"Ourselves?" Hawk asked, hands on his hips as if he were considering what to choose for dinner. "So it's bound to be obstinate? Opinionated? Fierce?"

He appreciated his friend's humor, even if he couldn't bring himself to smile. "It's bound to be much worse than that. Let's go."

He carried home in mind as he took a first step into the cave. His childhood on Atlantis. Magic. Love. The birth of his daughter. Meeting Ember. Her smile. Her eyes. Her caress. He would get home to her and set things right. He promised himself. But first...

The cave was cold, far colder than natural. The walls were smooth and gray, and already the darkness behind him swallowed the path they had taken.

"Portal?" Hawk asked, his voice uncertain.

Shep shook his head. "No." The space wasn't natural, but it wasn't a portal either. "This... this is magic I have never seen. Old." He reached out to touch the sides of the cave. It was spongy and reacted to his touch. In response the cave groaned. "It's alive," he whispered, awe mingled with unease.

A fine mist gathered around them, thickening with every step. Hawk made a noise between a wail and a squeal. Shep managed to find him, grabbing his arm to steady him and squinted. Hawk pointed. Ahead was a small boy with fair hair, playing dice by the side of a shore. Swindling, if Shep was correct.

"It's not real," Shep muttered, his eyes narrowing. But how could the same vision appear to both of them? Whatever this mist was, it fed on more than fear—it fed on memory, on thought, on the mind itself.

"It's me." Hawk knelt on one knee, eyes fixed on the boy as he swindled sailors much older and tougher than himself. One sailor finally shoved everything aside, and the boy scampered away. Hawk and Shep followed him deeper into the cave.

"Shortly after this..." Hawk began, but words weren't needed. They walked into the scene. This time, Hawk fell to his knees. The little boy was laughing until he ran through the streets.

The further they walked, the thicker the smoke became, choking the air. The boy paused, sensing something was wrong. He dropped the dice he was carrying, dipped his head, and ran around a corner—straight into the arms of an old man. The man grabbed him by the shoulders and turned him around.

"Don't look, son," the man said.

It was hard to see behind the man's bulk, but the boy wiggled free. Ahead, a house burned, its walls covered in graffiti—most of the word "witch" in angry, creative forms. Flames licked the structure, smoke curling into the cavern's mist, and the boy froze, wide-eyed at the sight of the inhabitants of the house. They'd been killed. Brutally, if Shep could tell. A man and woman's bodies lay in front of the doors, blood dripping onto the scorched ground. Hawk's parents.

The boy Hawk and the man stood together—the young Hawk with tears streaming down his cheeks. Shep knelt quietly, letting the scene unfold. The older man gripped the child's shoulders.

"It's not safe here." His voice was firm but gentle. He embraced the young Hawk in a hug. "You must take the ship and run, my grandson. Run!"

Hawk slowly stood, watching the boy shake as he made his decision. "The villagers were afraid of magic," he said, voice tight, wiping his nose with the back of his sleeve. "The ship was hidden, but my mother... she had herbs. Remedies. She healed them. Birthed their children." He pointed to a woman, clutching a small child at the back of the crowd. He pointed at all of them. "They did nothing."

"I'm so sorry," Shep said.

Hawk shook his head as the boy pushed his way through the crowd. The scene shifted, and the boy grew older. The mist revealed the ancestors Hawk saved on the ship. Hawk had always played it off, but sometimes he was too late, arriving to scenes of grim aftermath. He'd never faced Maryse directly, but the hellhounds had tested him time and again, and the loneliness he carried was evident in every motion, every glance.

Each vision grew harsher, more punishing, until they could see all that Hawk had saved. The families, the lives preserved, the love he'd nurtured. All of it.

Hawk's face had paled. The cave walls disappeared, swallowed by the dark mist that now surrounded them. Shep could feel them breathing in and out, alive and watchful. The mist turned black, and Shep's stomach fell.

"This will not be easy," he said, voice low, his hand brushing against Hawk's shoulder.

"Would you rather face it alone?" his friend said, stepping close.

Shep took a breath in. Would his friend judge him? His decisions? "No," he said.

The mist thickened, darkness pressing against them from every side. Only a faint wind drifted across their cheek, carrying dew that smelled of distant memories and old magic—not the harsh, ancient curse of the cave, but the light, pure magic Atlantis had once known.

Then he heard it: a baby's cry. He'd have dropped to his knees if he could. He knew this scene.

"Aurelia!" his voice tore through the fog, raw with agony.

He didn't need to see, but the mist showed him anyway. Aurelia's mother, dying in childbirth. Her face was as beautiful as the day he met her, yet pale and strained. Her breath came in shallow gasps. The midwife held their child. He couldn't bear to do it, yet the vision demanded he see it.

If the mist revealed anything, it was the truth he long avoided. He had left Atlantis not just to save it, but because he couldn't face this heartbreak. He'd abandoned his daughter for his own inadequacy.

His former self held her hands in his. He had known it as love, then, so he thought—but his idea of love had deepened since then. "Please don't leave us," he whispered, but she was already well on her way. Her eyes glazed, distant. He smelled the herbs in the room the midwife had frantically used to delay the inevitable. His hands shook. He hadn't confronted this memory in a long time.

She reached up, her hand shaky. "You will do great things," she said in a raspy voice, "and so will she."

He shook his head. "Not now." She was a mage, a fortuneteller, gifted at seeing the future. How had she not seen this? Or perhaps, she had—and chosen it anyway.

She tipped her head, coughing softly, then cupped his cheek. He leaned into her touch. "Now is all we have," she said, her voice gentle. "I forgive you. For all your about to do. For the feelings you don't have. For the terrible choices you'll have to make. Casius... look at me."

He remembered how unbearable it was, but he looked anyway. Her gaze met his—not in the past, not in the memory, in this moment. He knew it.

"You are a good man, presented with terrible choices. Perhaps the path will fill you with shame, unhappiness." She coughed again, turning briefly back to his younger self. "Eventually, you will face that shame. You will know that you did the best you could, as most of us do. You will know then, Casius, that you are forgiven."

He took a breath in. He'd forgotten all of it, dismissing it as the ramblings of a dying woman. The mist faded, revealing those choices—the curse, the murders, the years he spent alone and self-destructive. Hawk stood by his side through it all. Each scene, designed to wound him, seemed instead to pass, leaving him steadier with every step.

Eventually the dark mist cleared, and the cave walls appeared again.

"Was that all?" Hawk asked, but his pallor was a little green.

In front of them stood an altar. Standing behind it was the ghost of Aurelia's mother. He didn't lose his breath this time. She smiled and held her palms out to the basin on the altar. "To truly let go, you must bleed into it."

She floated around the altar, approaching him, like that last moment. She cupped his face with her hands and his skin frosted at her touch.

"Goodbye, Casius," she said, and her visage faded.

Hawk looked in the basin. It was coppery and empty. Next to it stood a sharp knife. "How much blood, do you think?"

Shep watched the last of her fade. "Let's hope not much," he said. He picked up the knife and sliced his arm, the first step to absolution.

CHAPTER 48

Shepherd and Hawk had been gone too long. The sun was nearly set. If they were going to set this group intention, it had to be now. Ember took a step closer to the portal, but Grace held her back.

"It won't help for you to get lost in there, too," she said.

Ember bit her lip. How much did Grace know? Her mother had cursed Shep with the blood sickness. He'd chosen it, but he'd chosen it for this—for Atlantis. She stifled a sob. *He was a good man. He did not deserve this.* What would he find on the other side?

The portal flickered. Ember froze, rooted to the floor. Magic flared within the cathedral, lighting up the beams and rafters, illuminating the mosaic on the floor and the beautiful frescoes above, but Ember didn't see any of it.

Aurelia clung to Grace. Paine stopped pacing. The fairies muttered something softly.

"The portal is moving," Grim said, under his breath. "Though whether away from them, or toward, I cannot tell. We are trying to hold it on task for a few more moments."

"Shep," Ember whispered, almost pleading as the magic flared. Inside the cathedral a soft rain pattered on the stained glass and thunder rumbled. Outside the dragons roared, Arcturus the loudest. She didn't know if their magic could pull Shep back, but they tried.

The portal shifted to face a different direction. Dark, far away mountains appeared. It flickered and moved as if going in fast-forwarded through a movie. Ember couldn't keep up, and finally Paine joined her. She had tear stains down her freckled cheeks.

"Was this worth it?" Paine asked, voice tight with frustration.

Ember pursed her lips. "Neither you nor I can make that decision," she said, sliding an arm around her friend. "It was up to them, and they chose."

"It's been ten minutes!" she cried. For a moment, the cathedral fell silent, and her cry echoed in the pews behind them.

The portal moved faster, floating through space and time. A hellhound brayed. Lightning flashed. They saw a cave entrance and then flashes of things they shouldn't. Ember saw her parents' accident. Sierra, lying in a coma. Her life, after—sad and dull. A chill broke out on her arms.

She looked around at all their stunned faces. Paine's mouth hung open. Aurelia clutched Grace's arm. Grim muttered under his breath.

Then the portal settled on Hawk and Shep on the floor, bleeding.

Paine screamed, but Ember didn't hesitate. She jumped forward, diving into the portal before anyone could stop her.

The first thing she noticed was the heat. Then she noticed the absence of sound. The storm from Atlantis was far away here, muted like a memory. Behind her, the portal shimmered faintly. She'd landed on her knees on rough stone and scrambled to his side. He lay by an altar covered in blood.

"What have you done?" she asked, taking his arm and binding it as best she could. "We have to get you back."

His eyes fluttered open. Clear. Deep. Just as they were on the first day she'd met him. There was nothing physical to tell her the curse was removed, but there was something different. An absence of fear. Of shame. Was that what Hell had done for him? If so... she could use a dose.

"My love," he said. His first words were nothing about the curse or the city. They were of her.

She propped him to sitting. "We haven't much time," she said. He looked around the cave.

"Everything is so muted now. I cannot even hear your heartbeat."

He pulled her into a kiss, and for a moment, she let herself fall into it. She pressed her forehead to his, a moment between them in the chaos. If that was all they ever had, she'd take it. It was more than she ever dreamed.

She squeezed his shoulder as she got up to sitting, holding herself back from asking what happened. She'd learn, in time.

Behind them, Hawk and Paine were rising also. Hawk's face had paled, but his lips were no longer the deep red of blood. The cave smelled of coppery blood, too much of it.

Ember held Shep up, letting herself take in the cave. The basin dominated the room, but along the walls were crude pictures drawn. Ones of feast and carnage. A series of pictures depicted a man being turned to a monster, the process long, drawn out and brutal.

"Did you go through all that?" she asked, her voice trembling.

His gaze followed hers, a lock of hair flopped in his face. "That, and much more." He struggled to stand on his own. His legs shook. "I did what I had to do, Ember. It was not always pretty. It was not always good. But I always had my goal of returning the city home. Returning magic... finding you." He met her eyes. Though his body trembled, his deep brown eyes were steady.

He lowered his voice as Paine and Hawk walked towards the portal. "I have had to face those parts of myself... to let them go."

Ember looked back at the basin. The blood inside had darkened and begun to smoke.

"That's what we leave here, then," she said. She turned back to him and nodded her head to the portal. "The future is that way."

"Yes, it is." He took her hand and struggled to walk, but with each step, he grew stronger.

"Is it over, then?" she asked, hesitating before stepping though.

He raised her hand to kiss it. "I've one more task here." He looked toward Hawk, who gave, a small, resigned nod from the edge of the portal. "I owe a debt to someone who helped me."

Hawk shrugged, though he winced as he did. "Leave a note," he suggested.

Shep's face brightened as he smiled. "An excellent idea."

Ember looked away as he wrote, in his own blood, a path forward—the way out and through.

CHAPTER 49

Ember and Shep stepped from the portal and into another kind of hell. She hadn't realized how boldly the stained glass tinted the church red, or how heavy the air felt now that they were back. Most of Atlantis slept in the town square, but a few people had taken refuge here before the curse fell. An older woman lay hunched over a pew in the back. A man in the second row snored softly, streaks of red and yellow light sliding across his face.

It was time.

Most of the fairies had left already to gather outside. Grim and Twilight remained, but they hurried out with Sierra. Aurelia paused long enough to hug her father. She held his shoulders and searched his face. A smile broke out on her face.

"It worked, then?" she asked.

He nodded, but he did not return her smile. "At a cost." He pulled her in for a quick hug. "As does everything."

Grace took Aurelia's hand and guided her out. The cathedral was emptied, leaving Ember and Shep with Paine and Hawk in the wide echoing space.

Hawk's usual humor was absent, but his face had picked up color. He leaned heavily on Paine.

"I think our cuts went too deep, mate," he said. He stumbled, and Paine caught him under the arm.

"You'll be okay," Shep said. "The hardest part is over. But it's all right if you stay here and recover. That was... deep." His eyes clouding for a moment.

"And miss the fun?" Hawk asked. "You go ahead. We'll hobble along, but they need you. You're the beacons. The keys."

Ember shook her head. Shep's arm rested around her shoulders, more for comfort than support. "I didn't ask to be a beacon," she said, but they slowly shuffled back toward the doors. She heard a song come from the direction of the square.

"No, often you don't. Like greatness, it's heaved upon you." Hawk smile this time, and it lit his face. The dark circles were gone from his eyes, and the red haze in the whites had cleared. "Its weight is heavy, but we will carry it with you. Go."

The song climbed in pitch and intensity. The fairies, she realized. A thread of worry touched her. What would the city do when it finally woke?

She tugged Shep's arm, urging him along, and they retreated without waiting for Hawk and Paine. They moved through the dim streets as quickly as Shep's strength allowed, not stopping to notice who slept where or the architecture or magic. She stepped over the cobbled path without wondering who'd built it or how many souls had passed over it.

A stray thought flickered through her—*Maybe they have a bookshop here.* Or maybe, someday, they could. Hope was not extinguished so lightly, she thought. And hope was everything.

They reached the square.

The fairies had gathered, just as promised. Ember had no idea how many fairies they'd freed, but both fairy and dragon covered every inch of the square. It was a sight so beautiful and magical it stopped her in her tracks.

The colors shimmered like living paint. Mist curled around her ankles and lifted with each note of the song. A soft hum vibrated through the air, through her bones, down her spine. It was the magic of love, the magic Atlantis has been built on. Somehow, the fairies had found it in themselves to forgive. Somehow her friends had returned the dragons.

Shep amplified the song, making it brighter. The tune soared up to the heavens, where they once were.

On the steps of the castle, Aura stood with Starling. They cut a powerful figure. Aura in white, her hair loose around her shoulders. Starling behind her, red wings fluttering in the rising magic. Grim and Twilight met them on the stairs, and together the four formed a quiet square of power. Javiar lingered in the shadows behind the Queen, watching her with an affection so plain it made Ember's chest tighten. What would happen between them, only time would tell.

Ember and Shep found their friends near the edge of the square. Hawk and Paine caught up with Sierra, Grace, and Aurelia. Sierra spun when she saw Ember and bounded toward her, grabbing both her hands.

"They showed up!" Sierra said, breathless. For a moment she looked like the girl Ember had played with, all flushed cheeks and wide eyes. There was magic in her, too.

"Who?" Ember asked, but she knew.

"The world!" She spun toward the gates. The flashing lights that had once signaled danger were muted, if they were there at all, and a gentle mist rose like a blessing. It felt like peace.

"We did it!" Sierra pulled her into a hug. Ember let herself sink into it for a heartbeat, let herself believe they fixed everything.

Around them, the people of Atlantis stirred from their enchanted sleep. Intention was powerful. Ember had always known that. It might be powerful enough to wake the city.

But was it powerful enough to save it?

Ember pulled back and met Shep's eyes with a wary, searching look. He kissed her forehead.

"One thing at a time," he murmured. A small smile tugged at his mouth. "Look, they're waking."

And they were. All around them, the people of Atlantis started to rise. They blinked at their surroundings, confused for only a breath before the fairies swept in to welcomed them home. Wonder lit their face, but none of them seemed surprised to see magic greeting them.

Across the plaza, Hawk's ship creaked and shifted in the wind.

He coughed. "Ahh, I missed her," he said. Paine watched him carefully, but Ember assumed the sickness left him, too, especially when Grace handed out pints from who knows where, and he downed his without hesitation.

"There will be more adventures," Paine said carefully.

"There will, indeed," Shep said.

They backtracked to meet Aura on the steps. She watched the city wake with tears in her eyes, but no one else dared address her. The steps were cool and slick, but at least they no longer had to step over sleeping bodies. The sun had set and left a long pink shadow cut by dragons and fairies flying by. Some of them darted close to the mainland and Ember's heart skipped a beat.

A low murmur rose over the crowd on the square as they realized what had happened and how long they had been gone. A mix of sadness and gratitude washed over them. Would they be welcomed home, or force to flee again? "Is it possible?" Ember asked, threading her fingers through Shep's. "To escape again? To run away?"

Shep shook his head, a steady grin on his face. "No. There will be no more running." He lifted Ember's hand to his lips and brushed it with a kiss. "This time, we face it."

Ember pursed her lips. She weighed the wisdom of asking the price, because there was always a price. This one, it seemed, was one they were all willing to pay. There was always a price to be paid for standing up for what's right and claiming your space. Sometimes it meant accepting that you would never quite fit in. Sometimes it meant letting your enemies say what they wanted even if it wasn't true, knowing the truth would prevail and their energy would one day find its way back to them. Sometimes it was a quiet, unshakable acceptance of yourself, and knowing you're doing the right thing. That you are, at your core, good.

It was worth all the gold in the world.

Ember shook her head. These thoughts were much too heavy for a night like this. Tonight was a celebration.

Aura sighed. "There is more to be done," she said. As if the city itself heard her, a path opened through the crowd toward the gates, as if by magic.

"There is." Javiar said. He touched her shoulder gently. "And we will do it."

A dragon roared overhead and Shep laughed, a sound threaded with a private joke. "No," he said, amused. "I do not think we will ride our dragons to the mainland today." He turned to the Queen, a mischievous look in his eye. One Ember loved. "Will we?" he asked.

Aura mirrored his smile, and it was a delight to see on her. "No," she agreed, "but I have another idea."

She led them down the steps of the castle to meet their fate on the mainland.

Chapter 50

The wind had died down and the sun set, leaving streaks of purple across the sky. Clouds drifted overhead, and somewhere beyond them Ember's bookshop waited. Her old life. Sierra put an arm around her shoulder. Shep walked on her other side. Aura and Javiar led the way, and Paine and Hawk walked behind with Aurelia and Grace.

The townsfolk murmured to one another as they passed, but none tried to stop them. It was as if they'd woken knowing what happened and what was to happen. Ember wished she knew as much.

"It's a beautiful city," Sierra said. Lights twinkled on inside homes and shops, warm and familiar, as if they'd never been silent at all. "I used to walk it. Float it..." She scrunched her face up in a laugh. "That was a joke."

Ember smiled. "It was hard without you," she said. "I buried them..." Her voice caught on the last word, and she remembered the rainy day she'd laid her folks to rest.

"I'm sorry." Sierra whispered. She rested her head on Ember's shoulder. It rose and fell as they walked.

Along the road, the fairies formed a glowing line to see them out. Some of them danced in the sky, turning the night shades of pink and blue and yellow.

The cobbled streets seemed to nudge them forward and the fairies gave them courage. Draco huffed above, a low rumble that vibrated the air, but he stayed behind. The Queen ordered it. Best not to overwhelm the people all at once. As it was, they had a few surprises up their sleeves.

The light around them darkened as the sun set further, but the fairies lit their way, humming a low tune that gave her courage. Ember doubted she would have to say much when the time came, but still she was not the same girl who had once skirted the city's edges. She would speak if she had to.

The gates rose ahead of them. She'd rarely approached the gates head on. They were made of a beautiful pearly white stone with decorations inlaid. So many carvings Ember couldn't tell one from another, but that's not what drew her gaze.

In front of the gates were Grim and Twilight. Starling hovered off to the side, flapping her wings. She winked at Ember.

"Are you ready?" Aura asked. She squared her shoulders and stared through the gate. There were less sirens and lights, but they were still there. There was a short path before the wards let up, and then they'd be on the other side.

Grim nodded. "We'll go together." He glanced at Twilight, who nodded. Her wings caught the low light, gleaming like molten silver. Ember wondered if she did that on purpose.

"It will be dangerous," Shep cautioned.

"Pft," Hawk said. "What isn't?"

They laughed, but Shep didn't waver. "We cannot promise they won't attack when we leave the safety of the city."

"No," Twilight said, her voice calm but steady as their laughter faded. "You can never promise that, nor predict it. You cannot control what others do—or how they react." They paused, as if recalling the terrible difficulties they'd been through. "But we can be honest and show up as we are. We can be strong for our peoples."

They all followed Twilight's gaze past the gates to the world beyond, waiting for their particular kind of magic.

"And you can forgive," Twilight added softly. "For that is the hardest thing of all."

"And if they aren't open to us?" Paine asked.

Twilight's eyes twinkled. "Then, we convince them."

"Let's hope it doesn't come to that," Aura said. "The gates, please."

They creaked just slightly as they swung outward on their hinges. They didn't lower the wards, but they'd be allowed through. Returning could be trickier, but that would be another battle.

Ember had forgotten the real world existed beyond the city. She felt the absence of magic as she stepped through. The wards kept it contained, and perhaps that was for the best. The rest of the world wasn't ready for that kind of power and love. Maybe someday they would be.

The island had nestled upon a grassy area. While the dragons remained behind patrolling Atlantis, Ember saw the normal birds of flight—seagulls and plovers nesting among the reeds.

The snow had melted. It wasn't quite spring, but winter was breathing its last cold sigh. Puffy clouds blocked the moon. Aside from the army at their gates, it could almost pass for normal.

Tanks and patrol cars formed a wide perimeter around the city gates. Any path they took would intersect them, and soon. They were a quarter mile off at most, and though Ember held her hand over her eyes, she could only see flashing lights. No one came to greet them.

"It's not Maryse, at least," Sierra said. A howl of wind blew past.

"No," Aura agreed. "But there is someone there."

As they walked closer to the shadowed lights, two figures emerged, with more behind them. Ember saw no weapons, at least none visible, but chest tightened anyway. Shep held her hand. Sierra held the other one.

A booming laugh cut across the field, one Ember recognized instantly. Then the wide figure of a man came into focus, a waifish woman beside him.

"It's Maryse," Shep said, awe in his voice. "Just not the one from our time."

Marching toward them were the younger version of Zyah and Maryse. Zyah wore a large, golden crown inlaid with jewels. His face was red and puffy when they met him, but his grin stretched wide.

"Your Highness." He bowed to Aura, who nodded her head. He touched the crown on his head. "I hope you don't mind—we borrowed this from the King." He winked, and somehow, Ember was at ease.

"And when you showed us the way back, well..." He exchanged a glance with Maryse. "We thought we could do more good here." He took Aura's hands in his. "What's done is done, and I am sorry for my failings. If I had known, then..."

Aura smiled, a wistful curve of her lips. Red lights washed over her face, making her look suddenly tired. "It is generally impossible to predict the future." She looked back to Javiar. "But we have done the best we could, all of us. We have held to our ideals and our principals. We've fought, and we stayed true."

"And here we are," Sierra said.

"Here we are," Maryse agreed, her layers of skirts and beads swishing and clinking with every movement. Ember thought of the first time she'd seen the woman in her parents' attic. That person had been hardened by life. This one before her... perhaps there was hope left.

Zyah took her hand. "And we have far still to go." He glanced back. "We have been working on a truce," he said. He released Maryse's hand and took the crown from his head, placing it on Aura's where it was far too big. "This, though, belongs to you, my Queen."

He knelt, but Aura shook her head.

"Stand, Zyah. I think it is where it should have been all along. I'm sorry."

Zyah shook his head. "As am I. But we will move forward from here. Atlantis is home." Maryse helped him to his feet.

Ember looked from one to the other. "But your future self..." she started.

Maryse only looked down. "She's gone," she said. That was the only explanation needed—or offered. Grace had explained the science. Maybe it had something to do with that, or maybe they'd traded places. Whatever the case, Ember didn't want to know more.

They all turned back to the city, glimmering in the low light. Ember felt hope stir in her chest—for the city, for the world, and her herself. She never thought she'd get over her parents' deaths.

They'd saved Sierra, but they couldn't come back. There was no magic for such things. She only had to let them go. Forgive.

It was not the woman in front of her who'd done it. That Maryse was gone. They had to start over.

Aura stepped forward and place the crown on Zyah's head as if it had belonged there. "I would like a place in your court." She nestled the crown firmly. "A place in truce negotiations."

"Of course," he agreed. When he shifted, Ember saw the army of police and military behind him. They'd come so far, but the journey was far from over. Returning Atlantis was a step, but only one.

"Release the wards," Zyah said softly. "Our people are no longer prisoners."

Aura paled, "But will they fight?"

Zyah shook his head. "I think not." Indeed, they'd dropped their weapons and were looking toward the soft lights of Atlantis. Some of the soldiers approached with men in suits—important ones Ember should have recognized, but such things had never concerned her.

"If you'll come with us..." One stepped forward. He was young, with the shadow of a beard. The Vice President, Ember recalled.

"You won't hurt them?" Aura asked.

"You have my word," the Vice President answered. He paused before turning and looked at Ember and the others, "and my thanks. We have known, for some time..."

Sierra sighed. "That may be a story for another time."

Zyah put a hand on Maryse's back to lead her after the others. She paused at the edge of the path. "Perhaps," she said, "there is a way to change your own path." Her eyes twinkled. Ember remembered them, when they burned with anger and revenge. It wasn't always possible to time travel to do it, but yes, you could change your path.

"Good luck," she said back. Maryse smiled.

"Now what?" Paine asked.

Behind them, curious Atlantians and fairies drifted toward the open way. Some stepped onto the grass as if touching a new world. Aura watched them, pride and worry braided across her expression.

"I still must protect them." She turned to Shepherd. "But you? Thank you for all you've done. I release you from service." She pulled him into a long hug. When she stepped back, his face was lit with surprise.

"My Queen," he murmured.

She touched his cheek. "You've done enough, Shepherd. Go."

"Thank you," he breathed. But when Aura turned to rejoin her people, they fell into step behind her anyway. Atlantis would need them. For a bit longer, at least.

And after that?

Well, that was up to them.

CHAPTER 51

The bookstore had changed, and it hadn't. The roof needed replacing, but it always needed something. The island was much busier now, serving as a stopping point on the way to the island of Atlantis. From the shop's front step Ember could just see the tops of the tallest spires, shimmering above the treetops. They'd bought her parents' old mansion back—or rather, it was given. The mysterious trust, though still mysterious, turned out to be a patchwork of ancestors and survivors more than eager to return things where they were.

But still, the shop was home.

Shepherd held up a romance book with a shirtless cowboy on the cover. "Bestseller?" he asked, raising an eyebrow.

"You better believe it," Ember said. "Put it right in the window display."

He'd changed in the months since their returned. Settled. His skin had more color now, and faint laugh lines creased his eyes. He looked older, but it suited him. He looked *happy*.

"Dad?" Aurelia came bounding down the stairs. She and Grace had settled in the upstairs apartment when she was in town, which was often enough. She'd been made an ambassador between Atlantis and the wider world, and it kept her busy. "I forgot to tell you—"

She ran into Ember first, pushing open the back windows by the reading room before giving her a quick hug. Ember remembered the days when Draco would start a fire in the grate for her. He was far too big to fit in the shop now, and often off with Arcturus, but he had a home with them, too. The dragons were enjoying their new freedom. Everyone was.

Aurelia's voice drifted from the front as she chattered about how Twilight had planned to write a romance book under a pen name and had asked for research material, which meant a stack of the most dramatic paperbacks they carried. Ember stood and brushed dust from her pants. It was too early in the season for a fire, but the air had picked up a chill. Tourists were rare in early autumn, but the island had become a hot spot and the bookstore especially. They'd do a brisk business all year.

She had already hired a new manager. Grim took his job very seriously, but he insisted on living in his own apartment off the beaten path. He'd be in five minutes before opening, making coffee and fluffing his wings—ready to guard the morning.

"They're settling."

Grace surprised her, standing at the bottom of the stairs and leaning on the rail. She was part fairy and part witch and tended to surprise Ember at every turn. She folded her arms and watched Aurelia perch on a stool to tell her father the plot of Twilight's book. He laughed as he stacked the books. He looked completely at ease.

"They'll be all right," Ember said with a smile. She ran her hand over the self-help display.

"And you?" Grace asked.

The old Ember would have said it wasn't about her. She had spent most of her life deflecting attention. She didn't need a self-help book to explain that. But in the last few months, she'd begun to realize that she was important, too. That she deserved to take up space. Have feelings—even if those feelings were fear. Shepherd had helped, yes, but mostly it was a change in her own heart.

She sighed. "I worry for Atlantis," she admitted. "I'm afraid for its people." She watched Shep laugh gently at something Aurelia said. He looked her way over the shelves and offered her a warm smile. "But there will always be fear, I suppose. And there will always be joy and love and happiness. I am trying to focus on that, Grace. I really am."

Grace laughed. "You forget I was raised in this world, too. I know how its darkness can pull." She surprised Ember by taking her hand. "But we'll push back."

"It's exhausting, sometimes," Ember admitted. They walked together to the front of the shop, the wood creaking under their steps.

"It is," Grace said, and nothing more. She didn't need to. The girl was wise beyond her years. Was it the fairy in her blood, the witch, or was it just her? Maybe she simply understood life better than most.

She slipped her hand from Ember's and crossed to the back, where she wrapped her arms around Aurelia and hugged her tight.

"Remember, we're going back today?" She nuzzled her face in Aurelia's hair.

Aurelia laughed. "That tickles," she said playfully, "but yes. We have treaties to prepare. Important stuff." She stood and let her father pull her into a warm hug.

"We appreciate you," he said.

"You've done enough," she told him. "Let the younger generation work too." Her grin made the tease land softly.

That was when Sierra burst through the door. She shared the house with Shep and Ember but was rarely home. She'd reconnected with that boyfriend of hers, and they were off exploring the world. Traveling suited her. "We got a postcard!" She held up a small rectangle.

"A what?" Shep asked.

Ember laughed. "They're a lost art, but we're bringing them back." She plucked it from Sierra's hand and read the back. "Exploring Mayan ruins. Parked the ship in the jungle. Paine ate a hot pepper and she's still sweating. See you soon. Love, Hawk."

"He's sending postcards?" Shep eyed the display behind the register as if he'd never noticed them before. Hawk and Paine had traveled all over. While Aurelia, Grace, and Aura had chosen to be envoys and broker peace, the two of them had chosen a different path. A long overdue adventure. Ember and Shepherd were somewhere in between.

"Where do you think they'll go next?" Sierra asked as she slid behind the register and started a pot of coffee, the rich scent filling the shop.

"I wish they'd come to the conference with us," Aurelia sighed, eyeing the coffee longingly. Sierra made it with extra sugar and cream and slid it over to her.

"Eventually we will all settle," Shep said, resting a hand on Ember's back. Outside, Draco let out a low roar. The bell above the door jingled. Their first customer of the day had arrived.

"Welcome," Shep said, turning to greet her. "To the Third Chapter."

The woman raised an eyebrow, but Ember laughed as the women went right for the romance he'd shelved this morning. She gave him a knowing look.

"Maybe it's time for a rebrand?" Grace suggested.

"The Bookstore of Lost Things," Aurelia said, pecking Grace on the cheek.

"I don't know," Ember said, thinking of her dad. "It has a certain charm as it is."

Shep winked, cradling a cup of tea in his hands. "Someone once told me the third chapter is when things get good."

Aurelia held her mug up. "To the Third Chapter," she said, "and many more."

"I'll drink to that," Sierra said, turning to brew her own coffee. The old bookstore had its charm, but it was time for new beginnings. Ember had a feeling Atlantis magic wasn't the only magic out there waiting for them.

"Who's this?" Grace asked, eyeing a book on the counter Ember had been reading.

"Oh." Ember held up *The History of Devil's Island*, the author's photo staring back from the back cover. "Legend says he's still around somewhere. I thought we might have a talk."

Aurelia wrapped her in a hug. "Rest a bit, will you? And take care of my dad."

She promised. They said their goodbyes. Aurelia, Grace, and Sierra were off to the conference, leaving Ember and Shep to settle into their life as best they could.

The bookstore hummed with activity. Customers wandered between bookshelves, browsing, laughing, pausing to ask questions. Rudy swept the sidewalk across the street, the rhythmic scraping of his broom blending with the faint chatter for the street.

And somewhere, just beyond sight, magic stirred again...

Acknowledgements

I was lax on my acknowledgements in the first *Atlantis* book—and for that, I apologize. Writing may be a solitary act, publishing is anything but. This series has been in my head for so many years, it's impossible to thank everyone who's shaped it, but I'll try to make a dent.

To my kids – Erin, Lily, and Danny—for inspiring me, for testing my patience, and showing me what love is. You are the meaning behind this book.

For my real life Shep—for protecting all of us. We might not have returned Atlantis, but we found our own kind of magic.

To my community, thank you for all your support. To the Bellingham Writers Group—still going strong after eight years! Thank you, Marjorie, for the wonderful idea of starting this group so we could share our work. Writing can be, indeed, solitary, and every time I've thought about giving up, this group has pushed me through. What began as a space to help others has given me so much in return—especially friendship and honest feedback.

To my friends and readers, thank you for your eyes, your heart, and encouragement. This book wouldn't have been possible without the motivation and occasional kick in the pants from my accountable partner, Lisa Ware, who is an amazing creative and human on her own.

And to my publisher Rowan Prose, thank you for your confidence, and for all your amazing work on this book. To Shakera Blakney for her amazing job editing. Thank you for making this book the best it could be, and for making my dreams come true.

Check out these other great reads from Rowan Prose!

Amy Cip is an author, blogger, people watcher, sci-fi junkie, website novice, eternal optimist, and introvert. She is the author of seven YA science fiction/fantasy/dystopian books. She resides in Massachusetts.
www.amycip.com

www.ingramcontent.com/pod-product-compliance
Lightning Source LLC
LaVergne TN
LVHW040134080526
838202LV00042B/2899